PAKISTAN, INDIA AND THE BOMB:

SPY VERSUS COUNTERSPY

A NOVEL

JAMES GLENN

Library of Congress Control Number: 2016908575
Create Space Independent Publishing Platform

ISBN-13: 978-1533341938
ISBN-10: 1533341931

1. India-Espionage and Nuclear Weapons-Fiction
2. Secret Intelligence Operations-Fiction
3. Nuclear Weapons-Fiction
4. Nuclear Non-Proliferation-Fiction

www.jamesglennauthor.com

Cover design and formatting by Debora Lewis
www.arenapublishing.org

Front Cover Photo: Delhi Gate, New Delhi
Front Cover Photo: Mikadun/shutterstock.com
Maps: Peter Hermes Furian/shutterstock.com

Printed in the United States of America

To our grandchildren:

Patrick, Andrew, Mike, Louis, Isabella, and Ryan.

May they live in a world they help to make more safe.

To Tim & Melissa,
With Best Wishes,
[signature]

The professional spy works best
In quiet secrecy. He operates
In highly stressful situations
With only his wits to protect him.

He depends on trust and integrity
As the basis for his relations
With his agents.

His secrets
May never be told
But are sealed forever.

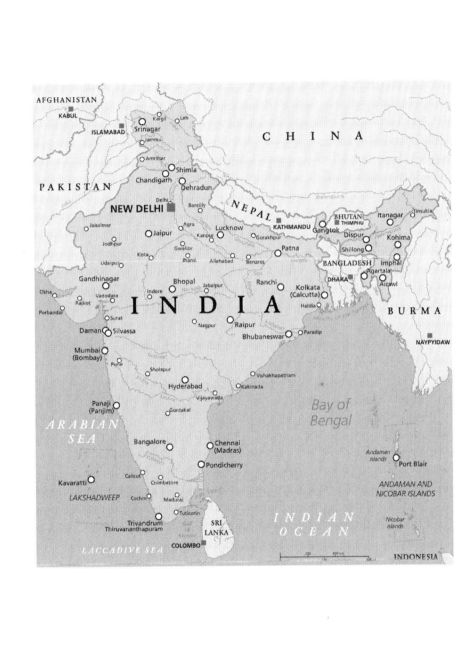

Contents

INTRODUCTION

This is a work of historical fiction. The story revolves around India's secret development of its first nuclear weapon and Pakistan's attempts to stop India's progress.

It is the early 1970's. The cold war between the Soviet Union and the United States continues unabated. India becomes a major battleground between the American CIA and the Russian KGB. They vie for India's influence, and, by extension, the influence of the emerging, non-aligned Third World Movement. The story portrays espionage by KGB, CIA, and ISI operatives in India at that time.

The Indian Intelligence Bureau (IB), Pakistan's Inter-Service Intelligence (ISI), the American Central Intelligence Agency (CIA), and the Russian Komitet Gosudarstvennoy Bezopasnosti (KGB) are known intelligence organizations. India's Prime Minister Indira Gandhi, Pakistan's Prime Minister Zulfiqar Bhutto, Homi Bhabha, Munir Ahmed Khan, and A.Q. Khan are known politicians or scientists. Their work and decisions influenced how and when India and Pakistan developed their separate nuclear weapons capabilities. They are, properly, part of this story. However, some of their attributes are the imagination of the author and may have little resemblance to actual facts.

The Rajasthan Canals Project, the Minerals and Metals Corporation, the Border Roads, and the River Valleys Development Board are actual organizations. Donovan Griffin's notional employer, The Earthmoving Corporation, does not exist.

No nuclear weapon has been exploded in anger since 1945. Yet, the threat of a nuclear explosion increases with the number of countries which have them. The initial five nuclear weapons countries have tried to control the spread of nuclear weapons to other countries with mixed success. Pakistan, India, Israel and North Korea also now possess nuclear weapons. Others, such as Iran, Saudi Arabia, Egypt, and Turkey may seek to develop them. The greatest future nuclear danger may come not from warring countries but from a terrorist organization not associated with any country. How does the world community combat that threat?

The Appendix gives a time line of Indian-Pakistani nuclear developments. The Reference section lists various books, autobiographies and web sites for the material of this novel.

James Glenn
Taos, New Mexico

Fictional Characters

Asaf Ali Khan, Muslim professor on leave from Pakistan's Lahore University. Recruited by his uncle to spy for Pakistan in New Delhi, India. He must both live a cover story for being in India and obtain India's plans to detonate a nuclear weapon. Ambika Nair Khan, his Hindu wife, Kumar, their son.

Graham Smith, the chief of station for the CIA in New Delhi. Melanie, his wife. Shamus, his second in command.

Donovan Griffin, an American territory sales representative for India and Ceylon for The Earthmoving Corporation. Emily, his wife, Matthew, their son.

Akbar Chaudry, the head of Pakistan's spy network for all of India, "Control", located at the Pakistan High Commission in New Delhi.

Colonel Bhandari, the Director of the Indian Intelligence Bureau (IB) in New Delhi.
> "One", head of the IB department for internal security.
> "Two", head of the IB department responsible for foreign intelligence.
> "Three", head of the IB department responsible for foreigners in India.
> "Four", head of the IB department responsible for military intelligence.

Shiree Saksena, graduate of Oxford University, Secretary of the Indian Government's Nuclear Power Commission and niece of Sena Saksena.

Sena Saksena, member of the Rajya Sabha, the upper house of the Indian Parliament, and uncle of Shiree.

<u>T.R. Nair</u>, member of the Lok Sabha, the lower house of Parliament, from Kerala State and father of Ambika Nair Khan, Ali's wife.

<u>Ravi Bhatra</u>, polo player and local entrepreneur.

<u>B.K. Mehta</u>, Bombay businessman and Parsi.

<u>P.I. Penkovsky</u>, a KGB agent assigned to the Soviet Embassy in New Delhi.

<u>Vladmir Yankovich</u>, Head of the KGB, the Rezident, at the Soviet Embassy.

<u>Two Star Air Vice Marshal Ahmed Anwar Khan</u>, head of the Pakistani Air Force, East Sector and uncle of Asaf Ali Khan.

<u>Hussein</u>, a diplomat to India from a Middle Eastern country.

<u>Wong Yonbang</u>, a Chinese Trade Representative.

Nomenclature

In this novel the foreign spies are known as Case Officers who manage their Indian Agents. For the sake of secrecy, the Pakistani ISI Case Officers are referred in official dispatches by pseudo identities. "Control" is the ISI representative responsible for Pakistan's espionage operations throughout India.

> Akbar Chaudry is the ISI Control for all of India.
> Asaf Ali Khan is referred to as Case Officer BAKRA.
> Pervez is referred to as ISI Case Officer BURKO.
> Shiree Saksena is referred to as Agent BOKARO.
> Ram Lal Dutta is referred to as Agent BALOO.

In this novel both the American CIA and the Pakistani ISI rate their official dispatches in terms of urgency or need for follow up:

CIA Messages: (1)	ISI Messages:
Critic	Critical
Flash	Urgent
Immediate	---
Priority	Priority
Routine	Routine

In this novel CIA professionals refer to the CIA as "the Company". Akbar Chaudry refers to the ISI headquarters in Islamabad, Pakistan as "the Factory".

(1) Kessler, Ronald. *Inside the CIA: Revealing the Secrets of the World's Most Powerful Spy Agency*. New York: Simon & Schuster, 1992. Print, page 35.

ASSIGNMENT: NEW DELHI

May, 1972
Lahore University
Lahore, Pakistan

The professor rested comfortably in his high-backed, soft chair as he graded his students' strength of materials test papers. From time to time he fully extended his arms and rose to his tiptoes, just to stretch. Boredom it was not. He was quite satisfied with the learning that he was imparting as demonstrated by the test results.

He reclined his chair against the floor to ceiling bookcase behind him. Swiveling, he visually caressed his collection of engineering texts, much as a gardener would contemplate his prize roses. Most in English, some in Urdu, a few in German. He expressed a sigh as he looked over to what he called his work table and his stacks and stacks on half-read professional magazines and his draft of a new engineering textbook. His office was not cluttered, just neat in an untidy way.

The telephone interrupted his concentration.

"Professor Khan."

"Ali, this is Uncle Ahmed."

Anticipating the next words, Asaf Ali Khan dropped his pen, straightened in his chair and pressed his phone closer to his ear.

"I have good news. The ISI has now approved your posting to New Delhi as our Science Advisor. Please finalize your preparations to leave the University. Tell Ambika that she will soon move to where she grew up. Remember what I told you about India developing an atomic bomb. I do not believe that the current ISI assessment is correct. I rely on you to give the ISI and me the latest and most accurate intelligence about India's plans. We must stop India from developing a bomb."

"Yes, Uncle. Thank you for your confidence. I will do as you ask. You can count on me."

Hanging up the phone, Ali wondered how his uncle gained access to the secret ISI reports or coerced the ISI to appoint him to New Delhi. He knew only that the air marshal believed that India was making faster progress on bomb development than the ISI reports revealed. Ali grimaced when he thought what action his uncle might take when India got closer to an actual bomb test.

Ali hastened home to give Ambika and Kumar the news. He wondered as he drove if he could do spy work for the ISI. After all, he was an engineering professor, not a professional spy.

———

May, 1972
Central Intelligence Agency
Headquarters
Langley, Virginia

Graham Smith strode into the Chief, South East Asia's office. Greying at the temples, with rimless glasses, wearing a dark blue pin-striped suit, white shirt and red paisley tie, he exuded confidence. As he approached the Chief's desk, the Chief came around to greet him with a broad smile and handshake.

"Graham, I am pleased to confirm your new assignment as our chief of station in New Delhi. This is an important position which acknowledges your success in your previous tours. You have been briefed about India's growing relationship with the Soviet Union. That greatly concerns us. We cannot allow the Communists to influence the world's largest democracy and leader of the non-aligned Third World Movement. We expect that you can learn what the Soviets are doing and counter the KGB's growing influence there. I rely on you to implement our strategic objectives for that country. Please give Melanie my best regards. I wish you both a successful tour."

"Thank you for your confidence. This is a challenging and exciting assignment. I look forward to getting back to the field."

———

May, 1972
The Earthmoving Corporation (TEC)
Headquarters
Dubuque, Iowa

The five young sales trainees stood to rigid attention in the first row of the otherwise empty auditorium as sales trainer extraordinaire Mark Baird burst in. The tension in the room was palpable.

This meeting culminated an intensive ten month sales training program. The men had worked in the factory assembling bulldozers, made production studies of equipment working in the field, compared competitive equipment, trained distributor salesmen, and evaluated distributor effectiveness.

They now eagerly awaited assignments to TEC's sales territories.

"Please sit, gentlemen."

Baird, a crisp, former Marine colonel with a strong jaw and crew cut, read off the assignments for four of the five who were assigned to district sales offices in the U.S. Their response was overwhelmingly enthusiastic.

"Now, Donovan Griffin."

Donovan, lanky at six feet, instinctively stood up, pushed his sandy hair back and replied, "Sir!"

The others chuckled.

"Donovan, we have had some difficulty finding a suitable sales assignment for you. You and your wife would prefer to live and work overseas. As Emily is fluent in Spanish, we have tried to place you in South America. Unfortunately, we have no open sales territories there. Our only open territory is that of India and Ceylon. Are you willing to take it? Our current sales representative there has just accepted a position as sales manager of our UK subsidiary."

"Yes, sir!" Donovan enthused.

"Donovan, you will work with our local distributors in those two countries to sell our earthmoving equipment to the government agencies which can obtain foreign currency. You will be stationed in New Delhi because that is where the Indian government decision-makers are. TEC will help you obtain the Government of India's permission to work there. You, Emily, and your son will have to obtain immunization against all of the diseases of that place. You will be living on the local economy just as the Indians do. You will find

3

too many people, no supermarkets, no peanut butter, no beef steak, only water buffalo, no fast food restaurants, no great sanitation, too few doctors, and a hot climate. Are you sure you want this challenge?"

"Sir, Emily and I have discussed this. She says that she will blossom wherever she is planted. If we are to be planted in India as our next adventure, we welcome it."

"Very well, then, Donovan...

Gentlemen, you have performed well over these several months. You have come together as a team. Remember the benefits of teamwork when you get to your sales territories. You are accepting responsible sales positions. You are fully capable of doing your assigned tasks. I expect only good news about you. I look forward to receiving your Christmas cards telling me how well you are doing...

Our next meeting will be a celebration at the Purple Passion Pub at 1800 hours. Dismissed."

The Pakistan High Commission

November, 1972
Pakistan High Commission
"The Palace"
Shantipath
Chanakyapuri
New Delhi

The driver turned off Shantipath, New Delhi's famous street of posh foreign Embassies and High Commissions, and drove the limousine into the long circular, gravel driveway leading to the main door of the Pakistan High Commission.

"Mom, Dad! Look! We're coming to a big pink and white palace!" Kumar, their five-year-old son, exclaimed as he turned to stare at the approaching, huge two story building with blue tennis-ball like turrets on the roof.

"Yes, son," his father replied. "This is our country's office here. We will meet my new boss in a few minutes. This is where I will be spending some of my time, when I am not visiting the Indian Institutes of Technology. It is, indeed, a beautiful building. This is the Pakistan High Commission."

"What's a High Commission?"

"A High Commission is another name for an embassy, an office of a different country. The British call their former colonies High Commissions, not embassies."

"What is a colony?" always inquisitive Kumar asked.

"Well, son, that answer will have to wait for another time. We have arrived."

With that question hanging in the air, Asaf Ali Khan, his wife, Ambika, and little Kumar scrambled out of the car and disappeared into the High Commission building. The driver agreed to wait for them.

The guard at the entrance welcomed and ushered them into the High Commission's spacious atrium, then phoned Akbar Chaudry to announce their arrival. Fatigued from their airplane travel, they pasted smiles on their faces, combed their hair and smoothed their rumpled clothes.

Looking around, they found a bubbling fountain in the center of the expanse. A large Pakistani flag decorated the wall to their left. The sign under the flag stated "Land of the Pure" in Urdu and English. Adjacent wooden chairs tastefully decorated with green and gold brocade cushions invited guests to sit. On the wall to their right a framed picture of Muhammed Al Jinna, the founder of Pakistan, imposed itself. Several luxurious, dark red, oriental prayer rugs added color to the area under Al Jinna's photo. A marble staircase beyond the fountain led to the second floor. Ambika detected a slight scent of curry.

Akbar Chaudry appeared at the top of the steps to the second floor, his face frozen in a smile. A tall, somewhat overweight man with a large moustache, heavy eyebrows and greying hair, he carried himself with the flair of a diplomat. He waved to the three as he slowly came down to meet them. Ambika noted his slight limp as he navigated the white marble steps. The head of Pakistan's espionage agency, the Inter-Service Intelligence, he shook their hands in welcome.

"Welcome to New Delhi, Ali. I am pleased to meet you and your family. I trust that your flight was uneventful and that you were not harassed at customs. What a handsome young lad Kumar is!"

"Thank you, sir. We had a smooth flight from Teheran and an easy time through customs. A very polite, rather intelligent Indian customs official took good care of us. Thank you for sending your car to pick us up."

Akbar half-bowed. "We are glad you are here. Please take the rest of the day to settle in and get comfortable in our guest house. Ambika, I would like my wife to show you the three houses we have available for your permanent residence. Please pick the one that you think will be most suitable. Perhaps we can get that organized tomorrow. While you ladies and Kumar are looking at houses, Ali and I can have a bit of a chat here at the High Commission. Ambika, is ten in the morning a good time for you to start? Yes. Then I'll have my wife pick you up from our guest house at ten. I'll also send a car around to pick up Ali. Good. Welcome again! We look forward to a good friendship."

He helped the three to find their way out to the waiting car.

"He's such a fine man," Ali remarked to his wife as he helped her get into the car. "We will do well here with his support."

"I hope so," she whispered, unconvinced.

Still a rigid smile on his face, Akbar waved to the departing car and turned back into the building. He nodded to the guard at the front door and slowly crossed the atrium. He paid no attention to the pain in his right leg as he climbed the stairs to the second floor. He nodded silently to Prime Minister Bhutto's portrait on the wall half way down the carpeted hallway to his office at the back of the building.

He told his secretary to make the next day's arrangements and moved to his large desk at the very back wall of the High Commission. Akbar settled his rather ample frame into his overstuffed chair. He again opened Khan's dossier lying on his desk.

Neglecting the file in front of him, and twirling a pen in his right hand, he mused about his newest spy.

I requested a professional spy for this assignment, and who did the Factory send me? A university professor! He is here because his uncle, the air marshal, believes India is making faster progress on bomb development than my intelligence reports indicate. My reports! How does uncle get them, anyway?

Now that I have met him, I see that Ali is a tall, lean, rather easy-going and mild-mannered, handsome professor with a straight nose and trim moustache. How willing is he to take the risks that a spy must take? I must determine his motivation and ability to do this dangerous work. He clearly will have to prove himself to me. Not everyone is cut out to be a spy. (1)

Akbar sighed, rubbed his eyes, turned to a rather high stack of secret intelligence reports and started to sign them.

(1) Paseman, Floyd. *A Spy's Journey: A CIA Memoir*. St. Paul: Zenith Press, 2004. Print. Paseman's Ten Axioms of Spying, page 281. "Axiom 1: Not everyone is cut out to be a spy."

ALI STAYS COMMITTED

November, 1972
Pakistan High Commission
"The Palace"
Shantipath
Chanakyapuri
New Delhi

The next day, Ali, with the help of one of the staff, found his way to Akbar's well-appointed office.

Two large pictures of rugged, snow-capped mountains overwhelmed the wall behind Akbar. Ali glanced at a number of plaques on the adjacent wall. One larger one stood out. It was the Army's commendation for valor in the 1965 war with India. Ali noticed a dark red prayer rug nestled between a sofa and two chairs in the corner.

"Please take a cup of tea and have a seat in the chair in front of my desk. We have a lot to discuss. This may take some time. Feel free to refill your cup anytime," Akbar said in his most welcoming and pleasant tone.

Ali poured tea, added two spoons of sugar and settled into the soft chair. It was the same kind of wooden chair with brocade cushions Ali had seen in the atrium. He placed his tea cup and saucer on the corner of Akbar's desk. He planted both feet firmly on the floor and placed each hand on a knee.

"Ali, I am delighted to have you working for me. We have some great challenges which we can together overcome. You have my full support for the tasks which you will be undertaking."

Not exactly true, but, that should put him at ease.

"Thank you for your confidence, Akbar." Ali sipped some of his tea.

"I have read your dossier. You have a fine record of accomplishments. You come from a landowning family in Sind. You obtained an engineering degree at Karachi University, then a Master's Degree at MIT where you specialized in strength of materials. You are a professor and research scientist on a leave of absence from Lahore University. That documentation has been properly backed up, should an Indian diplomat enquire in Lahore. You know, someone will."

Akbar continued. "I first want to confirm your cover work, the ostensible reason which brings you to New Delhi. Then, I will discuss your spying tasks. Our government has decided to implement a bold, ten-year plan to improve education at all levels including university education. We have about 20 universities but only three, those at Karachi, Peshawar and Lahore are anywhere near world class in engineering."

Akbar paused, raised his bulky moustache and sipped his sweetened tea.

"Your cover task is to visit the Indian Institutes of Technology campuses to study their curriculum and teaching process for undergraduate engineers. You will report your findings and make recommendations to improve our curriculum to your Dean in Lahore. You will write your reports here at the High Commission. I will arrange to send them directly to the Dean with a copy to the ISI. Before you leave today I will show you the office that you will use. You should be well received by the various IIT staffs you meet.

"Your Dean has arranged for an introductory letter from him and an official welcoming letter from the IIT Dean in New Delhi. Use both of these letters to introduce yourself to the IIT Deans at the various locations. The letters explain that it is in our two countries' best interests to share peaceful, country-building, educational information.

"Do you have the two letters of introduction?"

"Yes."

"Good. You are not a professional spy. You are not a diplomat. You are our Science Advisor. Your work with the IIT makes you legitimate in the eyes of Indian counterintelligence. Actually living your cover involves more work for you but it also affords you more protection. The Indian Intelligence Bureau will not look on you with the same suspicion it places on our Pakistani diplomats. Do you understand that?"

"Yes, Akbar, I do."

Akbar continued.

"We have arranged for two business cards for you. One states that you are a professor at Lahore University. Use that when you meet the IIT authorities. The second one introduces you as the Science Advisor at our High Commission. You may use that with Indian government officials. Remember, you do have diplomatic immunity as part of our High Commission delegation."

The ISI chief smiled and placed the business cards on the corner of his desk.

"In your first six months here you will schedule a visit to the IIT campuses at Bombay, New Delhi, Madras, Guwahati, Kanpur, Rookee, and Kharagpur. You will concentrate on two IIT locations because they give you access to your real targets, your covert agents. They are in New Delhi and Bombay."

Ali sat back and crossed his legs. He left the business cards on the corner of Akbar's wide desk. He noticed a large plaque with a camel, sword and spear on the other wall.

"Your IIT reports will assure the ISI that you are truly working your cover. We know from experience that someone who does not do his cover work always gets into trouble with the local security people. We do not want that to happen to you."

"I can assure you, Akbar, that I will conscientiously do my cover job," said the professor.

"Now, let us move on to the real reason why you are here. We suspect that the Indian government is developing an atomic bomb. Your secret work is to determine how much they have progressed in their bomb development. We need to know when they are ready to test their first nuclear weapon. Nuclear weapons development takes years, not months. You know from your discussions at ISI in Islamabad that India with a nuclear weapon gravely threatens our country. We have already fought three wars with India. India with a nuclear weapon tilts the military balance in their favor. We cannot allow that to happen."

Akbar moved forward in his chair. He folded his hands on his desk.

"Ali, please help me to understand why you, a university professor, agreed to take on this spy assignment. Spying is dangerous work, certainly not in your chosen field."

"My uncle is a marshal in our Air Force. He explained this opportunity for me to make a contribution to my country's security, but the decision to come here was mine. I have every confidence that I can do this spy work. Also, this position was attractive to Ambika. She may now see her father here in New Delhi. She has now returned to the place where she grew up."

Ali shifted his weight in his chair. Akbar scowled. He clenched his fists under his desk.

In a near-whisper he said, "Before I provide details about your secret assignment, I ask if you really are prepared to do the work of a spy. Frankly, I fear that you will fail. You will be challenged to obtain secret Indian government information. You will be committing treason against India. If you are caught, you and your family will be told to leave the country. Are you willing to work your cover and also manage agents? You will be doing two very different jobs. Are you willing to experience the intense stress of a meeting with your agent? Do you have the guts to do secret work? Do you have the stamina, the strength, to take the risks, and succeed? I am afraid that you will fail with disastrous consequences for you and your agents. I cannot tolerate your failure!"

Ali leaned forward, frowning, and replied, "I have thought long and hard about this assignment. I am committed to doing both jobs, and to doing them well. My cover story is perfect. I will be well received by the IIT staffs. As for spying, I have been well trained by the ISI."

Ali's boss sat back in his chair and crossed his arms over his chest.

"Please recognize that we are working in a hostile environment here. The splitting up of the old British India into a new, smaller India and new country, Pakistan, created an enduring rivalry and lasting bitterness between the two new nations. As a result, all Pakistanis here are looked on with suspicion..." (1)

Akbar continued, "Yes, I know that you met your wife when you both were graduate students at Georgetown University following your MIT degree. You broke tradition by falling in love and marrying. Does your wife have unspoken thoughts about your work against her native country, even thoughts to turn you over to the Indian authorities?"

Ali replied, as forcefully as a university professor could, "I have also held many discussions with Ambika about what it will be like to do both assignments. She has agreed to support me fully. I respectfully look to you for guidance in the secret work I will be doing."

Akbar relaxed and placed his arms on the chair's arm rests. He tried to use his most fatherly tone of voice.

"Frankly, Ali, I do not see that you have the necessary characteristics of a spy. You are too mild-mannered. You are not internally driven to succeed at all costs. You are not accustomed to prodding and sweet talking and, yes, intimidating another person to do what you want him to do. You do not seem to possess a certain inherent deviousness that a successful professional spy must have, a passionate but quiet deviousness for a cause which some would define as patriotic. You are here because your uncle wants independent reports of India's progress in developing a nuclear bomb. You did not request this job. You were pushed here by your uncle. I do not doubt your ability to work with the IIT universities. I do doubt your ability, your motivation, to spy for us. I do not want you to start to work with our agents, then fail or have second thoughts. Ali, it is not too late for you to change your mind. Why not return to Lahore, now, before you become too involved here and cannot quit? We will understand."

Ali replied, grimacing, "Akbar, I told you I am willing and able to do both assignments. I am not going back now that we have just arrived!"

Akbar scratched his nose and ran his hand through his thick, greying hair.

"Not only will your uncle and our ISI receive your reports of your secret meetings with your agents. Prime Minister Bhutto has also requested copies. So, if you make one mistake, just one mistake, I will send you home immediately and the person at the highest level of our government will know about it. Are you willing to take that risk?"

"Yes, Akbar. I am."

"All right, Ali. We understand each other. I ask you three questions."

"Are you willing to break the laws of India in order to conduct your spy work here?"

"Yes, I am."

"Are you willing to lie, to be deceitful, if necessary, to protect your agents, and to obtain the information you need?"

"Yes."

"Have you been sufficiently trained by the ISI to do this spy work?"

"Yes, I have."

"Then, I will include in my notes of our meeting that you are fully aware of the risks of spying and totally willing to do this secret work. Agreed?"

"Yes, Akbar. Agreed. Let's get on with the briefing."

Akbar sighed, and then continued.

"After you have fully developed your cover work, we will assign two agents for you to manage. One is new. The other has been with us for some time. One is here in New Delhi, the other in the Bombay area. Both are very sensitive and demand special handling by someone who knows what he is doing.

"Let me give you some background now about the one who has been with us longer. Our man in Bombay is about your age. He is from an old Muslim family. When Babar Panwar was about 9 years old and living in his native India, the India-Pakistan partition occurred in 1947. His father, mother, aunt, and uncle decided to migrate to the new Pakistan. They took him and his two sisters with them.

"They packed up what they could carry and became part of a large Muslim group trekking from their village in Gujarat toward Hyderabad in the new Pakistan. They got as far as Surat when they were attacked by a large group of Hindus from Pakistan coming the other way. His mother, father, and uncle were brutally killed. His aunt rescued Babar and his two sisters and retraced their steps, never to try again to cross the new border. They did not go back to their village but moved further down the Indian west coast where they finally settled. They lost their identification papers in the flight. They applied for new identities. The astute aunt then registered Babar Panwar as Ram Lal Dutta. So he is known today. Ram Lal Dutta is a Hindu name."

Akbar frowned. "Ali, you were still a boy in what is now Pakistan when the partition occurred. You were not aware of the mass slaughter of Muslims by Hindus and of Hindus by Muslims when millions of trekking migrants encountered each other as they crossed paths. Thousands of Hindus and Muslims were massacred. The deep animosity from that terrible time lingers on both sides. That is why we work in a hostile environment in India today, and why we cannot allow India to get the bomb." (2)

Akbar went on, "I was a teenager when the partition occurred. My father and uncle owned and operated three cotton textile mills near Indore. My family decided to migrate to the new Pakistan. My uncle and his family stayed behind in India to run the mills. My family managed to walk to Lahore where we started a new life and a new cotton mill. On the way we witnessed firsthand some of the useless slaughter. I still have nightmares from that time...

"Dutta has an engineering degree from IIT, Bombay. He works in India's Trombay Nuclear Research Lab, the center for India's bomb development. It is a few kilometers outside Bombay. Dutta has access to the visitor guest register of the scientists who visit Trombay. We have indications, not hard intelligence, that Trombay is developing a plutonium implosion bomb similar to that dropped on Nagasaki by the Americans in 1945. We also suspect that Trombay has divided this bomb into three or more parts, and has assigned other Indian nuclear facilities to develop and build the components.

"You will meet Dutta once a month in the Bombay area at a time and place you decide. He will give you a list of all of the Indian scientists who have visited the Trombay Lab during the last month. When we know who visits, and where they are from, we can deduce whether they are discussing peaceful uses or bomb development. Moreover, we may deduce from the visitors list when the scientists move from bomb development to bomb building. That is critical for us."

Akbar pushed his long hair back from his forehead.

"We also know that the plutonium given off as a by-product at the Trombay Lab must be processed many times over for it to cause a devastating explosion. India already operates a plutonium reprocessing plant. About six to ten kilograms of highly enriched plutonium is enough to produce one atomic bomb.

"I will have information for you about the agent in New Delhi at another meeting. We expect to turn both of these agents over to you when the timing is right, but in about six months' time. Again, Ali, your task now is to develop your cover story. Make it strong enough to withstand the scrutiny of the Intelligence Bureau...

"Young man, we are sitting here in my comfortable office discussing your meeting with Dutta in just six short months. You may think that preparing and actually meeting an agent is as easy as sitting here calmly talking about it. First, you will spend several hours preparing for the meeting. Then you will experience the anxiety and stress of carrying out the actual meeting.

"You will meet Dutta at night, after dark. You will drive to the meeting site, first assuring yourself that you have not been followed. You will pick him up, talk while still driving, and drop him off some minutes later. You will struggle to concentrate on what he says while you avoid creating an accident while you drive. You will be under tremendous stress.

"Just one last time, Ali. Are you sure that you want to do this dangerous spy work? It is not too late to return home now."

Ali sighed. "Yes, I am sure, Akbar."

"Again, you are here to run two already recruited agents. We do not expect you to spot, assess, or recruit new agents. Please stick to your assignment.

Remember, we Pakistani's are high on the Indian Intelligence Bureau's counter-spy list. So, when you meet your agents, you must always be very careful and use the best spy tradecraft.

"Live your cover story for the next six months. Now, let me introduce you to our Ambassador. He has approved your work here and wants to meet you."

(1) Talbot, Ian and Singh, Gurharpal. *The Partition of India*. Cambridge, 2104. Print, pages 154-175.

(2) Ibid, page 2. "Communal massacres sparked a chaotic two-way flight of Hindus and Sikhs from Pakistan and Muslims from India. In all an estimated 15 million people were displaced in what became the largest forced migration in the 20th century. The death toll remains disputed to this day, with figures ranging from 200,000 to 2 million."

AKBAR'S DOUBTS

ADMIN
ROUTINE
16 November, 1972
TO: ISI, Islamabad
Attention: Head, India
Ref: Case Officer BAKRA

Case Officer and his family arrived safely at his new assignment. They will stay in one of our guest houses until they decide on a permanent home.

Although subject is not a professional spy, he confirmed that he has been well trained by the Factory to do the espionage work which I will assign to him. I reviewed the risks that he will face as an ISI Case Officer. I agreed that he is well qualified to perform his cover assignment. I told him outright that I doubted that he will be successful as a spy. I doubt his motivation to do this work. I doubt his ability to cope with the stress of managing an agent. He has been pushed here by his uncle to obtain a separate assessment of India's progress in nuclear bomb development. I told him that if he makes one mistake, places one of our agents in jeopardy, I will immediately send him home. He confidently stated that he can do both his cover work and his assigned spy tasks.

He understands that he will not spot, assess, or recruit agents.

I reviewed his dual roles in some detail. First, he must develop his cover so that the Indian authorities will not suspect him of his second, more important spying assignment. Unfortunately, it will take him six months to develop his cover before he can perform any work for the ISI. As far as I am concerned, that is wasted time.

Again, he strongly stated that he is both willing and able to conduct spy work. I will hold my evaluation of him until he actually performs as a Case Officer.

At our first meeting, subject's wife appeared rather uncomfortable about her husband's new intelligence assignment. Resigned, perhaps, and wondering if her professor husband really can do spy work, or, fearful that he will be caught doing it. I cannot yet tell whether she is emotionally capable of supporting a spy. I question his wife's motives for returning to her native country.

Signed,
India Control

AMBIKA'S FEAR

November, 1972
Pakistani Guest House
Haus Khas
New Delhi

Ambika was pleased to note that the guest house was furnished and clean.

Located on the second floor above a retail store, it consisted of a combined living-dining room, kitchen, bath and two bedrooms. The overstuffed sofa and two chairs in the living area showed wear but were clean and comfortable. Ali perused the books on the bookshelf, noticing that they had been segregated into English or Urdu sections. The dining area table had been previously set for four people. The small kitchen held a refrigerator, stove, sink, dishware and cooking utensils.

Ambika and Ali brewed tea while Kumar guzzled cola and crackers at the dining table.

"Ali, I really liked that house in Green Park. It is on a quiet street and near the IIT campus in Haus Khas where you will be conducting your interviews with the students and professors. Please tell Akbar that we would like to live in that one."

Kumar piped up, "Yes, I liked that one, too. I liked the tombs down the street. My new friends and I can play bandits and soldiers there."

"Well, then it is two votes for Green Park. I will tell Akbar."

No servants here. Ambika cooked a nice dinner from the food in the refrigerator. Kumar quickly found his bed and fell asleep before his head hit the pillow.

Ambika stood staring out the window onto the street and the park below, imagining Kumar playing with new friends. Ali found a travel book about the sights of New Delhi and read it quietly in a nearby chair.

Suddenly, the emotions which Ambika had controlled all day overwhelmed her. The realization that they were actually in New Delhi on a difficult and dangerous assignment hit her like a freight train. Tears came to her eyes and soon grew to sobs.

Ali got up and put his hands on her shoulders.

"My dear, what is the trouble?"

She turned around to face him.

"I want to go home!" she exclaimed. "I want to go back to Lahore, to my friends, to my house, to my things, to the park where Kumar loved to play with his friends."

"Now, Ambika, we have talked this over and over. In fact, you are home in your own country, in New Delhi where you spent time growing up. You can wear your lovely saris and move about freely here. No more long skirts, baggy pants, and long-sleeved tops with dupatta scarfs. No, we will return to Lahore when my work here is finished."

"I do not care about what I wear as long as I can be with you and Kumar. I love you. I am afraid for you, and for Kumar and me. You are a university professor. You are no spy!"

"Yes, I love you, too, my dear. I have been well trained to do this ISI work. It is very important to my country that I do this."

"Your uncle made you come here. It was his decision, not yours."

Ali soothed, "Yes, my dear, he did ask me to take this assignment, but as I have told you many times before, the actual decision to come here was mine."

"You gave up your comfortable job at the University to do this risky assignment. If you fail here, you will have a hard time returning to the University. Your uncle will see to that."

"Both you and Akbar seem to think that I will fail as a spy. You are both wrong. I will *not* fail here."

Her eyes widened and her jaw dropped as he let slip that Akbar also thought that he would fail as a spy.

"What! Akbar told you that he expects you to fail?"

"Yes, he did. But, I convinced him to let me try to do this secret work. He agreed."

"Please, let's go back home, now, while we still can. I have a feeling that something terrible will happen to us here."

"NO! We are here and we will stay here until my work is completed. Then, we will return to Lahore and the comfortable life you crave. Remember, you were the one to point out that you could see your father when we are in New Delhi. Does that not count for something?"

"Yes, but now I realize that I would rather have a successful husband in Lahore than to have you fail here. I cannot even think of the disgrace and shame if you do not succeed here...If Akbar thinks you will fail, he will not support you, and, you *will* fail!"

Ali soothed, "Akbar promised to give me his full support, no matter what happens. I believe him. He *must* trust me to succeed in this spy business. Akbar surely does not want me to complain to my uncle that he is not supporting me. My complaining to Uncle Ahmed would hurt Akbar's standing with the ISI."

He hugged and consoled her, "My dear, we will return to Pakistan when we are finished here and not before. Just today I pledged to Akbar that I will not fail him. Neither will I fail you."

With that he kissed her, took her hand and led her to the bedroom.

Head down, she followed slowly in his footsteps.

THE INDIAN INTELLIGENCE BUREAU

November, 1972
Indian Intelligence Bureau (IB)
Undisclosed Location
New Delhi

Colonel Bhandari, the head of the Indian Intelligence Bureau, looked out his window to see the panoramic sweep of New Delhi at his feet. In his fifties, he still held the swagger and demeanor of a former Indian Army officer. From his plush leather chair on the top floor he could swivel around to get a clear view of the Parliament building in the foreground and the bustling traffic around the India Gate further away. The rising sun gave the sandstone buildings a special red glow. He was content to sip his freshly brewed black Darjeeling tea for a few more minutes as he ruminated about the day ahead. His "reports" would be showing up this morning, one by one, to brief him about recent security developments. This afternoon after his sparse dal-based vegetarian lunch and daily walk he would brief three of the Lok Sabha parliament members about the recent demonstrations in Kashmir and the Chinese border incursions in Ladakh.

He surveyed the room in which he sat, pleased with what he saw. His roving eyes were often attracted to the three objects hanging on the opposite wall. On the right, a picture of sparsely-clad Mohandas Gandhi at his proverbial spinning wheel.

We do not let you down, Gandhi-ji. We are always vigilant to protect our country. You would be proud of what we have accomplished in just 25 years!

His gaze moved to the painting on the left, of Major General Sir Charles MacGregor, the head of the Intelligence Department for the British Indian Army at Simla in 1885. Bhandari, the historian, knew that the General had established the Intelligence Department to track the Russian incursions from the northwest frontier. Because of the work which Sir Charles initiated the IB could boast that it was one of the oldest intelligence services in the world.

In the middle was his favorite, India's national emblem. It was framed on the wall directly in front of him as he sat in his chair. Every morning as he came into his office he bowed to the three lion Ashoka design, one looking left, one looking right and one looking out. Standing, mouths open as though roaring, the three lions stood majestically on the 24 spoke Ashoka Chakra wheel at the base. The Colonel knew that the blue Ashoka Chakra represented Buddhist symbols and was impressed in the center of the flag of India.

Each day he touched the words under the emblem, "Truth Alone Triumphs", and muttered to himself a prayer to uphold the truth this day.

His gaze moved to the wooden and silk flower design brocade settee and two arm chairs below the wall hangings.

He had recently had the honor of hosting Prime Minister Gandhi for tea, sweets and an informal discussion about her security arrangements. He proudly gave her what advice he could, not knowing her staff that well. She was thrilled to see the Gandhi picture and surprised to see the painting of General MacGregor. She hadn't known that the IB boasted such a long history. She asked where he had bought the low hand-carved teak coffee table and two chokies which sat in front of the settee. She wanted to buy a set of them for her own home. He also told her where she might find the incense he was burning in her honor.

He said a small prayer of thanks for the two ceiling punkas which constantly moved the sometimes stale air around his office. Keeping up with the times, he did recently have air conditioning installed for the top two floors. He still preferred the old system of punkas and desert coolers, though and feared that he was spoiling the 4th floor employees to the detriment of those on the 3rd and 2nd floors. Those poor sods did not yet have air conditioning. He jotted a few lines in his notepad to provide air conditioning for them in the next budget.

Finally, his eyes rested on the large carpet which covered much of the floor of his expansive office. It was a floral design specially made near Varanasi. He did not care a whit about the design. He only cared that the colors of the flag of India, green, white and orange, dominated the carpet. He had insisted on including the six-foot diameter Dharma Chakra Wheel of Law in the center of the carpet. His subordinates knew better than to set foot on the Wheel as they approached his desk.

He was curling his graying handlebar moustache when three knocks on the door interrupted his musings. He knew it was Three.

"Enter," he boomed.

"Three" appeared at the door. He was short, with slightly greying black hair, dark brown in complexion, and was somewhat stooped for his age. When he was out on the streets doing surveillance, he was sometimes mistaken for a poor beggar. He often bragged that he was the average Indian that no one could remember or describe, just a typical blend in the crowd guy. But, those who knew him knew that he was the best head of the IB's domestic counter-intelligence service in the history of the department.

"Come in, Three, and make yourself a cup of tea. Let's take the end chairs. They're more comfortable."

Three poured tea, added two spoons of sugar and milk and moved to a chair. Colonel Bhandari poured a second tea for himself, moved to his chair and placed his cup and saucer and note pad and pencil on the coffee table. The two men settled in comfortably.

"Now, Three, tell me what you have discovered about our foreigners. I am most interested in knowing what those two curious Russians were up to."

"First, Colonel, let me give you a summary of the new foreign entrants during the latest reporting period. We obtained the names and details of 229 foreign passport holders from our immigration officials and border police. None was a tourist. Of that total 105 were diplomatic and the other 124 were technical, business, legal or NGO. Many were on multiple entry visas. We noted those for whom we already have set up dossiers. We have decided to set up new dossiers on the following newly arrived diplomats:

Three new Polish diplomats. Two of them are women. One of the women is a grandmotherly type, the other rather young and beautiful. We have no titles or job descriptions for them yet. We are suspicious that they are intelligence types looking for targets in our government.

A new Pakistani science advisor.

A Chinese trade representative.

"We also noted but did not open a dossier on a new American USAID Assistant Director and a new American officer for their Calcutta consulate. We have decided that the others are low on our list and not worth spending time on now, unless their actions cause us to take notice of them in the future."

"What do you know about the new Pakistani? Maybe we should consider him for a more intensive screening?" Colonel Bhandari asked.

"We know little now. He is 36 years old and born near Hyderabad in Sind Province. He was 11 when India and Pakistan were partitioned. It is interesting that his name is Asaf Ali Khan. Of course, you, the historian of India's independence movement, recognize Asaf Ali as one of our Indian independence leaders during the British times. Our original Asaf Ali was a barrister who protested in the British courts about the British-imposed rules over his people. Like Khan, the original Asaf Ali was a Muslim. This Asaf Ali, I expect, has had some previous army experience. Like other Pakistani diplomats, he is undoubtedly well connected back home. I suspect that he is ISI."

"Let's give him thirty days to get settled. Make a note to have one of our surveillance teams check his movements then. Perhaps you could use what they report."

"As good as done. It is ironic that Pakistani and Indian diplomats today talk to each other in English, our common language. We know that Khan speaks excellent English from the customs report. Your instruction to the customs authorities continues to pay off. We consistently get more information about some of these diplomats of higher interest. The Palam Airport customs officer who interviewed Khan reported that Khan spoke English with an American accent. That says to me that Khan was in America at least for a two-year master's degree which he also likely has obtained. Or, he may have been a family member of a diplomat assigned there. If so, and it's a big if, he will be comfortable with the American diplomats who are here. I would expect him to reach out to Americans as friends and possible professional associates. The customs official also noted that Khan's wife was wearing an expensive Indian-made Punjabi outfit.

"Now, let me turn to the more interesting non-diplomats who arrived recently. All are on two-year, multiple entry visas. None deserve our scrutiny, yet. We have not made dossiers for them. They represent where our country is in its development. A Japanese engineer from Komatsu has been assigned to the Hindustan Group in Bangalore. A Mercedes process engineer arrived to work at the Tata truck facility in Jalalabad. Doctors Without Borders have a replacement for one of their family doctors working in Calcutta. An American-based international corporation has assigned a new sales representative here.

"Colonel, you asked about our two Russian diplomats. They arrived six weeks ago, their purpose unknown. In keeping with our policy we put them at the top of our list for surveillance. We have followed them off and on in ten to twelve hour shifts. We rotated the Kism and Weja surveillance teams here in Delhi so the Russians did not suspect they were being under surveillance. The Koti team followed them on their travels. We have no indication that the Russians were aware of our surveillance.

"They visited the tire facility in Faridabad, the diesel engine piston plant in Nagpur and the car assembly plant in Poona. We concluded that they wanted technical information about car manufacturing. They also met here in New Delhi with a Fanuc robot rep, a Japanese national based in Singapore. He flew in for a two-day meeting with them at the Oberoi Hotel. The Russians talked with him and the others they met during their visits in English. Their technical English was rated very good. The Russians flew yesterday to Tokyo. Fanuc is in Japan. At least, their ticketed final destination is Tokyo. The plane stopped in route in Bangkok and Hong Kong."

Three continued. "I think they're KGB, possibly 4th or 6th Directorate. The Russian Autovaz car company would not have either the inclination or foreign exchange to send someone out of country to learn from competition."

"Good work, Three. Considering that the Russians are currently in great favor with our lovely prime minister, I am grateful that the Russians were not aware of your surveillance. These two obviously were not any threat to our national security. Do you have anything else of interest for me?"

"Yes, Colonel, I do. We're getting feedback from the diplomatic cocktail circuit that a foreign intelligence service is trying to recruit one or more of our high ranking military people. We're not sure whether it's the Pakistanis or Chinese, or even the Israelis. You remember the drubbing we gave the Pakistani military last March when East and West Pakistan split into two. Cocktail gossip says that the Pakistani generals are angry and want to know more about our military preparedness. They possibly fear that we are developing a nuclear weapon. They will develop one, too, if we do. I request that "Four" step up his observation of our military leaders. He could focus on the higher Army types who are also Muslims."

"I will tell him. By the way, perhaps you should give the Chinese trade representative the same 30-day review as Khan. What is his name?"

"Wong Yonbang, Colonel. I will add him for review."

The Colonel jotted Wong's name on his note pad.

The Colonel stood. "Remember, Three, you are responsible for looking after the foreigners in our midst. I am here merely to advise you. I am always available to you. You are doing excellent work."

"Thank you, Colonel. I appreciate your confidence." Three quietly left.

Colonel Bhandari returned to his chair at his desk. His thoughts turned to the atomic bomb. He remembered that China had some years before successfully tested a nuclear weapon. Perhaps 1964? China became the fifth UN member to have a nuclear weapon. Ironic, the countries with nuclear weapons were the ones with permanent UN Security Council seats. First, the Americans, then the Soviets, then Britain, then France and finally China.

He meditated. *I wonder whether Prime Minister Gandhi has made a decision to develop and test a nuclear weapon. I hope not. Three is correct that once we do, Pakistan will follow. We certainly have the technical know-how. We have been doing nuclear research and development for the last twenty years and operating those nuclear reactors in Trombay since the early 1960's. We do not need to spend valuable government money on such foolishness as a bomb. We have other priorities from our latest five-year plan.*

I must get Two to give me an update on Pakistan's possible development of a bomb.

He made a few notes on the notepad.

A single knock on the door interrupted his thoughts.

"Enter," the Colonel bellowed.

"One" entered. Ramrod straight, with a turban and full beard, the six foot Sikh came forward and bowed slightly. Colonel Bhandari knew that One was also wearing a bracelet, carrying a comb and a concealed knife, as required of all Sikhs, known as the fiercest fighters in the Indian Army.

"I'm glad to see you, One. Please take some tea and join me in a comfortable chair."

"I trust that I am not late for our appointment, Colonel. You seemed deep in thought as I entered."

Colonel Bhandari again hauled himself out of his desk chair and moved to the one opposite.

"One, you are a most perceptive person. That is why you are so good at what you do. You keep me and our government up to date about our internal security problems. You describe them well, though our meek politicians are too often loath to address them."

The Sikh replied, "We can only do our best, provide sound information and leave the policymaking to our elected leaders. I learned that well in the Army."

One and the Colonel settled in the two facing chairs near the settee.

"So, please give me a briefing about the Naxalites and the situation in Kashmir, as well as any other trouble spots you see."

"Sir, we are tracking the Communist Party of India-Marxist. The CPIM calls for class struggle and violent revolution. That message is gaining traction in West Bengal."

"As I recall, One, the CPIM split from the original Communist Party of India sometime in 1964."

"Yes, the CPIM accused their CPI brethren of bowing to Moscow's instructions. The Soviets were developing a closer relationship with our leaders and did not want the local Communists to hamper that. Moscow essentially told the CPI to behave. The CPI has stated publically that their objectives can be met peacefully through the vote."

Always the historian, the Colonel replied, "The CPI has been here since the 1920's. That was shortly after Lenin took power in Russia. Interesting, the CPI has recently supported P.M. Gandhi and her Congress Party. They are legitimate, not revolutionaries. So, please tell me what the CPIM is up to."

"Sir, Charu Majumdar, even in death, continues to grow in importance as a spiritual leader of the CPIM. That incident four years ago in the small village of Naxalbari has blossomed into a large threat to our government. Majumdar preached to the lower classes to overthrow the land owners and the corrupt politicians. The tribespeople in the countryside are taking up his teachings by advocating a revolution. Majumdar decreed that the CPIM should assassinate their class enemies. He targeted businessmen, land holders, university professors, politicians and police officers."

Colonel Bhandari grimaced, furrowing his brows. "What happened to Majumdar? You said that he is dead."

"Yes, sir. He was captured last July and died in jail. The police are now looking for Kanu Sanyal, a CPIM member and avowed Communist. We believe that Sanyal has solicited help from the Communist leaders in China.

"Sir, when you talk to the Prime Minister and members of parliament about this issue, please be your usual forceful self. Here is a white paper to use in your discussions. We clearly describe the situation and strongly recommend a twofold policy to eradicate this threat before it grows into a horrible monster. First, prosecute the lawbreakers. Second, answer to the complaints of the underclass. We cannot redistribute land but we can initiate programs to educate the poor and provide housing, sanitation, water and jobs. If they are revolting because they feel oppressed, we have to relieve that oppression."

One passed the document to his boss.

"If we do not stop this violence now in West Bengal, we predict that it will spread to other rural areas in India. That could be a fire of such conflagration that the government may not be able to put it out. We see this as the number one short and long term threat to our country. It is not going away tomorrow."

"Thank you, One. You have done excellent work here. I agree that this is a serious situation. I will compel our politicians to take note and do something before the situation spreads to other parts of the country and becomes unmanageable."

The older man pressed on, "Now, what is happening in Kashmir?"

"We continue to see the usual street demonstrations by the Muslim community which are weather and tourist related. No one wants to demonstrate in Kashmir's cold winter. The tourist season starts in May and lasts through August. No one wants to turn off the tourists, so there are no marches then. Now is again the time for a few demonstrations. The rabble-rousers are funded by the Pakistani authorities on the other side of the Line of Control. If we throw the current trouble-makers in jail, new ones will arise. We find it more prudent to encourage these troublemakers to be peaceful though we put the rock-throwers in jail for a day to cool off."

"One, can you give us a solution to our Kashmiri problem?"

"I have none because there are no good options to negotiate. As you know, the Maharaja of Kashmir, a Hindu, tried to align all of Kashmir to India at the time of the partition. But, most of his people were Muslims. Their demonstrations started the first Indo-Pakistani war. Now we have a partition along the Line of Control. Part is Pakistani-controlled; part is Indian-controlled. Neither India nor Pakistan is willing for Kashmir to be an independent state. India is unwilling to evict the Muslims from its region. They make good businessmen and they pay taxes. Pakistan wants total control over all of Kashmir. India refuses. We have a perpetual stalemate."

Colonel Bhandari stroked his mustache.

"One, you have as usual given me a lot to meditate over. Do you and your staff see any other possible threats?"

"One more, Colonel. We know that some influential Indians in the Madras area are providing money to their cousins, the Tamils, in Ceylon. As you know, the British over one hundred years ago imported people from south India to work in Ceylon. The British called them Tamils, people from south India. The Tamils are concentrated in northern Ceylon. The current Tamils want more autonomy from their government in Colombo. The more money that flows, the more the Tamils increase the pressure on their own government in Colombo. We can soon expect more pressure on our government to stop the money flow from India."

The Colonel wrote a few lines on his notepad.

"We are done, then. Thank you, One. And, remember, you are responsible to report and make recommendations about our internal threats. I am here always as your advisor. Please know my door is always open to you. Please keep me informed. I do not like surprises and neither does the Lok Sabha."

"You know, Colonel, I am always available to you. At your service."

One rose, half bowed, turned smartly and left the room, closing the door quietly behind him.

Moments later, two knocks on the door interrupted the Colonel's scribbling. He knew that it was Two.

"Enter," he bellowed.

"Two" appeared in a brown safari bush shirt and matching brown slacks. The retired ambassador ambled awkwardly to the edge of the Wheel of Law but was careful not to touch it as he placed his cane on the carpet. He gave the Colonel a half-salute with his free hand.

"Mr. Ambassador, please take a cup of tea and find your chair. I am most interested to hear what you have learned about Pakistan's attempts to develop a nuclear weapon, and the recent incursions of the Chinese army in Ladakh."

Two found his usual chair. The Colonel plodded after him.

"Colonel, Ladakh first. The Chinese Army has withdrawn from its forward positions. They are no longer on territory we consider ours. That is good news. We believe they have departed for the winter months and will be back in the spring again to bother us. As you know, the Ladakh part of Kashmir averages over 14,000 feet above sea level so is not a very hospitable place. Our Army has decided to push forward now to the line we consider our boundary. We'll be in so-called Chinese territory. When spring comes, we will move back part of the distance to our old boundary. By so doing, we are establishing a new boundary between us. Perhaps the Chinese will not force us to retreat further to our original line. Come spring, we may, just, reach an unofficial stalemate. We would welcome a new boundary we both can live with. By the way, I am informed that our Border Roads has a project to buy several earthmoving machines to improve the Ladakh roads. When completed, the Army can then move troops around faster where they are most needed.

"Now, Pakistan. As you know, Munir Ahmed Khan is the key to Pakistan's development of a nuclear bomb. He was working for the International Atomic Energy Agency in Switzerland. He has now returned to Pakistan and is the head of Pakistan's Atomic Energy Commission. We know from his public pronouncements that he favors Pakistan's building a nuclear weapon using plutonium, not uranium. Pakistan has several operating reactors which may provide the spent plutonium. Pakistan is now negotiating with a French company for a large reprocessing plant for its spent plutonium. That fits with Khan's preference. Our latest intelligence report states that

Pakistan will build a bomb, and it will be a plutonium device, but that it is years in the future."

"Tell me, Mr. Ambassador, why would a country prefer plutonium as the fuel for a bomb?"

"Because it is an easier path. Plutonium comes as a by-product of a nuclear reactor which uses natural Uranium U-238 as the fuel. U-238 is not fissionable. That is, it cannot be used for a bomb. Of course, the plutonium has to be processed to a very high degree of purity for it to be used in a bomb. Once plutonium is extracted, it is a rather straightforward if laborious process to refine it to bomb purity. A Uranium bomb also requires a high degree of purity. But, in the latter case, it is the fissionable Uranium U-235 which is needed for a bomb. U-235 is found in nature but at less than one percent of all of the natural Uranium. So, many centrifuges must be used in cascades to separate the scarce U-235 from the abundant U-238. I am told that the Uranium process is both more complex and technically difficult. Of course, I say this as a diplomat, not as a scientist."

"Has Pakistan signed the Nuclear Non-Proliferation Treaty?"

"No, it has not. The five permanent UN Security Council members, America, the U.S.S.R., China, England and France, all now possess nuclear weapons. They were the ones who sponsored the NPT in the first place, stipulating that other countries may develop nuclear power only for peaceful purposes. At last count about 140 countries have signed the NPT. Israel, Pakistan, North Korea and a few others, including India, have not.

"The problem with the NPT is that as soon as a country gets the technical know-how for peaceful uses of nuclear power, it is a small if rather laborious and time-consuming step to build a bomb. The International Atomic Energy Agency is the global inspector but is allowed to inspect only those sites that the host country declares as nuclear. So, a country can still develop a bomb in secret without the IAEA or world knowing about it."

"Thank you. Now, please give me an update on our perpetual question. What about the two hostile countries we face? China already has a nuclear bomb. Pakistan may be building one. What would happen if China threatened us with a nuclear weapon? Perhaps over Ladakh? What if China actually uses it against us?"

"Our intelligence estimate states that China will not use a bomb except if her soil is attacked. Through diplomatic channels we also know that the Chinese leaders do not consider Ladakh a territory worth fighting over. Frankly, neither do we. A nuclear weaponized Pakistan would use a bomb on us only if it feels it is pushed into a corner by India. We have warned both our politicians and military leaders numerous times not to push a hostile Pakistan into a corner."

"Do you have any other noteworthy foreign intelligence to discuss?"

"No, Colonel. We have the usual ongoing complaints from our overseas Indian nationals about discrimination, but nothing worth bringing to your attention."

"Thank you, Mr. Ambassador. Please keep me informed about the major foreign issues you are tracking so I may pass our concerns to our politicians."

Two departed, his cane in the crook of his arm and his IB embossed cup and saucer still in hand.

Donovan and Emily Move In

November, 1972
J Block
Green Park
New Delhi

"Sahib, the household goods are just now coming!" Har Saroop exclaimed from his perch on the flat roof of the newly rented house.

Donovan and Emily had decided to rent this recently built three-bedroom bungalow in a newer part of New Delhi. Donovan from here had convenient access to Mehrauli Road and the Ring Road to his office in Old Delhi. They felt safe behind a six-foot brick wall which totally enclosed the compound. The house had enough amenities including a fireplace in the living room for the few cold months, a small patch of grass in the front, and a driveway to the garage and maid's quarters in the rear. Best of all, it was affordable on Donovan's rupee salary.

Donovan trapped the soccer ball Matt and he had been kicking across the lawn. He nudged it toward the recovering banana tree at the edge of the flower garden along the wall. He was told that the front gate was often open during the house's recent construction. A stray cow wandered in and had been found feasting on the banana leaves.

They strolled the thirty feet to the front gate, opened it, and looked down the street.

Two bullocks ambled along at a snail's pace, one behind the other. Each pulled a cart with an ocean-going wooden crate. The heads of the bullocks swayed back and forth with each slow step, drawing the Griffin containers foot by foot closer to the house. A cowbell attached to one of the bullock's necks tinkled in cadence to their rhythm. A thin Indian man in a white dhoti garment and a white turban walked beside each bullock holding the bullock's reins in one hand and a long stick in the other.

"Dad! Our furniture is coming but not on a truck!" five-year old Matt exclaimed.

"Yes, son, no eighteen wheelers here."

The first cart passed the front gate and the driver skillfully backed the bullock and cart into the driveway. Donovan read on the side of the crate:

DONOVAN GRIFFIN

THE EARTHMOVING CORPORATION

NEW DELHI, INDIA

The driver stopped the cart adjacent to the verandah and proceeded without a word to remove the end of the large crate. The second driver hunkered down, flatfooted, beside his bullock just outside the gate to wait his turn.

The wooden crates had been specially-built to accommodate the Griffin's furniture by carpenters at Donovan's company. The carpenters had placed heavy tarpaper over the top and sides to prevent rain from damaging the contents.

The two drivers easily took instructions from Har Saroop, the newly-hired cook and titular head of the servants. Har Saroop spoke English well and acted as the translator with all of the servants. Ram, the gardener-night watchman, also helped unload. The servants dispatched the furniture quickly to the proper places in the house under the watchful eye of Emily, the M'em-Sahib. Matt immersed himself in the box containing his toys. He excitedly showed them, one by one, to Mary, the ayah. He'd been cooped up for weeks in one room at the Claridge's Hotel without them.

As they put the last of the furniture in place, Ram, through Har Saroop, asked if he could take one of the oceangoing crates. Wanting to keep a servant happy, and having no further use for it, Donovan agreed. Donovan figured he might break up the wood for firewood. Ram was visibly overwhelmed, almost in tears. He repeatedly thanked both Donovan and Emily in his own tongue.

Emily surveyed the furniture. Everything in place, she smiled, turned to Donovan and gave him a big hug.

"Well, dear. We are home. At last, we have our familiar, if used, things. Now, all you have to do is to connect the refrigerator, stove and three air conditioners we brought with us." She poked him in the chest with her finger.

"Yes, love, I will get Har Saroop to help me organize the kitchen appliances and place the three air conditioners in the bedroom windows. The refrigerator is easy as we brought a transformer for it. We just plug it in. I will have to get propane tanks for the stove. Remember, I had to pay baksheesh in American dollars from my Travelers Letter of Credit (1) in order to clear the new air conditioners through customs."

"Har Saroop is a gem. He has already showed me the open meat market just around the corner. I held my nose and swatted the flies away as he led me through the stalls. I was amazed to see a butcher sitting on a raised platform cutting meat with a cleaver he was holding between his toes. I had Saroop buy some water buffalo for tomorrow's dinner. That is, if you can get a propane tank for the stove by then."

Donovan looked lovingly at his petite, curvaceous, blonde wife. He admired her courage by agreeing to come with him to such a different place as India. He wondered sometimes if their marriage would hold up to the continuing stress of living in such a demanding place.

"I've arranged for the propane man to come this afternoon. We should have a working stove before tomorrow's dinner. You will soon have a kitchen that works. That will be necessary because I leave on Thursday for Bombay and Colombo."

The couple sat down and held hands on the sofa in the living room. They sighed simultaneously.

"Well, love, we are doing it. We are here in a totally different and strange place. This is what we were dreaming about when I took the TEC job and we moved to Dubuque."

"Yes, dear. We knew that we had to start somewhere in this big world. We just did not contemplate India. Now that we're here, I am finding daily living quite challenging. Mind you, I am up to it. After all, this is the excitement we both were looking for. I just hate your traveling so much."

"When I asked you to marry me, you said 'Yes, but just don't be a traveling salesman.' Fortunately, our mutual desire to experience the adventure of living in a foreign land helped to overcome your objection. I am good at what I do and will excel even in this difficult environment. That involves constant travel."

"Yes, I know, dear. We have been here only for six weeks and you have already visited all of your distributor offices around the country and even visited your distributor in Colombo twice."

"Love, I have to go where I can obtain sales. Ceylon is a great opportunity. The River Valleys Development Board there wants to buy eight large bulldozers. I am working hard to get that order. I also am working on an order right here in New Delhi for the Rajasthan Canals Project. Problem is, I cannot get any business until the project is funded with U.S. Dollars, Yen, or British Pounds. Venkey told me just last week not to spend any time on the Beas Dam Project because it will not get any foreign exchange to purchase imported equipment."

"Please, dear, remind me why you visit Colombo over a weekend."

"Ceylon uses a Buddhist Poya calendar which is out of synch with our seven-day week. So, I can work in Bombay for a few days, fly to Colombo to work our normal weekend, and fly back through Madras to work another few days there. That makes me more efficient."

"Well, dear, if that is what you want to do. Some may think you are crazy to want to work all the time."

"My persistence will eventually get us out of here to a better position with TEC. Please bear with me on this."

"Yes, dear, I am with you for the long haul."

Needing to change the conversation, Donovan said, "Love, when you are ready for guests, I'd like to invite Venky and Sharda over. They have been so kind to us when we were stuck at Claridge's waiting for our household goods."

"I'd also like to invite Claus and Elna. They were so gracious to us after we met them at Claridge's. Matt loves them as his stand-in grandparents. We can play bridge with them after dinner."

"Emily, are you comfortable being in charge of the servants?"

"Trust me, I will be the best M'em-Sahib ever!"

As promised, the propane man pedaled into Donovan's driveway that afternoon on his tricycle. Five bright, red propane tanks nestled on a wooden platform between the two back wheels.

Donovan started the conversation.

"I see that you have full tanks of propane. I would like to purchase two tanks and obtain refills on a regular basis. How can I do that?"

"Sahib, we do not sell the tanks but rent them. In order for you to become a customer, you first have to give me two empty propane tanks."

"I do not understand. We are new here so do not have empty tanks to give you."

Shaking his head back and forth, he replied in singsong English, "That is a very big problem, Sahib. I can fix, but later. I return by six o'clock tonight." Without a further word he turned the tricycle and rode off.

Sure enough, he showed up that night with two empty and two full tanks.

"Hello, Sahib. I have found two empty tanks for you. Here they are. But, they have cost me some rupees." As he smiled from ear to ear, he showed his missing front teeth.

The newly wise Donovan pulled some rupees from his pocket and paid the propane man baksheesh. Donovan took the two full tanks and fitted one of them to the stove. Emily was delighted.

One evening a few days later Donovan took a different route home from his office in Old Delhi. He was surprised to see his wooden crate with his name, TEC, and New Delhi in the middle of an open field not three blocks from his house. Donovan recognized Ram's wife and two small children crouched in front of the crate, cooking something over an open fire. Ram and his family were living in Donovan's crate.

(1) Credit cards had not yet been invented. Donovan used a U.S. $5,000.00 Travelers Letter of Credit (L/C) to pay for his business expenses. When he needed local funds, he took the L/C to an Indian or Ceylonese correspondent bank and cashed a dollar amount from the L/C. The bank issued him money in local currency. He accounted to TEC for his expenses monthly. He requested a new L/C from TEC's corporate headquarters when his L/C was almost exhausted.

CALCUTTA DEMONSTRATIONS

November, 1972
American Embassy
Shantipath
Chanakyapuri
New Delhi

Graham Smith sat upright in his cushioned chair. He never slouched although he himself confessed that he was adding grey hair and a small paunch. He looked up from his desk to see Jenny's full figure gracing his open door. He caught a scent of her perfume.

"Jay Jay is here to see you, sir," she advised.

"Come on in, Jay Jay," Graham replied.

A rather disheveled Jay Jay appeared with a paper in his hand. He stood on one foot and then the other in front of Graham's desk. He wiped his free hand on his shirt and then through his short crew cut.

"You need to see this, Boss. It just came in over the scrambler. It is a PRIORITY from Pete in Calcutta. One of his agents just reported about a mass demonstration two weeks from now. The three largest trade unions are organizing it. The CPIM has not been invited to participate but the CPIM intends to turn a peaceful demonstration into a riot. Pete is asking for instructions. Here are the details."

Still standing, Jay Jay handed the paper to Graham, nodded and turned to leave.

"Thanks, Jay Jay. But, wait a minute."

Jay Jay stopped, turned and faced Graham. He looked down at his feet as though his shoes were untied.

"You have been working overtime for the last four days. You transmitted many internal documents from that recently held Third World Movement conference. Please take the next two days off. Get some rest. Spend some time with your two wonderful kids and your wife. If anything urgent comes up, we will call you."

"Boss, I really appreciate that. Thank you. I will do so beginning tomorrow. But, first, what would you like to advise Pete?"

Graham's eyes moved to the message from Calcutta.

"Let me read the dispatch, then I will draft instructions for you to send to Pete."

"OK, Boss. I will not leave here today until I have sent Pete your response."

Graham looked up.

"Jay Jay, you are the most dedicated person in this building. Thank you for your total commitment!"

"That's my job, Boss."

Jay Jay walked out of Graham's office with a somewhat bouncier step.

Graham made a few notes as he read the dispatch. He picked up his phone and dialed a direct number.

"This is Colonel Bhandari."

"Colonel Bhandari, this is Graham Smith at the American Embassy. I may have some interesting information for you."

"I am always delighted to talk to you, Mr. Smith. Of course, I know who you are. I am still thankful for the information you gave me a few months ago about the plot in Kashmir."

"I have just been informed that the three largest Calcutta trade unions are planning a mass demonstration two weeks from today. The Calcutta police are already aware of the peaceful demonstration as they have given permission for it to take place. The demonstration will, as usual, demand social justice, higher pay and protest inequality. What the police do not know, perhaps, is that the Communist Party of India-Marxist plans to turn the peaceful demonstration into a riot. The demonstration is planned to end in the downtown financial district. My source says that the CPIM has targeted three of the banks in the district. As the demonstration ends, CPIM hit squads from within the demonstrator ranks will attack the banks and cause as much destruction as possible both outside on the street and inside the banks."

Graham paused to catch a breath. "I thought you should know about this CPIM plan."

"Mr. Smith, we will be sure that the Calcutta police are forewarned. I sincerely appreciate your sharing this information with us."

Colonel Bhandari made a few notes on his ever-present note pad.

"By the way, Mr. Smith. I see that your agency is getting very bad press even from a few of the prime minister's cabinet members. Would you like me to put in a good word with her about your ongoing cooperation with this office?"

"Thank you for your thoughtfulness, Colonel. No, I would rather have those closest to the action be given whatever credit may be due. In this case, the Calcutta police should receive credit, assuming they are able to upset the CPIM's riot plans."

"Very well, then."

Colonel Bhandari hung up and immediately called One for an urgent meeting.

Graham drafted a message to Pete suggesting that Pete tell his local police contact about the CPIM's intentions. Jenny carried the message to Jay Jay for immediate transmission.

Graham mused about his conversation with Colonel Bhandari, confident that the open sharing of information would keep them indebted to each other.

Vietnam Breakthrough

January, 1973
Late Evening
American Embassy
Shantipath
Chanakyapuri
New Delhi

Jay Jay roused Shamus from a deep sleep. He urged Shamus to pick up and hurry the boss over to the Embassy, now. Jay Jay had just received an "eyes only" IMMEDIATE for Graham.

Shamus apologized to Graham as the two raced through the wide, almost empty New Delhi streets in Shamus's car. Neither could understand why Jay Jay refused to call Graham at home. Perhaps Jay Jay wanted both Shamus and Graham to be present to read the IMMEDIATE message. Lucky for them, Shamus and his wife lived next door to Graham and Melanie in the Diplomatic Enclave.

The Marine guard at the Embassy was ever awake. He quickly recognized and passed both men through the main door. The two men signed in and sprinted to the Embassy's message center where Jay Jay was still working.

Jay Jay told everyone who would listen, "I communicate with the world." Tonight, he was. He used all of the transmitters and wires on the top of the building.

"Thanks for coming in so quickly, Boss. Here is the message. It is quite long. Perhaps you and Shamus can read it in the conference room. I'll wait in case you need to send an immediate reply."

"Thanks, Jay Jay. We'll read it and write a response now."

"Of course, Boss."

"Shamus, this is a message from the Saigon Chief of Station."

Graham sat in one of the plush conference room chairs, holding the lengthy message in both hands. Shamus stood looking over his shoulder, trying also to read the message.

"What's up with Saigon?" Shamus asked.

"There has been a breakthrough in the Kissinger-Le Duc Tho negotiations. It seems that they have finally agreed for us to pull our troops out of South Vietnam by sometime next March. There is no mention of the North pulling their troops out of the South. As a result, the Saigon Chief is, correctly, I think, predicting that the South's situation will deteriorate quickly as we get closer to that deadline. He wants to get our Company people (1) out of harm's way, and fast. He plans on pulling them out in stages, beginning with the ones in the northern part of South Vietnam and Camranh Bay. He wants us, Bangkok, Seoul and Manila to take some of them for up to two weeks, temporary quarters, until Langley can find a more permanent place for them. It sounds like a good plan. You know what will happen as soon as our soldiers leave. It will be mass panic and a lot of retributions."

Shamus sat down in the chair next to Graham's so he could better read the message. "There will be no place for us'ns to hide. Not to be cowardly, but it is better that we get our people out before the last of our troops."

Graham pointed at a line about halfway down the printed page. "The Saigon Chief does not say how many will be coming our way. Nor, does he say when. Where could we bunk, say, a total of twenty of our own?"

"Let's forewarn three of the best hotels in town to expect our guests sometime over the next three months. We can use some of those blocked rupees to pay for the rooms. We can never in a lifetime use all of the Indian rupee payments for the tons and tons of wheat and rice that USAID has shipped here."

Shamus reflected for a second, then continued. "Also, we should not count on them being here just for two weeks. Let's plan on their being here for three months. The grapevine tells me that most of these poor guys, once they get used to the good life of the pools and bars of the Taj, Oberoi, or Kismet Hotel, will be yanked back home where they will be given a hug, kiss, and their separation papers. After all, they are now part of a war which is now over. I hate to say it, but, for many of them, their usefulness with the Company is over."

"As always, I value your advice and thoughtfulness. Tomorrow, please tell Jenny to forewarn three of the best hotels. Please arrange for rupee payments in advance. I will make sure that these men have valid three-month tourist visas before they arrive. I will also ask the Saigon Chief to give more details on a timetable and to send us the first group he pulls out. They will have cooler weather evacuating to Manila or Seoul in the summer months."

Graham wrote a reply to Saigon and gave it to Jay Jay for transmission.

Graham and Shamus nodded to the Marine as they left the building. Jay Jay sent Graham's reply to Saigon and left soon thereafter.

As the two drove back together to their adjacent houses, Shamus asked, "Say, Boss. Do you think Christopher will come this way? I am sure that our people in Laos will also be pulled out."

"Let's see who is sent to us. Both Melanie and I would be ecstatic to see our son again in a safe place. He wasn't satisfied with a stint in the Marines. He needed more interesting and risky work, much to his mother's chagrin. He's just like me in that regard. It has been almost two years since the Company assigned him to work with the Hmong tribesmen. It's about time for him to rotate home anyway. Shamus, I am not going to tell Melanie that Christopher may come here. She would get her hopes up, perhaps for no reason."

(1) Karnow, Stanley. *Vietnam, A History*. New York: Penguin, 1984. Print, page 547, 616-617. The CIA's Phoenix Program badly battered the Communist South's political organization by breaking down the Vietcong's rural structure.

ALI'S PROPOSAL

January, 1973
Pakistan High Commission
"The Palace"
Shantipath
Chanakyapuri
New Delhi

When Ali appeared at the open door of his office at the High Commission, Akbar looked up from his paperwork. He produced his most affable smile.

"Come in, Ali! I have been expecting you. Let's go into my conference room where we will not be disturbed."

The two entered a sparse, small room. Akbar closed the door. The room held only a table and six swivel chairs. A faded carpet covered the floor. The room was devoid of any other decoration. No paintings, no pictures, no portrait of Prime Minister Bhutto. One small window faced the Ambassador's private residence in the back of the property.

The two settled into two chairs opposite each other across the small table.

"First, Ali, tell me. Is that rental house in Green Park suitable?"

"Yes, the house is very suitable, Akbar. Ambika is making good friends in the neighborhood. We have enrolled Kumar in the Delhi Day School. He comes home with good stories and school papers every day. Of course, Ambika is delighted to be so close to her father who is here in New Delhi about half of the time. He, as you know, must also visit Kerala to keep ties with his voters there."

"How are your visits to the IIT campuses working out?"

"I have visited five so far. I am impressed with what I have found. I have met great professors who know their material and how to teach it and very engaging students. When I say that I am a professor at Lahore University, some of the students do not recognize that Lahore is in Pakistan, no longer in India. I do not tell them otherwise. I have done my best to write fair evaluations. I trust that my Dean has received them. Getting to the IIT campus here is easiest. It's about a ten-minute drive from my house."

Akbar swung his swivel chair to the right and left. He looked Ali straight in the eye.

"Yes, you have been working hard on your cover. You are writing very useful and detailed reports about the IIT Universities. I just received a message from your Dean who is impressed with your reports, as am I. He also advised that the Economic Counselor at the Indian High Commission in Islamabad called him. The Indian diplomat said he wanted to talk to you. The Dean regretted to tell him that you were on a sabbatical assignment in New Delhi for some months. The Indian seemed satisfied. Ali, I told you that an Indian official would check your University background."

"Still, Akbar, I am anxious and excited to get to work on my real assignment. Please tell me when I can start."

Akbar sat back in his chair and crossed his arms.

"I certainly appreciate your willingness. We may turn the Trombay agent over to you in May. We have not yet gotten the full commitment of the agent we would have you handle here in New Delhi. We are still not sure that this agent will cooperate with us. By May, we will know if the New Delhi agent is ready. By then, you will have an impeccable cover. The IB will not bother you."

"Akbar, I will willingly wait until May to start working with the agents but I do ask you now for a favor. Will you allow me to contact the CIA person at the American Embassy here? He may have more information about India's program to develop the bomb. I will suggest to him that we share information for our common good. I will do so as the Pakistani Science Advisor, not as an ISI spy."

Akbar coursed his hand through his tousled hair.

"The CIA spy would immediately see through your Science Advisor story. You would be revealing to a foreigner, an American CIA agent, that you are also a spy. He might, for some favor of the Indian government, expose you to the Indian authorities. No, I do not think that is a good idea. Let's not complicate our original plan. Besides, even if I allowed you to do so, how would you contact him? You cannot just walk down the street to the American Embassy and ask for the CIA officer. Your Pakistani cover would be blown by the Indian security around that Embassy."

Ali moved forward in his chair.

"I will wait for what we called in the Army a target of opportunity. I will find, somehow, an American who does not work at the Embassy, someone who can act as a middle man for me."

"I do not like this idea, Ali."

Ali leaned toward Akbar, his forearm on the table.

"Consider this, Akbar. We already have unsubstantiated indications, only indications, that the Trombay Lab is developing a nuclear bomb. Pakistan cannot do much to stop it short of all-out war. But, if we can convince the Americans that India truly is developing a bomb, we may be able to get the Americans to stop it before an explosion occurs. Look, the CIA agent may be able to prod the American Ambassador to ask Prime Minister Gandhi if she has yet approved a nuclear test. If she says no, and it then happens, she will have lied to one of the most important foreign diplomats in New Delhi. There will surely be bad repercussions from the Americans. If she says yes to his question, she will then suffer consequences from the Americans *before* a bomb blast, just to force the Indians not to set off a bomb. Either way, the Americans may be able to stop the P.M. from approving a test. They would at the least be mad at the P.M. And, she would know it."

Akbar sat back and stroked his chin, pondering whether such an action might cause Ali to be kicked out of the country, thus facilitating his preference to acquire a more professional spy.

"Hmmm. That might be worth your contacting the CIA agent. Ali, I agree. Just be sure that you achieve *one* and *only* one outcome. Get the American Ambassador to ask P.M. Gandhi about a bomb before it is set off. We do not want other complications to our plan."

"Thank you, Akbar."

Ali left the High Commission, thinking about how and where to find an American, any American.

AKBAR'S REACTION

ADMIN
ROUTINE
28 January, 1973
TO: ISI, Islamabad
Attention: Head, India
Ref: Case Officer BAKRA

Subject is working his cover. He has been well received by his Indian counterparts and has sent regular reports back to his home contact. He has not attracted the attention of the Indian Intelligence Bureau. He seems to be clean at this time.

At our 22 January meeting subject asked me if he could contact the CIA person at the American Embassy here. His purpose would have the CIA officer convince the American ambassador that India is, indeed, developing a bomb. He wants to get Ambassador Moynihan to call out Prime Minister Gandhi about the bomb before it is detonated. I agreed, on one stipulation. That his contact with the CIA person does, indeed, result in the Ambassador calling out the PM before bomb detonation. If his contact produces other results, I reserve the opportunity to send subject home immediately and request a professional replacement from the Factory.

Signed,
India Control

SHIREE MEETS RAVI

February, 1973
IAF Polo and Riding Club
Delhi Cantonment
New Delhi

For some reason, Shiree's mare refused to leave her stall. No matter how much her mistress coaxed and pulled, Namaste was not budging. Shiree wondered if it might be due to the injection to help her conceive a new colt.

She then realized that someone else was also leading out another horse just four stalls away. She turned to see a handsome young man in a bright yellow shirt with the number 2 on front and back leading a thoroughbred towards her.

"Sorry, I believe my horse has spooked yours. I see you are riding a nice Indian half-bred," he said. Shiree was surprised to hear his American accent.

"She won't come out of her stall. Perhaps after you pass, she may be more willing. You are dressed to play polo today."

He noted her excellent English accent.

"Yes, we are playing against the Gurgaon Polo Club. If you wish, after you have exercised your horse, come to watch the rest of the game."

"I just may do that. I love to watch polo matches. I first need to get my horse properly prepared for her dressage event in two weeks' time."

"I hope to see you later, then... Shiree." He slowly walked his horse past Namaste's stall.

Shiree knew he'd noticed her name on the stall door but wondered what his might be. He appeared about six feet tall, lean, and had long black hair, a small moustache, a straight nose and wide smile. She liked his sparkling eyes and wondered if his thoroughbred might be a good match for her mare.

As she pondered, her horse left her stall without further prompting.

Shiree had watched Ravi make the winning score a few minutes before the end of the sixth and last chukker, and he'd invited her to join him for a quiet lunch at the IAF Polo and Riding Club's restaurant. Part of the old hangar, a relic of World War Two, had been converted into what an Englishman would have called a tea and crumpets palace. There were tables for perhaps forty people at one end of the hangar. An attendant in a mock Indian Air Force uniform waited on them.

Over a curry lunch Shiree learned that Ravi Bhatra, unmarried, had graduated in Electrical Engineering from the Massachusetts Institute of Technology in Boston, spent two years with a communications company in Canada, six years in the Indian Air Force, and had worked for the past four years in one of his family's new corporations. Ravi, she found, was in charge of developing television in India for his new Bharat Communications Company. Shiree sensed his excitement about the prospects for his new business.

He enthused, "I learned a lot about television and the new mobile car phones when I worked in Canada with Northern Telecoms. I have maintained contact with my old boss since I returned to India. He asked me to represent his company and sell their equipment here. I agreed, and set up my own company with my family's backing.

"The television industry in India is still in its infancy. The Telly, as you would say in England, is provided only by All India Radio and now available only in Bombay and Amritsar. In 1965 All India Radio started to broadcast TV signals as a test. The All India Radio is wholly owned by the Indian Ministry of Information and Broadcasting. I sell and install the transmitter equipment to send TV signals through the air. Sometime in the future, we will also be able to provide transmission by low orbiting satellites. Of course, there is also the possibility of getting TV in color. The marketing possibilities are enormous! Of course, at some point, the Ministry will have to separate TV from its radio operations. That must happen. I do not know whether our government, so set on socialism, will allow private TV programming and private TV operators. That's why I am excited to sell and service the equipment that the government needs. Think about it! We have 640,000 villages in India, none with even one TV set."

Ravi learned that Shiree had grown up with her uncle after her parents died in an automobile accident. She attended Oxford University in England for a degree in International Relations and Economics. She had been in her last semester at Oxford when her uncle told her to come back to India to marry immediately after graduation. The family would arrange for a suitable husband. She had been adamant that she would pick her own husband. Her uncle immediately stopped financing her education. That had been traumatic, especially since Shiree knew that her uncle was, after all, sending her money that had belonged to her dead parents. She had been investigating a loan from the University when an angel, Diana, an Oxford alumna, met her and gave her the remaining money she needed. Shiree felt a great obligation to Diana, but Diana refused to allow Shiree to repay her. On graduation Shiree returned to India, but not to be married. She then wasted three years doing nothing useful. That had made her totally despondent. Finally, she'd obtained a job with the Nuclear Power Commission. She sheepishly admitted that her job had been arranged by her uncle as he was a member of the Rajha Sabha. He had simply pulled some strings, as they say in England, and she'd gotten the job. She glowed when she told Ravi about what great progress India was making in nuclear power.

Ravi found her about five feet seven inches tall, unmarried, and quite attractive. She had all of the right curves, a warm, round face, dark, intelligent eyes, black hair pulled back in a bun, sparkling white teeth, and a delicious smile.

Before they parted, Ravi gave her one of his new, rather heavy and cumbersome mobile car phones and taught her how to use it.

"Shiree, this is a demonstration model which the Canadian company provided. You may call me on this phone from anywhere in New Delhi. It is made by an American company called Motorola. I have set up one transmitter station just for your phone and mine. If you are outside the transmission area, the phone will not work. I am sorry that the phone is so bulky. It will not fit into your shoulder bag. It is intended for use by one car driver to talk to another car driver, so the weight of the phone is usually not so much of a problem since it will always be kept and used inside a car, except for you and me here."

They agreed to meet the next week at the Lotus Blossom Tea House in Chandni Chowk. In the meantime, they would try to stay in touch on their mobile car phones.

DONOVAN PLAYS TENNIS

March, 1973
Gymkhana Club
Safdarjung Road
New Delhi

It all started at the clay tennis courts of the historic Gymkhana Club on Safdarjung Road. Donovan was scheduled to have a tennis lesson with his tennis teacher, Prem, at 10:00 A.M. He arrived on time. Two others also were waiting. Prem introduced Donovan to Kuldip, another tennis instructor, and Asaf Ali Khan, another student. Prem asked if the four might play a set of doubles. Mr. Khan and Donovan wound up playing the two Indian tennis pros. Mr. Khan played well, more than making up for Donovan's deficiencies. Still, the two foreigners chased the balls all over the court. It was a rather one-sided match.

At the end of the match Mr. Khan invited Donovan for a spot of lunch at the Kashmiri Lounge. Donovan figured he'd lost at least three pounds chasing the pro's balls. They washed up, changed clothes and found a table at the Lounge.

The Lounge exuded an elegant atmosphere. Tan linen tablecloths covered the tables which were decorated with silverware, white linen napkins, and fresh garden flowers. Colorful print drapes hung from ceiling to floor. On two sides floor to ceiling windows allowed the guests to look out onto the tennis courts below. The waiters wore tan riding pants, white shirts, red jumping jackets and white gloves topped off with high white turbans. One never knew how they kept their turbans on when they bent over to pour coffee or tea or a beer.

The lunch conversation with Mr. Khan was more interesting than Donovan anticipated. They made the usual banter about time in New Delhi and families. Donovan remembered that a person with the family name Khan must be a Muslim. The two men found that they both had five-year old sons in the same class at the Delhi Day School. They lived at opposite ends of the same street in the Green Park subdivision. They shared what they did in New Delhi and exchanged business cards.

Donovan found that Mr. Khan was attached to the Pakistan High Commission as its Science Advisor. He was a professor on a leave of absence from Lahore University to do research on the Indian Institutes of Technology. Donovan excitedly talked about the Rajasthan Canals Project and the order for TEC bulldozers and scrapers he had just received.

By then they were calling each other by their first names.

Donovan advised that he and Emily were holding their own, excited and somewhat astonished that they could successfully live on the local economy, unlike Americans on official or diplomatic duty with American PX privileges. Ali confessed with lowered eyes his diplomatic status.

After a rather large lunch Donovan ordered coffee and Ali ordered tea. They reflected on the tennis match of the morning.

Donovan was about to get up and leave when Ali moved a bit closer and whispered confidentially, "This has been a very opportune time for me to meet you. Do you know anyone at your American Embassy?"

Donovan replied that he knew the USAID officials and the Economic Advisor through business dealings. He knew others socially and spiritually through his international church.

Ali continued. "Please find the proper person at your Embassy and tell him that the Indian government is in the process of developing an atomic bomb. If your friend wants to know more, please have him contact me."

Donovan looked perplexed. "How do you know this?" he asked incredulously.

"Never mind how. It is true. Your government must learn about this and be concerned."

"Why are you telling me? Perhaps you should go directly to the American Embassy and seek out the correct person yourself."

Ali replied smoothly, "I am a Pakistani. I cannot go directly to the American Embassy. The Indian security people who watch that Embassy would wonder what I was doing talking to the Americans. Unlike you, I am in a rather hostile country. Pakistan and India have already fought three wars. I need someone like you, Donovan, to be my, how you say, go-between, with the proper American Embassy official."

"All right, Ali. Let me find the right person and get him in contact with you."

They shook hands and went their separate ways. Ali left with a great smile.

Donovan drove to his office in Old Delhi. He always had to concentrate on his driving because, thanks to their British upbringing, the Indians drove on the wrong side of the road. He especially paid attention when circumnavigating the roundabouts or traffic circles. He wanted to turn in the opposite direction as he entered each traffic circle.

He drove with unsettling thoughts about his conversation with Khan. He wondered what he was getting into. He asked himself how he would explain this new development to Emily.

DONOVAN'S CONFESSION

March, 1973
J Block
Green Park
New Delhi

"What!! You promised to find the name of the CIA person at our Embassy and give it to a Pakistani? Why? What were you thinking?"

Head down, Donovan held his wife's hand and directed her to the living room sofa. He'd known he'd have a difficult time explaining his meeting with Khan. At least, he'd waited until Matt was in bed and the servants were no longer in the house.

He described his conversation with Khan.

"Love, I will get the name and give it to the Pakistani that I played tennis with at the G-Club today. That is all I promised."

"But, how will you find out who that is? We have met a lot of Americans since we've arrived, but I doubt that we have met this person."

"I will ask Hugh when we play bridge with him and Sarah next week. Hugh surely knows who the CIA person is."

"Dear, I do not like this. We have nothing to do with spying and need to keep it that way. You could be putting us in jeopardy with the Indian government. Please promise me that you will get the name and do no more. We need you here, not in some Indian jail!"

"Yes, love, I promise. I do not need this distraction. You know how hard I'm working to make a name for myself with my boss in Singapore and at the home office. I need to bust my sales quota to get their attention and get us to a new assignment in a better place. That large order we received from the Rajasthan Canals Project will do it for this year."

USAID HELP

March, 1973
Greater Kailash Colony
New Delhi

Hugh and Donovan were good friends. Hugh was the USAID officer at the American Embassy. They enjoyed both a business and personal relationship. Donovan enjoyed telling Hugh that his USAID dollars funded Donovan's activities. Hugh and his wife, Sarah, had two children, one a year younger and one a few months older than Donovan and Emily's Matthew. The children attended the same Day School. The two wives shopped together at Connaught Circle and sewed much of their kids' clothing over coffee once a week. The couples played in the same bridge group and attended the same international church.

Emily and Donovan had been invited to play bridge with Hugh and Sarah at their house. Mary, the ayah, stayed home to look after Matt.

Toward the end of the evening Donovan mentioned to Hugh that he had met Mr. Khan, a Pakistani diplomat, at the Gymkhana Club. Khan told Donovan that he had some secret information to pass on to the proper person at the American Embassy, and wanted to find out who that might be.

"Perhaps Mr. Khan may be looking for an Embassy person attached to the CIA. Hugh, can you tell Mr. X, whoever he is, to contact Mr. Khan directly? He can be reached at the phone number of the Pakistan High Commission."

"Sure, I can do that."

DONOVAN BECOMES ENTANGLED

April, 1973
Donovan's Office
Old Delhi

Donovan happened to be in his office when he received a phone call from a Mr. Smith. "Donovan, this is Graham Smith. Hugh, my Embassy associate, says you'd like to meet me. How about lunch tomorrow? I'll treat you to a good lunch at a Punjabi restaurant around the corner from your office. Is noon good for you?"

"Yes. Do you know where my office in Old Delhi is located? You do. OK. I'll see you then."

The next day Graham Smith appeared in a bush shirt, rumpled slacks and a Panama hat. He carried a ready smile and a twinkle in his eye. His brown hair was starting to turn grey. He wore rimless glasses and sported a small, well-tailored moustache. He had a tan sufficient to pass as a native of Northern India. Donovan immediately took a liking to him.

They walked to the restaurant which was just a few blocks from Donovan's office, mingling with the foot traffic on the sidewalk. Graham repeated, "Nay, munkta" to the many shopkeepers who tried to lure them in both Hindi and English into their shops. The two turned a corner to see the nearby Jama Masjid looming in the distance.

"You know, Donovan, the Jama Mosque is the largest in India. Melanie and I toured it a few months ago. I recommend you add it to your sightseeing list. It was built in the mid-1600's by Shah Jahan, the same Mogul emperor who built the Red Fort here and the Taj Mahal in Agra. It can hold 25,000 worshippers on the outside courtyard. I remember that the two minarets you see so vividly from this distance are 40 meters high. Not surprisingly, lots of Muslims live in this area."

"Thanks, Graham. It's so close to my office in crowded Old Delhi. I will tour it with Emily and Matt someday."

As they entered the restaurant, the proprietor greeted Graham in Punjabi as a member of his own family.

Donovan found himself in a small room crowded with perhaps eight square tables and chairs. Each table was set for four persons with red and white checkered cotton table cloths. Glasses and silverware wrapped in paper napkins showed their eagerness for the next customers. Several photos of Sikh leaders paraded along the back wall. Punka fans danced in rhythm slowly from the low ceiling. A lovely aroma of spices swirled around the room. It was a very comfortable place.

They were ushered to a corner table toward the rear and the kitchen, perhaps Graham's usual one. Donovan learned over a lovely curried chicken and rice lunch that Graham grew up in northern India where his parents were Christian missionaries. He learned Punjabi and made life-long Indian friends as he was growing up. He was delighted to return to his country of birth as an American official.

"So, Donovan, what brought you to India?" Graham asked.

"After graduation from grad school I joined The Earthmoving Corporation's sales group in Dubuque, Iowa. By then I had married Emily and we had our first son, Matthew. Emily and I both wanted to live and work overseas. She already had a wonderful summer experience teaching school children English in Costa Rica. I had previously worked in Mexico. We knew we'd enjoy the challenge and excitement of living and working in a different culture. I got my chance when TEC's sales territory for India and Ceylon opened up. We took this opportunity and are glad we did. I can boast that I have just received an order for TEC equipment from the Rajasthan Canals Project here. Our Matt, now five, is thriving. Emily expects our second child in August, right here at the Holy Family Hospital. We love the Roman Catholic nuns who faithfully run that oasis for the sick and needy."

Donovan related his encounter at the G-Club with Khan. The two had five year olds in the same Day School class and lived on the same street in Green Park. Graham furrowed his bushy eyebrows when he learned what Khan had said to Donovan about India's building a nuclear weapon.

"Donovan, I'm dubious that this information is correct. We have no such information. You may be assured that if we did, we would be *most* interested and very concerned. In this wonderful world only a handful of nations have developed an atomic bomb. Of course, the U.S. and U.S.S.R. were the first, but our government has no interest in allowing other countries to develop their own bombs. The fewer countries with the bomb, the less chance that some country will actually use one."

Graham asked Donovan why Ali chose him rather than coming directly to the Embassy to talk to a U.S. government official. Donovan replied that Ali evidently looked for an American to introduce the right person at the American Embassy to him.

After a few seconds' thought Graham said, "This is what I'd like you to do. Contact Khan and tell him you have spoken to the appropriate American Embassy person. Tell him that we'd like to know some details about India's bomb development. For example, where is the work being done? By which agency? You know, a few scientists in a lab cannot do it by themselves. They first need a design, then they need to obtain equipment to process the fuel, and most important either a source of uranium or plutonium. Ask him to give us some details. By doing so, he will be establishing with us his *bona fides*, that he knows what he is talking about. We do not want to know his source of this information, at least at this stage."

Donovan remembered his promise to Emily.

"But, Graham, why don't you contact him directly? Just call the Pakistan High Commission and ask for him. I'm just a territory sales rep for The Earthmoving Corporation. I don't know anything about bombs, and surely don't know anything about the kind of high level government intrigue that this seems to be! Besides, I promised my wife that I would give Mr. Khan's message to you and do no more."

Graham sipped his tea and replied, "It would not be wise for me to contact him directly. For one, I'm fully occupied trying to determine what the Soviets are doing to influence the Indian government. I am not focusing on what the Indian government is up to. Oh, yes, we follow the local politics but do not get involved in that as much as you would think from reading the *Times of India*. And, be aware that we get what we call fool's calls at least three times a week. We sometimes have difficulty determining whether they are a hoax or a prank."

"But, Graham…"

"You also have to understand that the Pakistanis are being supported by China at this time. It would not be wise for me, an American official, to contact him directly. That might raise eyebrows with his coworkers at his High Commission."

Graham wiped his lips and mustache. "Besides, you just said that Ali wants you to be the contact for us. Ali likely expects that you, not I, will follow up on this with him. So, Donovan, please contact him in the next week to get more information, then contact me and tell me what he says."

"How am I going to do that? I won't be so bold as to meet him at the Pakistan High Commission."

"You'll find a way, I am sure. You both live on the same street. Begin with high tea at your place for him and his family. I doubt that he drinks alcohol."

A dejected Donovan slowly walked back to his office as he tried to determine what to say to Emily. He pushed a stray cow away from his parked car then entered his office building. He immediately immersed himself answering telexes and organizing his next appointments with his customers.

WINDFALL

April, 1973
American Embassy
Shantipath
Chanakyapuri
New Delhi

Graham moved from his desk to the adjacent conference room with the Reports report in his hand. He needed quiet time to contemplate what it said.

The Reports group at headquarters regularly evaluated the field CIA personnel on a country by country basis. Graham was pleased that he and his case officers had received an excellent grade for spotting and recruiting new agents. Headquarters complimented Graham for the useful intelligence the new agents were providing. Headquarters was critical, however, that Graham and his team were not spending enough time on Covert Action to combat the KGB's "active measures" programs. (1) Graham had, indeed, performed some CA activities which Reports had counted, just not enough. He had also prodded the Embassy's public relations officer to sponsor 45 Indian politicians on a trip to the U.S. last winter to observe the national election. He had written articles in the local newspapers about the U.S. support of India's democracy. He gave speeches to local Indian service groups promoting the American form of government, ideals and society. His motto always was to tell the truth. That showed the difference between the Soviets and the U.S.

Graham's attitude about CA was clear. He knew from experience that CA worked only when it was part of an overall country strategy which included political, economic and social programs. Covert Action without the other, coordinated programs too often failed. (2)

The original reason for CA was to destabilize or overthrow existing governments or regimes opposed to U.S. interests. Unfortunately, the resulting regime was sometimes worse than the original government. Sometimes the CA effort exploded publicly in large newspaper headlines chastising the CIA and the U.S. for its interference. Graham did not like Mrs. Gandhi's ideas about socialism but would continue to support her legitimate government.

Graham preferred to ask the help of his more visible associates to combat the Soviet's increasing influence by highlighting the American-Indian relationship. The Ambassador repeatedly told Mrs. Gandhi that the U.S. supported her and yet cautioned her on relying too much on the Soviet Union. The Embassy's military attachés regularly warned about increased Soviet military influence. The agricultural counselor talked about India's increasing need for farm mechanization and the U.S. suppliers' support of the 'Green Revolution'. The USAID director regularly popped up on the radio and in newspapers extolling the imported U.S. food assistance program. He also issued press releases about U.S. financing of large infrastructure projects. The economics counselor conferred with Indian government officials about economic matters, especially India's development of better reporting systems to track the economy. The U.S.-based Ford and Rockefeller Foundations were often in the news for their assistance in fostering India's Green Revolution in agriculture.

The Reports group did not allow Graham to count such effective, non-CIA sponsored activity.

Graham was completing his response to Reports when Shamus poked his head into the open conference room doorway.

"Hey, Boss, do you have a minute? I have an interesting situation."

"Please come in, Shamus, and have a seat. I was just finishing a report back to headquarters about our results of the last six months. We received excellent grades for recruiting new agents, thanks to you and the team."

"That's good recognition, Boss, and you know that we all were involved...."

"What can I do for you?"

"I played polo last Saturday, this time with the IAF Team. I was lucky to use a borrowed speedy Arabian as one of my horses. After the match... by the way, this old man scored two goals... a man came up to me to ask about the Arabian. I told him what little I knew of the stallion's breeding. He was very interested, and introduced himself as

Hussein. He is a diplomat here in New Delhi with one of the Middle Eastern embassies."

Shamus shifted his weight in his chair. Graham suspected that he was nursing a sore leg that had possibly been caught between two horses at the polo match.

"He indicated that he really likes Arabian horses, Turkish Delight, and Turkish coffee. He noted my American accent and clearly wanted to have more conversation. I was unusually uncomfortable. I did not quite know what to do, as by then I was greatly in need of a shower. I suggested that I or one of my American Embassy associates contact him. He wrote his home phone on his card and gave it to me. Boss, would you like to follow up with him?"

"Yes, I will, Shamus. But, are you sure that you do not want to call him? After all, he did make contact with you."

"No, I have enough to do right now. I got the distinct impression that Hussein was really looking for another American, you, the Boss. Please call him."

Shamus gave Hussein's card to Graham and left the room.

Graham finished his response to Reports, considered all of the tasks he had set for himself, sighed, and picked up the phone to call Hussein.

(1) Gilligan, Tom. *CIA Life: 10,000 Days with the Agency.* Boston: Intelligence Book Division, 2003. Print. Gilligan wrote an excellent chapter entitled, "Covert Action Charade", pages 223-232.

(2) Shackley, Theodore. *Spymaster: My Life in the CIA.* Dulles: Potomac Books, 2006. Print, page 39, "...no covert-action operation mounted by an intelligence service has much chance of success if it is not solidly supported at the highest levels of government and coordinated with the leadership's other means of persuasion-diplomatic, military, propagandistic."

GRAHAM'S NEW INTEL TREASURE

April, 1973
Hussein's Home
Nizamuddin East
New Delhi

"Welcome to my home, Graham. Salaam Aleichem!" Hussein bowed gracefully.

As tall as Graham, thin, with black and grey salt and pepper hair, a mustache and half beard, Graham judged Hussein as about the same age.

"Aleichem Salaam, Hussein."

A broad smile showed on Hussein's face. "Ahh. You have had some experience with my part of the world. May I ask where?"

"Yes, I've had some exposure to Middle Eastern customs. A few years ago I had the pleasure of being assigned to my country's embassy in Ankara. Here, I brought you some Turkish coffee and two cezves. Unfortunately, I do not have any Turkish Delight sweets!"

Hussein took the gifts, a twinkle in his eye.

"Ahh. Ankara, a rather bleak and stale city. I preferred Istanbul and Izmir. Now that you have brought coffee, I suggest we boil up some Turkish coffee with the two cezves you brought."

Hussein led Graham through the house into his small kitchen.

"I see that my friend Shamus told you about my tastes. By the way, he is a very fine polo player. For an older man, he is very bold on his Arabian horse. I have made sure that we will be alone in the house. So, our conversation will not be overheard."

Graham wondered, though, whether the house was bugged.

The two made coffee.

"Hussein, please remind me how to brew a good cup of Turkish coffee."

"Easy, Graham. Put finely ground Turkish coffee, just enough to make one serving, in a small copper coffee pot, add cold water and cardamom, bring the cezve, the coffee pot, to a boil, stir if adding sugar, and when boiling pour into a demitasse cup. If done correctly, the foam should build up on the top of the coffee in the cup."

The aroma of coffee enveloped the kitchen as they compared Graham's living in Turkey and Indonesia and Hussein's living in Turkey and Iran. Their small talk about where they had been assigned previously led each of them to the silent conclusion that they were both in the espionage business. Hussein poured the steaming coffee into his demitasse cup from his cezve like a pro, as did Graham. The coffee foamed perfectly. Hussein strolled with his cup and saucer to his high ceiling living room. Graham followed.

"Hussein, I am going to guess that your Embassy provided locally-built living and dining room furniture. But, you have lovely tapestries and this is a beautiful carpet. Is it from Tajikistan?"

"Yes, the Embassy provided the furniture but I brought the tapestries and carpet with me. No, the carpet is from Afghanistan, believe it or not. It is rare to see such a high quality carpet from that country. Most of the wall hangings are from Iran bought when I was stationed there. My round brass coffee table in the center of the room is from China."

The two settled into elaborate, stuffed arm chairs at the far end of the high-ceilinged living room. The wall hangings gave Graham a warm and comfortable feeling.

"Graham, I would like to get right down to business, as you say in your country. You see, I was educated at Stanford University in your California, so I can speak some American slang. May I speak freely and confidentially? From one professional to another?"

"Yes, of course."

"I wish to offer you secret information which I believe you will be very interested in. For this, I wish to be paid by you."

Unsurprised, Graham sat back in his chair, balancing his cup and saucer on his lap. "Tell me what kind of information you have to offer. My government may be interested."

"I am managing a Soviet agent. This man was recruited by my organization when he was visiting my country on official business. He is KGB first directorate now stationed here in New Delhi. His name is Uri and he is running three Indian agents for the KGB. He is feeding his KGB Rezident here in New Delhi the intelligence he gets from these three agents. He is also quietly feeding me the same intelligence. He pays these three agents from KGB funds and I pay Uri personally for his sharing of the agents' intelligence with me. His KGB boss does not know that I am receiving the same secret information or that I am also paying Uri for it. Uri's motivation is only money."

Graham sat straight up in his chair, almost upsetting his coffee, intrigued.

"Hussein, this is all well and good. But, what can your government possibly do with India's secret information?"

"Ahh. Graham, you must understand we are Bedouin. For centuries we are accustomed to trading our horses, our food, our hides, sometimes our women with outsiders. We do this naturally. Why not also trade secret information?"

Hussein stroked his mustache with his free hand. "You see, I obtain secret information from Uri, the Russian KGB man. For this my government pays money to his private account in Switzerland. He does not know or care what I do with the information as long as he is paid. I trade the information he gives me with my Chinese contact here for more money than we pay the KGB man. Everybody wins, as you say in America."

"What secret information is Uri providing to you?"

"One of Uri's agents is the secretary for the Communist Party of India. Uri gets regular reports about CPI activities and funding requirements and in return he provides the CPI lots of rupees. My Chinese contact is very interested in the ways that the Russians are subsidizing the CPI. Of course, the Chinese are subsidizing the more revolutionary, breakaway Communist movement here in India, the CPI-Marxist."

Graham carefully and slowly sat his coffee cup on the side table. He immediately realized that Hussein was offering him access to some of the CPI's most secret information, one of his major priorities.

"Another of Uri's agents is a key engineer at the Hindustan Aeronautics in Bangalore. HAL, as it is called, is an Indian government corporation under the Ministry of Defense. HAL has a number of aviation-related contracts with foreign aerospace agencies including Airbus, Lockheed, Boeing, Israel Aircraft, Russia's Ilyushin and Tupolev. HAL now also assembles MIG-21 jet fighters under license from Russia. This agent regularly gives Uri confidential engineering information that the Western aerospace corporations have transferred to HAL under their separate licensing agreements. So, you see, the Russians are now obtaining the latest technology from Boeing, Airbus or Lockheed to use in their own products. My Chinese contact also uses this same technical information for his country's own product development."

Graham recognized that this commercial espionage might be of interest to the economics counselor at the Embassy... and to Boeing and Lockheed.

"The third agent is a newspaper reporter here in New Delhi. Uri gives him *Pravda* news releases to publish in his paper as the reporter's own under his own name. The news releases preach the usual Russian line about peaceful coexistence, the peaceful intentions of the Russian Bloc of countries and the warlike belligerence of the Western powers."

Graham already had a list of Indian reporters who regularly wrote the Russian story line. This information might confirm what Graham already suspected.

"Graham, I thought this information may also be useful to your government, inshallah, for a fee. My government pays Uri separately, unknown to his KGB boss. So, too, I wish to be paid by you, unknown to my superiors. Is that acceptable to you?"

"I will have to see some of the intelligence. Then, I may be able come to an agreement with you."

Hussein finished his coffee and sat the cup and saucer on a side table. "I thought you might require some proof. I have copies of last month's intelligence from all three agents. Here, please develop this film then tell me whether you wish to receive this information on a regular basis. I am sure we can come to an agreement if you think this information is useful to your government."

"Thank you, Hussein. We will talk again. By the way, how did you know to find Shamus and me?"

"That was easy. I asked Uri to give me the names of the CIA people here in New Delhi. I saw Shamus' name on the list of polo players last Saturday. I stayed after the match to meet him. Here we are."

"Hussein, I will be in touch, soon. I will try to get you some Turkish Delights for next time."

"Thank you, Graham."

Shaking his head in amazement, Graham quietly left Hussein's house. He ruminated about the possibilities of working with Hussein, knowing that he had found a treasure trove of information. He thought that Colonel Bhandari at the IB would be delighted to know about the KGB's infiltration of the CPI. No, the Colonel would likely roll up the CPI man and make Uri *persona non grata*. That would destroy Graham's new source.

After reviewing the intelligence Hussein provided, CIA Headquarters approved making him an agent and gave him an appropriate code name, WINDFALL. Hussein became a prolific producer of secret information of great interest to the American government. Graham kept him well supplied with Turkish coffee and Turkish Delights.

SHIREE AT WORK

April, 1973
Rajya Sabha Conference Room
Parliament Building
Sansad Marg
New Delhi

"Now be sure to distribute your notes in the next few days. You know that our Prime Minister herself is most interested to see what progress we are making in nuclear power."

Shiree Saksena turned in her chair to face her uncle. "Yes, Uncle, I will sit down at my typewriter just now to type the first draft of the meeting notes."

Sena Saksena, a most distinguished member of the upper house of Parliament, the Rajya Sabha, kissed his niece on the cheek, bowed gracefully, and left the room.

Shiree sat alone with her thoughts. The other members of the Nuclear Development Commission had already left. She carefully placed her notes in her briefcase. She resolved to type the meeting notes while they are still fresh in her mind. She can then quickly disseminate the notes to the Commission and Prime Minister Gandhi.

She sat, motionless for a few moments, as a wave of fatigue washed over her. She thought back over the past years that had brought her to this work as Secretary to the Nuclear Power Commission. She often thanked her uncle for this job. She had graduated Oxford University only with the financial help of another Oxford alumna after Uncle Sena told her to come home for an arranged wedding. She knew in her heart that an arranged marriage was not her karma. She boldly refused.

She got up from the conference table and walked down the hall to her nearby small office.

She had her own dharma, her right way of living, her rule of life including a desire to be loved for who she was, not to be pawned off to a strange man for a dowry. She fanatically watched the Bombay movies over and over, as she found that the music and love stories appealed to her heart. Perhaps she was too westernized.

As she opened the door to her closet-like office, her thoughts turned to Ravi. She expected that he would by now be arriving in Toronto to start his six-month training program with that Canadian company. She reveled in his talking about the many opportunities he saw in India about the nascent TV and car phone industries. She realized, again, that she missed his smiling face and sparkling eyes.

Her notes in hand, she sat down and began to type.

T.R. FUMES

May, 1973
Joint Conference Room
Lok Sabha
Parliament Building
Sansad Marg
New Delhi

T.R. was still fuming, even if now only internally. He sat alone in the joint conference room, the other attendees of the joint Money Committee having picked up their papers and left.

He tried to settle himself. He plied his papers into his briefcase. He reached out for his cane, elevated it, and came down hard with it on the table in front of him.

"Dammit! Dammit! Dammit!" He exclaimed aloud, to no one. He preferred to swear, which was not often, in the King's English, because it is so much more, well, special. Meaningful.

His thoughts turned again to the meeting which had just ended.

The great actor that he was, he wobbled to stand upright, leaning on the back of a chair, and orated to the empty room, "Now, Shri Sena Saksena, you and your Money Committee in the Rajya Sabha received the same briefing from the IB's Colonel Bhandari that we in the Lower House did. I convinced my Money Committee to provide substantial rupees for development in the areas in West Bengal where the farmers are taking pitchforks and axes to government buildings. Some government workers have already been killed! My money bill to spend one crore of rupees per troubled district on local schools, road improvements, sanitation and clean water was passed by the Lok Sabha and sent to your Upper House. What's one crore, only ten million rupees, compared to all of that money we waste on building fighter jets and tanks. We know that twelve districts already would qualify for the money. That is twelve too many! Unfortunately, your Money Committee did not approve our plan. You did not reject

71

or amend it. You just forgot to include it in our new budget. So, we sat here this afternoon to arrive at a compromise on spending. Some compromise."

He straightened, picked up his tattered briefcase and cane, and shuffled out of the room and down the long hallway to the door of the building.

As he walked, he thought to himself, *Sena, I know you were educated at Oxford University. That does not make you any more English than I, a farmer from Kerala who attended Trivandrum University.*

Those damn Communist Party of India-Marxists must be fomenting the insurrection. Why can't they be sensible like their larger Communist Party of India brothers? The CPI has stated it will create the revolution by the ballot, not the gun. Yes, Lenin and the Communists took over the Tsar's Russia in 1918. They used the gun and Marxist teachings as their bible. What do the Russians have now? A new aristocracy to rule over them. They were all serfs with the Tsar. They are still serfs.

The Communists also took over China in 1949. But, they were not really believers of Marx-Lenin. They used the word "Communist" as a rallying cry. They simply won a peasant struggle against their overlords and the corruption of government officials. Their bible was Chairman Mao. So, what has changed there? Only the names of those in control have changed, not much else since.

The Russians and Chinese both say they practice Communism. But, neither looks out for the poor or needy, or the average citizen. Both governments are absolutist and corrupt.

One would think that Communism is one philosophy, one creed. But, the Russians and Chinese cannot even get along with each other. The Russians are suspicious of the Chinese along their common border. The Russians favor India, the Chinese favor Pakistan.

As he exited the building, T.R. forced a smile on his face and gave the guard at the door a cheerful goodnight. He plodded to his car parked nearby.

Well, my associates here in New Delhi call me a communist. I have not even read the <u>Communist Manifesto</u>. I am just fighting for the poor and lower castes of our society. If that makes me a communist, so be it.

He turned the key in the car door, slowly heaved himself in, turned on the ignition and drove off to Green Park to meet Ambika and Kumar for dinner. He would have to tolerate Ali and his endless talk about his most recent visits to the IIT campuses, but he knew that seeing his daughter and grandson, his most cherished loved ones again, would be worth the chatter from his son-in-law.

ALI'S NEW ASSIGNMENTS

May, 1973
Pakistan High Commission
"The Palace"
Shantipath
Chanakyapuri
New Delhi

Akbar Chaudry was his most ebullient as he again hosted his newest spy.

"Welcome, Ali. Please take a cup of tea from the tray and we'll settle into the adjacent conference room. I have some interesting files to show you."

Ali made a statement which he had practiced several times. "Thank you for making my stay so pleasant so far. We are very happy with the house you provided. Green Park is a nice, newer development. You also made sure that our servants were not IB employees. My wife has been delighted to be able to see her father so often. Of course, T.R. dotes on his only grandchild, our Kumar. I have worked hard to develop my cover story. I am ready for the next step. I look forward to using my ISI intelligence training at last."

"I understand from your Dean that you are continuing to give very useful reports about what you have learned at the IIT Universities. You are doing your cover work well. You should know that an Indian diplomat in Islamabad again contacted the Dean to try to reach you in Lahore. The Dean said that you were on a temporary assignment in India for the University. When the Dean said that you had already sent several reports, he requested a copy. The Dean regretted that he could not share your work with someone not on the University staff. The inquirer seemed satisfied. I am sure he sent a clear message confirming your cover story back to the Indian IB."

Akbar closed the adjoining door to his office behind him and pointed to one of the arm chairs at the table. On the table sat two manila files, one rather thick and another rather thin.

"Let's get down to business. First, I have good news. Our Prime Minister Bhutto has finally decided to allow our scientists to develop a nuclear bomb! He believes that the Indians are well on their way to having their own bomb. We cannot be left behind in this race."

The two settled into two chairs opposite each other.

Ali replied, "I am not surprised. My uncle has been pushing our politicians to allow us to develop a bomb. A nuclear weapon in our possession would upset the current military balance in our favor. If India gets the bomb first, they will dominate us."

"We, of course, want to give our P.M. the latest and best information about India's plans and progress. Ali, your mission here has become very important. I have every faith that you can pull it off."

"With your help and support, Akbar, I will get a timetable for India's first nuclear bomb test. Then, our government can determine how to respond. I am ready to get to work with the two agents."

Akbar pushed the two files toward Ali. "Here are the files on the two agents. You already know about Ram Lal Dutta, the Trombay Lab engineer. His file is the thick one. You will meet him next week in Bombay. The instructions about a time and place are in the file. Pervez, our current case officer running Dutta, will meet you first. He will introduce you to Dutta and explain how and when to contact him.

"Dutta is working for us because he wants to provide useful information about India's bomb development. He has the highest motivation, revenge, for the Hindus' killing his parents in 1947. We pay him a few rupees each time we see him, but money is not his motivating factor. You can get a good feeling about who Dutta is by reading Pervez's contact reports in the file."

"I cannot begin to understand what he and his family went through back then."

"You know, Ali, that some agents are motivated to spy for idealistic reasons, some to obtain money, some to enhance their egos, and some because we can blackmail or otherwise threaten them. (1) Those like Dutta are the best, most productive agents for us, for they have the highest motives for breaking the law of their own country."

Akbar pointed to the thin file. "Now, this is the file on our new agent in New Delhi. She... yes, this agent is a woman... I can tell from the astonishment on your face that you do not welcome this. Ali, you have spent enough time in the West. You know that the traditions between Muslim men and women must change. Look at the repression women face in Saudi Arabia. That is no longer either fair or desirable. Both you and Ambika know that your woman, your wife, is not your slave. So, think of Shiree Saksena as an agent to be used, not in any sexual way, but to fulfill your spying objectives."

Ali pushed his chair back from the table and held up his open hands. "But what will my Hindu wife say about another Hindu woman as my agent?"

Akbar sat back in his chair, scowling.

"Your wonderful Hindu wife already knows that you are here for two reasons, not just to study the engineering curriculum of the IIT Universities. She met me, not our Ambassador, on your first day here. She has accepted the fact that you have been fully trained by the ISI and are now starting to work for the ISI. Indeed, you have been sent here primarily to work for the ISI. Ambika is living in our provided house with provided servants...in fact, provided everything. She has accepted your ISI association because she wanted to see you succeed and to visit her father here in India. She knows that he cannot visit her in Pakistan."

Ali sat upright and moved forward in his chair.

"Yes, we have talked about her reservations about my spying on her native country. She sometimes feels she is a foreigner in her own country. She no longer believes in the old Hindu rites and traditions. That's why... how I was able to marry her. Her family just about expelled her when she told them she was going to marry me. Fortunately for me, she loves me and dotes on our son."

Akbar folded his arms on his chest.

"You must decide how much information you share with your wife. For your own safety I recommend you say nothing about your woman spy, or, for that matter, the man in Trombay. The less she knows about the details of your actual ISI work, the better for both of you."

"Yes, Akbar. You are correct. The less Ambika knows about what work I am actually doing for you, the better."

"Now, back to Shiree Saksena. She is the niece of Professor S.L. Saksena, a member of the Rajya Sabha, the Upper House of Parliament. For years her uncle has been a big advocate of India's nuclear power development. Shiree is the secretary for the Nuclear Power Commission here in New Delhi. The Commission periodically reviews India's progress in nuclear development and gives its report directly to Prime Minister Gandhi and a few other select politicians including Professor Saksena. The Commission updates all of the India's nuclear activities, including peaceful nuclear reactors and nuclear bomb development in a report for the government's policy makers. Shiree's uncle got her the job there."

"Surely, she has some credentials or previous work to enable her to understand what the Commission members are discussing? The very words used by the nuclear scientists are not the stuff of daily vocabulary. How can she be the reporting secretary if she does not understand the discussions?"

Akbar pointed to the thin file.

"It is all in there. We know that she is 27 years old, unmarried, and a graduate of Oxford University in England where she studied International Relations and Economics. We know that she has also at least once turned down a family-inspired marriage. We can assume that she is very smart and westernized. We believe that her uncle found someone to tutor her in the jargon of the nuclear scientists."

"You said before that she was not yet fully recruited. Is she fully committed now?"

Akbar replied in his most fatherly tone of voice, an expression of patience on his face. "Shiree has been recruited by an American woman married at one time to a Pakistani businessman of some wealth. This woman, Diana, lives in London for most of the year. She is also frequently seen in Singapore, Hong Kong and the French Riviera. Diana is well connected to the American politicians because she donates generously to their political campaigns. Most of her money comes from her husband's funds, through her own checking accounts, mind you."

Akbar continued, matter-of-factly, "Please bear with me as this is a complicated situation to explain. Diana is also a graduate of Oxford University. Diana met Shiree when Shiree was a student at Oxford. Shiree was in her last semester at the University when her uncle told her he had arranged a marriage back in India as soon as she graduated. Shiree said she would marry for love but not because the family arranged it. Upon learning this, the uncle cut off all of Shiree's funding for the University. That's when the older Diana helped Shiree financially to finish her Oxford degree. Diana lost contact with Shiree after graduation but Diana had given Shiree a business card so Shiree could contact her in the future. Shiree never forgot Diana's help."

Akbar got up and poured himself water from the pitcher on the side table. He took a long drink and sat back down.

"Diana married one of our country's businessmen some years ago. Of course, the husband is a good Muslim as well as a very successful and aggressive businessman. About two years ago, he broke the news to Diana that he was taking a second wife. To sooth her feelings, he advised that he would keep the new, younger wife in Pakistan, and visit Diana when he was in London. He was not concerned if she continued to jet around the world, even if she wanted to have an affair now and then. Diana exploded. She demanded an immediate and costly divorce and she got it.

"Ali, this is where it gets interesting for us and the ISI. Last year, Shiree contacted Diana in London to ask for a person-to-person meeting. Diana flew to New Delhi and met Shiree who said that because of her new job she had access to India's nuclear development programs. Shiree was very concerned that India was in the process of developing a nuclear bomb. She told Diana that her uncle wanted a bomb, but that she disagreed with him. She asked Diana to go to the Americans she knows at their London Embassy to tell them India is developing a bomb, so that they would force the Indian government to stop."

Akbar moved forward and put his arms on the small table.

"Diana told one of her American Embassy friends in London of Shiree's information about an Indian nuclear bomb. The American laughed. He said that the lady had fancy dreams or hallucinations. He stated that India was a leader in pursuing a peaceful path among those nations not aligned with the West or the Soviet Union. Of course, India would not develop a nuclear bomb. Diana was humiliated by the arrogant, know-it-all American Embassy representative."

Ali frowned.

Akbar continued. "In the following few weeks Diana worked with a Pakistani lawyer in London to finalize her divorce. When Diana told him about the humiliating conversation with the American official, the lawyer suggested she take her story to a friend of his at the Pakistan High Commission in London. Diana talked to an ISI officer who did not laugh at her story. He told her to go back to Shiree and say that any information Shiree would give to Diana, Diana would pass on to the American government officials in London. Diana realized that the information would wind up in Pakistan, not America. Nevertheless, Diana agreed with Shiree that India should be stopped from developing a bomb. Even though Diana was tricking Shiree, Diana justified it for the greater good. Our ISI man promised Diana that our government would use Shiree's information to find a way to stop India's nuclear bomb development."

Akbar took another long swig of water, as though it were a strong scotch although he did not drink alcohol.

"Diana has now met Shiree in New Delhi on two further occasions, in October of last year and in February this year. Each time Shiree passed information about India's nuclear bomb plans to Diana and each time I subsequently met Diana in Bombay before she returned to London. I passed on the information to the ISI in Islamabad.

"Please understand that Shiree has the best of intentions. She is motivated by the highest ideals, and we must always play to those. You must always tell her that she is doing the right thing, that because of her information the Americans are becoming aware of India's mistaken plan to make a bomb. Tell her that it is a big mistake that we all want to stop. No matter that she is naïve, or so westernized that she wants to have her independent way. She is clearly too trusting of Diana and too reliant on Diana's friendship."

Akbar chuckled. "Ali, Shiree thinks she is working with the Americans. In our profession we call this a "false flag" recruitment.

"Now Diana wants out and India is getting closer to finalizing the bomb. We need someone here in New Delhi who can meet Shiree more frequently to get the latest information. That's where you come in. Diana will be back in New Delhi in June and has already arranged to meet Shiree then. At that time Diana will introduce you to Shiree and say goodbye to her. You will then meet Shiree about once a month. Your contact with her will usually be a brush contact. She will pass her written information to you while you hand her your new requirements as well as a time and place for your next meeting. You need not even speak, just pass the documents.

"Please take your time to review both files. You have all of the information you need there. Of course, you cannot take the files out of this room. I will be in my office if you have any questions."

Ali picked up the thin file and started to read. Akbar got up and left, closing the door softly behind him.

(1) Crumpton, Henry. *The Art of Intelligence, Lessons from a Life in the CIA's Clandestine Services*. New York: Penguin Books, 2012. Print, page 74. "...the ingredients of a recruitment operation: MICE. This stood for money, ideology, compromise, and ego."

AKBAR'S DOUBTS

ADMIN
PRIORITY
10 May, 1973
TO: ISI, Islamabad
Attention: Head, India
Ref: Case Officer BAKRA

I acknowledge receipt of your two messages about Case Officer BAKRA. I do not think I am being too harsh on him as he has yet to produce any intelligence. In fact, I have scheduled him at last to meet his first agent later this month. He will meet his second agent for the first time in June. It is high time that we get some real production from him. As always, as and when I receive it, I will forward his intelligence, whatever that may be, to you via courier.

He is now due for his six-month review. I rate him 'Unsatisfactory' as he has not produced anything of intelligence value. You may say that he has proven himself in his cover role. That is meaningless to me, as he has not advanced our ISI mission here, or started his real assignment for the ISI.

Thank you for agreeing, if reluctantly, with my decision to allow BAKRA to contact the CIA person here. BAKRA has not yet met the CIA man. Contacting CIA was his idea. I recognize that the CIA person may turn him over to the IB. If so, BAKRA will be expelled from India.

As you know from my comments, I still doubt that BAKRA is capable of succeeding as a spy. I will continue to give him my full support even as I am dubious about him. Should he fail, it will be his own fault.

Signed,
India Control

AFTERNOON TEA IN GREEN PARK

May, 1973
J Block
Green Park
New Delhi

"Welcome, Ali. Please come in. We're glad you and your family could visit us."

"Donovan, this is my wife, Ambika, and our son Kumar. This is Mr. Griffin with whom I played tennis at the G. Club."

"Ambika, please call me Donovan. Meet my wife, Emily, and our son, Matt. I believe Matt and Kumar are in the same Delhi Day School class."

Both families sat around the Griffin's new dining room table. Ambika asked where they had obtained such a lovely set. Emily, pleased, replied that they had just bought the teak dining set from Kumar Furnishers on East Park Road. The carving on the chair backs and table siding was of the Mogul arch. Emily had given Mr. Kumar a design for the arch, and he willingly complied. She explained that they also bought the credenza to go with the set.

Emily offered iced tea or ice water and lime, nimbu pani, to drink. She brought out three kinds of cakes she had purchased at the bakery at Connaught Circus. The cook had made cucumber and tomato sandwiches under Emily's tutelage. Har Saroop was delighted to be able to take home the bread crusts. He also set out fresh strawberries with cream and powdered sugar.

When the two families had finished the refreshments, Donovan suggested that the boys play on the front lawn while the ayahs watched from the front verandah. Emily called Ambika to the kitchen to get some advice about cooking Indian recipes on her imported stove. Donovan suggested that he and Ali move with iced tea to the somewhat remote and separate office at the front of the house.

They could hear Matt and Kumar kicking a soccer ball back and forth.

Once settled comfortably, Donovan started the conversation where they had left off at lunch that day at the Gymkhana Club.

"Ali, I met the intelligence person at the Embassy. I told him of your statement about India building a nuclear bomb. He seemed more dubious than curious. He suggested I ask you for more details. He wants to believe you but has no other corroborating information from others. He says to tell you that he does not want to know about your sources, but would like information which he can check."

"With whom did you talk?"

"Graham Smith."

"Right on. I know about him. He's with your CIA."

Ali reflected for a moment, and then he said, "All right. Please tell Mr. Smith that the bomb is being developed at the Trombay Atomic Energy Lab. Mr. Smith will tell you that his government has known about the Trombay Lab since the late 1940's. Trombay has always led India's research about peaceful uses of nuclear energy. However, in 1948 Prime Minister Jawaharlal Nehru tasked Homi Bhabha to develop a nuclear weapon. You may not know that it takes YEARS to develop nuclear technology either for peaceful purposes or for bomb-making. India's nuclear weapons development has not been a priority until recently. What is new is that the Indian government under the leadership of its current Prime Minister Gandhi has started a new initiative. The Indians are now in a hurry to develop and test their first nuclear weapon."

"Wait a minute, Ali. I will have to take notes to give this information to Graham". Donovan pulled out a lined pad and pencil from his desk and scribbled some notes about what Ali had just said.

"Please continue."

"I already told you that I am a Professor at the Lahore University. I am on a leave of absence from the University to do research on the IIT Universities here.

Please tell Mr. Smith something about me and Ambika. I obtained a Bachelor of Science Degree in Engineering from Lahore University. Following that I obtained a Master's Degree in Engineering Materials at MIT in Boston. I then obtained a Fulbright Scholarship for a Master's Degree in International Studies at Georgetown University in Washington, D.C. where I met Ambika.

She was in the same program and we fell in love. I am a Muslim from Pakistan while she is a Hindu from India's Kerala state. We married over the objections of both of our families."

Ali settled more comfortably in his chair.

"I obtained this assignment in New Delhi because my uncle is an air marshal in the Pakistani Air Force. He obtained permission from my government at the highest level to send me here because he is worried about the possibly misleading information that our spy agency, the ISI, is giving him about India's progress in making a bomb. He does not trust the ISI. He thinks that India is far more advanced in its development of the bomb, and that the ISI is way behind in their assessment. He wanted an independent confirmation. I am not an ISI spy. My uncle insisted that I work with the ISI to find out what the Indians are really doing. I report directly to my uncle and our Prime Minister about India's progress. My analysis is that India is getting close to finalizing its bomb design. When that happens, India's next step will be to build the components and then assemble them and prepare for a detonation. If I am right, Pakistan will have to take drastic steps to counter India's obtaining its first bomb."

Ali took a sip of his tea. He continued.

"We are fortunate that at least here in India the politicians decide and fund such sensitive projects as atomic bomb development. In my country the military is in charge of such a project. Once India gets a bomb, our generals will go all out to develop and test an atomic bomb of their own. Or, they may decide on something stupid and bomb India's nuclear facilities."

Head down, totally absorbed, Donovan continued to write.

"Donovan, don't you see? India with a nuclear weapon upsets our military balance, our equilibrium, in India's favor. Pakistan can't accept that. That is why the American government must be told about this newly approved project. Perhaps the Americans can stop the Indians from developing a bomb. If not, Pakistan will as a minimum also have to develop a nuclear weapon. Or, if the generals have their way, they may start another war with India. That makes this part of the world much more dangerous."

Ali shifted his weight uncomfortably in his chair.

"Here is one more complication for your friend, Mr. Smith, to consider. Please tell him that Ambika's father is T. R. Nair, a representative from Kerala state in the Lok Sabha, the lower house of the Indian Parliament. T.R., as he is affectionately called, is a communist and very much an Indian nationalist. He advocates strong central government control and a public works budget to help the poor and lower castes. He knows that I am here to visit the IIT Universities and report on their educational process. As he has visited us at home over the months that we have been here, I have told him in very flattering terms about my visits to the various IIT locations. I have shared a few of my reports to my Dean at Lahore with him. I have told him nothing about my other reason for being here. Still, he suspects that I am a Pakistani spy. He and I now get along famously but forgo any political discussions or sharing of state secrets. He dotes on his only grandchild, Kumar, who Ambika and I have given him."

Suddenly, Donovan stopped making notes. He carefully put his pencil down on his desk. He looked at Ali with a puzzled expression on his face.

What was he getting himself into?

"Ali, when we played tennis, I had no idea that you and I would be involved in a nuclear weapons race between India and Pakistan. I told you over lunch at the G. Club to tell someone at the American Embassy. Now, we both know that the person you need to talk to is Graham Smith. I want you to contact Mr. Smith and leave me out of this intrigue. I am just a private American citizen. I am not in India in an official government capacity. I have no clout with my own government. I cannot help you with this!"

Ali's brow furrowed in concern. He was about to lose his American contact.

"Donovan, please understand! I got you involved as an interested third party. I knew that if I went directly to Graham Smith with my story, he would not believe me. He would dismiss me as another, how-you-say, foreign kook wanting to make trouble where there is none. I'm sorry to inconvenience you, but this subject for my country is a matter of survival. I was looking for another American to tell Graham my story, and you conveniently crossed my path."

Donovan sat back in his chair.

"I do not like this one bit. I do not have diplomatic immunity from prosecution as do you. I have enough to do just working to obtain equipment sales for my company. I do not have the time or ability to continue to be in the middle between you and Graham."

Ali grimaced.

"I can sympathize with what you are saying. I am here because my uncle wants an independent evaluation of India's bomb development capabilities. I am a university professor doing spy work. So, you see, we both are now in uncomfortable situations. I assure you, I just want you to get me and Graham together, and then you can leave us. Will you do that?"

"O.K., Ali. I will arrange for you two to meet then I wash my hands of this whole affair."

"Please tell Graham what I have told you about my concerns and especially about my background, including my relationship with my father-in-law. Then, please arrange a secret meeting for me and Graham, right here in your home. I'd prefer, as would he, that it be at dusk or after dark, after the servants have left, and after your son has gone to bed. We do not want to involve the families, just us three."

Donovan nodded in the affirmative.

He continued, "Here is how we can arrange the meeting. We may have to use the wives for communication. Both Ambika and Emily must know that we need to meet. First, you contact Graham and get one or more evenings when he is free. Ambika will invite Emily over to our house for tea one afternoon next week. Ask Emily to give Graham's free dates to Ambika. After I check my calendar Ambika will tell Emily what date we will meet."

"I'll arrange this meeting, then it's between you and Graham. I have a sales quota to meet and construction equipment customers to serve. I do not want to risk my stay here with the Indian government. I cannot be part of a plot to harm India."

Relief on his face, Ali replied, "Thank you, Donovan for your hospitality."

The two families reunited for good byes.

Donovan and Emily saw the Khan family safely out the driveway gate. The Khans strolled down the street to their home. Donovan and Emily headed back to their bungalow.

After their first discussion about Ali Khan, Emily had agreed, reluctantly, after some prodding and pleading to host the Khan family at their home. Donovan now wanted to share his latest meeting. He was not sure that he could oblige her and still fulfill his promise to Khan.

He suggested that they could talk about his discussion with Ali after dinner and after Matt was in bed.

She did not wait.

As they walked back to the front door, she stopped in the middle of the driveway, put her hands on her hips and said, "My darling, Donovan."

Donovan immediately knew he was in trouble. She only used that phrase when she was about to cry or chastise him for some wrongdoing.

"That was a lovely time. I enjoyed getting to know Ambika and Kumar. We may try to car pool our sons back and forth to the Day School."

She gave Donovan her most convincing smile. Her teeth shone like diamonds.

"Now, through no fault of your own, I sense that you are getting deeper and deeper into an international intrigue. Please remove yourself from this mess as soon as possible. Matt and I need you here, at home, not in some Indian prison. Now, let's have supper."

With that, she strode through the front door and made a bee-line toward the kitchen, leaving Donovan alone outside, wondering how he could get himself out of this predicament.

THE IB INVESTIGATES

May, 1973
Indian Intelligence Bureau
Undisclosed Location
New Delhi

Colonel Bhandari had indigestion. He vowed never again to eat that mango dish his sister served every time he visited. The only bachelor in his family, he had two other sisters and brothers whom he seldom saw. They were off working elsewhere while his loving sister and her husband lived near his home. He delighted to visit them. His niece and nephew loved to see their uncle who always brought them sweets.

He was reminded of the family planning billboard sign near their house. It read, "Do Ya Teen Bacha-BAS!" "Two or three children-STOP!" Unlike his own parents. He smiled, thinking that his sister had, indeed, stopped at two.

He moved from his huge desk to refill his tea cup.

At home that morning Colonel Bhandari had looked at himself, fully clothed, in his mirror. He'd reviewed his greying black hair, always groomed, his still youthful clean-shaven face, his curly moustache, his white tailored pants and jacket. He knew that he was just a bit too fat around the midriff because he did not get enough exercise. He had spent twenty years in the Army and almost ten at the IB. He sometimes considered retiring before he got either too fat or senile. Truth be told, he enjoyed the daily excitement and satisfaction of defending his country. Even the P.M. herself acknowledged his good work. What would he do after he retired?

Three knocks on the door interrupted his reverie. Three, again.

"Enter!" he bellowed.

Three appeared at the door. The two men went through the ritual of greetings and getting a cup of tea and settling into the two most comfortable chairs in New Delhi. Three reviewed the recent foreign newcomers to India but made no suggestions for new dossiers.

The Colonel flipped from page to page in his notepad.

"Ah, there it is. My notes from our meeting of last November. Now, Three, please tell me what you have learned about Ali Khan, the Pakistani science advisor, and our Mr. Wong, the Chinese trade representative."

Three pulled his notes from a full briefcase although he already had a full report for his boss in his head.

"After our meeting last November, I asked Two to check Khan's background in Pakistan. One of our IB staffers in Islamabad contacted Lahore University to confirm Khan's story. The Dean replied that Khan is a professor there, now on a leave of absence in India to do studies on university level engineering. Khan's regular coursework had been transferred to another University professor. He also said that he had started to receive Khan's rather lengthy and very useful reports of his findings here in India."

"That is a sound report. But, there are many Khans in Pakistan. Do we have the right one?"

"Yes, sir. Khan's bio at Lahore University shows that he did graduate studies in America. He returned to Pakistan to serve for three years in the Army. What he did on Army duty is not known. He worked for his uncle's export-import business in Karachi for a few years before becoming a professor at Lahore three years ago. He teaches courses in engineering materials."

"Could he have been recruited by the ISI when on active Army duty?"

"Yes, that is certainly possible."

"Well, Three, what have YOU learned since November about Khan?"

"We have confirmed that he has visited at least four of our eight IIT locations. According to those whom he has met, he has asked many questions about our engineering courses. He is interested in how we select students for our engineering programs. He has asked about how our corporations value our IIT graduates for employment. It all seems legitimate. He, his wife and son are renting a bungalow in the Green Park enclave near the IIT campus in Haus Khas."

"Three, that is a good report. Did you make Mr. Khan "King for a Day" as I suggested last November?"

"Yes, sir. We put a surveillance team on Khan for a day last December. Our team tracked him in the morning to the IIT Campus where he first met with a group of engineering students in one of the classrooms. He then met two of the professors at the campus cafeteria over tea. We saw Khan making notes on his clipboard as he talked to the students and the professors. Khan then drove the two professors to lunch at the Moti Mahal Restaurant. He returned to campus to drop the professors then returned to his home in Green Park by mid-afternoon. We have also pieced together his activities at the other IIT locations by talking to those whom he has met over the last six months. Based on that, he certainly seems legitimate."

Three caught his breath. Three always confessed to his staff that a meeting with Colonel Bhandari always took his breath away.

"We will follow Khan again for a full business day sometime in November. As you know, our Delhi surveillance teams have been busy following known Russian and Chinese spies. Khan is lower on our priority list at least for now."

"Three, you and your staff have always done well in prioritizing your foreign targets. How would you rate Khan now as a threat?"

"I give him a C rating. I would rate him at a lower D except that he is, after all, a Pakistani. I will make him King for a Day again in the fall."

"Very well."

The Colonel made a few notes on his ever-present note pad.

"Three, I have another question for you to add to Khan's dossier. You will not be able to answer it today. My question: What amount of time would it take a Pakistani college professor to visit all of our IIT Universities, obtain what information he needed, report back to Lahore, and leave India? To answer my own question, I would say that it would take no longer than a year. Mr. Khan arrived here in November, 1972. I would expect him to leave us by November, 1973. If not, why not?"

Three made a note on Khan's dossier.

"So noted. You have a great ability to ask the critical questions that always lead to more digging on our part. Useful digging, I may say."

"Now, let's turn to Mr. Wong. What have you learned about this Chinese trade representative?"

Three shifted his weight unobtrusively in his chair. His old leg wound was bothering him. He hoped the Colonel did not notice his quick grimace.

"He showed a diplomatic passport at entry. That says he has connections with the Chinese Communist leaders. He has been buying Indian goods for export to Hong Kong. He has established contact with several wholesale outlets in New Delhi, Calcutta and Varanasi. On each visit he buys various crafts and carpets for export. He opened two bank accounts here in New Delhi. One is a trading account which he uses to pay for the goods he buys and sends to Hong Kong for sale there. The second account pays for his daily living expenses. A Hong Kong bank sends him regular money transfers. He has purchased more goods each month. Likewise, his trading account here has received more money each month. He is buying mostly expensive goods. We talked to a few of the owners where he made purchases. They do business with him only on a cash basis. They say his English is good enough to make the transactions. They usually arrange for the shipments to Hong Kong for which they are paid extra."

"Do you know where he has taken up residence?"

"Yes, per your request we did put a surveillance team on him for a day last December. He rented a house in the Sundar Nagar enclave. The landlord provides a housekeeper, cook, and night watchman as part of his rental contract. Wong does not go out much when he is in town."

"By that do you mean that we were not able to put one of our IB staffers in his house as a servant?"

"Yes, sir. The landlord has already provided the servants and pays monthly for their salaries."

"What grade have you given Mr. Wong?"

"As you know, we give the A grade for those we consider direct security threats. We suggest that a lesser B grade is appropriate. We do not know his full intentions and are basically suspicious of any Chinese who is here on a long term visa. We must keep a better track of his comings and goings. You know how much more closely aligned China is now with Pakistan. Could he be sent here to do us harm? We do not yet know."

"Three, I would like you to do two favors. First, please tell One about Mr. Wong's travels. He may have already encountered him in

Calcutta. Also, please have one of our Calcutta surveillance teams trail Mr. Wong next time he flies to Calcutta. We may be very interested in their report."

"Yes, Colonel, I will do so. Is there anything else?"

Colonel Bhandari searched his notes on his notepad.

"What ever happened to those three diplomats from Poland that came to us on the same week with Khan and Wong?"

"Oh yes. The older lady turns out to be the wife of the new security man at the Polish Embassy. For some reason they do not have the same family names. The young and beautiful lady turns up at the Gymkhana Club for drinks and conversations three to four nights a week. So far, she has not developed any relationships I would consider dangerous to our national security although she and several men are having fun. We noted on her dossier that she has added weight since her arrival. Perhaps she drinks too much alcohol."

Three chuckled, as much as an Indian counterspy may chuckle.

"Thank you, Three, for a thorough report. Remember, you are responsible to keep track of the foreigners in our midst. I am here merely to advise you. You are doing a great job."

"My pleasure, Colonel."

Three raised himself slowly from the most comfortable chair, put his teacup and saucer on the side board and quietly closed the door behind him.

ALI'S FIRST RESULTS

May, 1973
Pakistan High Commission
"The Palace"
Shantipath
Chanakyapuri
New Delhi

Ali showed his credentials to the guard at the entrance and found his way to Akbar's second floor office at the back of the High Commission.

"Please come in, Ali. Tell me about your first trip to visit Dutta. Did the turnover go smoothly? Of course, you will have to write a complete report for the file later."

Akbar pointed for Ali to take a seat in the chair across from his desk.

Ali described his first encounter with Ram Lal Dutta. As arranged, Ali first met Pervez who showed him where to pick up and park the car to be used for his future meetings with Dutta. Pervez explained that Ali and only Ali would use that car.

Pervez showed Ali how to navigate the streets of Trombay then told him how to meet Dutta. Ali would have to recognize Dutta from others on the crowded streets.

"Akbar, the transfer went well. I sat in the back seat while Pervez drove to the pickup place. It was dusk, almost dark. He saw Dutta, pulled over to the curb, and asked Dutta to get in. Pervez introduced me to Dutta as his new case officer. Dutta gave Pervez a list of the visitors to the Trombay Lab during the last month. Pervez gave Dutta an envelope with some rupees in it. We agreed on a date, place, and time for my next meeting, and for an alternative meeting that same night."

Ali settled back in his chair.

"Dutta said that two weeks ago four scientists from the Pune Lab visited Trombay. They spent three days secluded in one of the conference rooms. Dutta had not seen their names on the guest register before. At previous times, only the boss from Pune had met with the Trombay scientists. Dutta thinks that the new scientists may be part of the build team and that the bomb design phase may be over. We will have confirmation only when other new names from the other Labs show up on the Trombay guest register."

Akbar replied, "The visit of the new scientists is very important. I must immediately tell Islamabad about this. Of course, this is an indication, not hard intelligence, that the bomb-making has already started. I am not surprised."

"Although he has tried to find out several times, Dutta still does not know where the spent plutonium from the reactors is being sent for reprocessing. He was totally in control and very interested to actually see my face. So, too, was I to see him sufficiently to recognize him at our next meeting on the crowded street. Before he got out of the car, Dutta wished Pervez a safe return to Pakistan. This list from Dutta gives the names of the new Pune and other scientist visitors."

"Good work, Ali."

"On a personal note, Dutta said that he had been asked about a possible marriage to an unwed lady living in his same house. He told the match maker he was interested in someone else."

"This is an interesting turn of events," noted Akbar. "Dutta certainly is a very eligible bachelor. If Dutta does get married, it may be to a Hindu girl. Such an arrangement may complicate our relationship with him and his usefulness to us."

Ali had read about Dutta's situation in his rather fat file. At 34 years old, Dutta was certainly an eligible bachelor. Ali was surprised to read that the Lab had obtained government funds over the years to build a self-contained village about three kilometers from it. The village included apartments, shopping, services, schools, its own electricity source, two cinemas, and a large park for exercising and strolling about. Dutta lived in a Lab-provided flat in the Deepak House, one of many apartment buildings built exclusively for the Atomic Research Lab's scientists and their families. Ali had read that the Deepak House was named after a classical Indian raga. As one would expect, many of the students, coming from scientist families, graduated and went on to one of the IIT Universities for further study in engineering. Some even went off to study at Oxford or MIT.

"Akbar, Dutta and I have set regular meetings for Monday evenings at places Dutta does not usually visit. We do not want our meeting to be witnessed by someone who knows him personally. I will fly Indian Airlines on Monday afternoon to Bombay, check into one of the hotels near the airport, have dinner, get the car, meet Dutta, use the car the next day to go to IIT Bombay for my university meetings then fly back to New Delhi on Tuesday afternoon or evening. Dutta will use the local commuter train to travel from the Trombay Station to another of the stations toward Bombay. I will pick him up at the station, and talk with him in the car for a few minutes while I drive to the next station where I will drop him off. The commuter trains are always overcrowded on week nights. Dutta will have no problem blending in with the surrounding crowds."

"A good plan," Akbar smiled at his new spy. "Nice work, Ali, for your first meeting with your agent."

Ali got up from his chair and turned toward the open door.

"Just a minute, Ali. Please come back."

Ali sat down, somewhat perplexed.

"Do you know why we prefer car meetings at night with our agents?"

"No, I never gave it any thought."

"You know that we are working in a very hostile country. To avoid detection, we must take the most secret and secure ways of meeting our agents. We find that either short car meetings at night or daytime brush contacts are the most secure for both our case officers and our agents. We must use the best tradecraft when meeting our agents including watching for surveillance. Now, were you a British case officer here in New Delhi, you and your wife would do a lot of entertaining at local restaurants. You would have a large circle of friends including a few agents. As part of your monthly routine you would openly take your agent and his wife to a lovely dinner at one of the better restaurants. The IB would think you were having a good social time. You and your agent would know better.

"If you were a Russian case officer, you would disguise your agent meetings within lively after working hours' parties at your home. You would have invited numerous local dignitaries, one of whom would be your agent. You would find time to talk to your agent privately and quietly amid all of the noise of the party. We find that the Americans also use parties for meetings with agents. The only difference is that the Americans drink scotch and bourbon while the Russians drink vodka."

Akbar chuckled.

"So, you can always tell who the Russian spies are. They are the diplomats who drink too much vodka at those parties and show up at their embassy rather late in the morning with large liquor hangovers!"

Akbar added, more seriously. "So, please understand, Ali, that your car meetings are the best and most secure method of meeting with your agent. Please remind Dutta that these car meetings are the safest way to meet."

Akbar warmed to instruct his university professor further.

"Here's another question for you. Do you know how our recruitment of spies in this hostile India is different from what the British, Americans and Russians do?"

"No, Akbar."

"The other case officers all use the typical three phase spot, assess and recruit process. They initially know very little about their potential agents. They start only with a list of needed information and a target list of government agencies which have that information. They have few actual names of people who work there. They have to dig a lot to learn about the individual, his motives and his past before they can even pitch recruitment to their potential agent. We do not do that. We have the advantage of already knowing a lot about Indian individuals in places of power, people who have access to the secrets we need."

"I don't understand," Ali said.

"Think about this. You know that millions of our current countrymen and women moved to Pakistan in 1947. Their allegiance now is to the new Pakistan rather than to the old India which no longer exists. They still know many people who stayed in India. They are for us, for the ISI, a great resource because they can so easily introduce us to their old friends, family and acquaintances who stayed here. Our unique style of recruitment is truly relationship recruiting.

"For example, we needed a spy at the Atomic Research Lab in Trombay. We found Dutta only after contacting several people in a great chain of people who ultimately led us to him. By the time we had identified him, we already knew everything about him because of the relationship chain which caused us to find him in the first place. So, you see, although we are in a hostile country, we do have the advantage of old pre-partition relationships to find and recruit so many good spies. That, of course, helps to keep our country safe."

"Thank you, Akbar for a very revealing lesson."

With that Akbar returned to his paperwork as Ali quietly got up and let himself out.

Akbar wondered if perhaps Ali would turn out to be a successful spy after all, yet warned himself to keep careful watch over his secret meetings.

AMBIKA'S NIGHTMARE

May, 1973
J Block
Green Park
New Delhi

The dry heat of the day was oppressive. The sun glowed like a white orb radiating the city, the dust from the Rajasthan Desert only 125 miles away casting it as an eerie white apparition through the haze as it set. The usual vehicle pollution was no match for the desert dust.

An exuberant Ali opened the front gate and pulled his car into the driveway.

"Ambika, Kumar, I'm home!" he exclaimed.

The cook emerged first, took Ali's overnight bag and briefcase, closed the gate, and disappeared into the house. Kumar raced out to meet his dad, almost knocking down the cook.

"Dad! Welcome home!" Kumar exclaimed, jumping into his father's arms.

A weary Ambika appeared at the front doorway. She did not venture into the late day brilliance.

"Son, here is a set of toy soldiers for you to play with. They are made out of metal and nicely painted. Now, go, play in your bedroom while I talk with your mom."

Kumar barely stopped to show the toy soldiers to Ambika before he raced into the house.

As Ali approached Ambika, she withdrew into the living room. He embraced her and kissed her gently. She seemed unmoved.

As she pulled away, Ali looked at her closely. Dark rings circled her eyes and the usual red spot was absent from her forehead.

"My dear, what is wrong?"

"I have just spent the last two days not knowing whether you would come home to me or would wind up in an Indian jail. I am relieved that you are home but I am exhausted from worrying about you. I did not sleep at all last night. I was on edge all of yesterday and most of today. I had to apologize three times to our servants for yelling at them for no reason. I cannot stand the stress of knowing you are in danger, not knowing that you are safe. I did not anticipate so much anxiety for your safety."

"Ambika, please know that my business in Bombay went very well. I just saw Akbar. He is pleased with my work so you should not have been so concerned or upset. Please have a little faith in me, in my ability to do this work!"

"I cannot help myself. You went off to Bombay like you were a knight ready to kill a dragon. I stayed behind, struggling to keep a level head and imagining all sorts of terrible things happening to you. I expect I will feel this way every time you go to do your work for Akbar. I love you and want you to succeed, but you have to recognize that I will have some unsettling times when you are away on his business."

"I love you, too, my dear."

He held her tight as she sobbed on his shoulder.

Akbar Still Doubts

INTEL
URGENT
23 May, 1973
To: ISI, Islamabad
Attention: Head, India

Case Officer BURKO turned over agent BALOO to Case Officer BAKRA on 21 May. Case Officer BAKRA said that the turnover went smoothly.

Agent BALOO said that four different scientists from the Pune operation met at the Trombay Lab two weeks ago. They had not shown up on the list of past visitors.

Agent BALOO advised that the presence of the four new scientists may be the first indication that India has progressed from bomb design to bomb manufacture. If so, this is another step closer to India's explosion of its first nuclear weapon.

Agent BALOO had already told us that the bomb components will be made at three or four different sites and assembled at the Trombay facility before being taken to the Rajasthan desert for detonation.

Agent BALOO is a long-time agent with a Distinguished rating. We can rely on the intelligence he gives us and on his judgment.

We are asking our other agents with access for more specific intelligence to confirm that the components for India's first nuclear weapon are, indeed, now being built.

The names of the four scientists are attached. Please determine if you have any record of them and advise.

C. O. BAKRA is scheduled to meet Agent BALOO monthly.

I still have my doubts about Case Officer BAKRA although he did succeed In meeting his first agent. As you know, the turnover of an agent to a new case officer is a very sensitive moment. I must keep a close watch on BAKRA as he finally begins to give us some intel production.

Signed,
India Control

GRAHAM IS DUBIOUS

June, 1973
J Block
Green Park
New Delhi

The sun had set and darkness was enveloping Donovan's household compound as he prepared to introduce Ali to Graham. Donovan made sure that the house was quiet. Matt was in bed. The cook had gone home for the night and Mary, the ayah, had retired to her apartment above the garage. The night watchman had not yet arrived to guard the house from evil spirits and robbers. The rest of the house remained dark.

Emily was quietly reading in the bedroom at the back of the house. She, the M'em-Sahab, had set out a most welcome container of iced tea and three glasses on Donovan's desk in the office at the front of the house. The cook had boiled the water and made ice in their American refrigerator.

Donovan turned on the indoor lights and the punka fan in his office. The punka swished silently, moving the hot, dry air around the office.

The house remained eerily quiet.

Donovan's heart raced as he heard the front gate open and close. Graham arrived first. Donovan greeted him with a solemn handshake and motioned for him to pour some iced tea. As he did, Ali appeared in the doorway.

"Ali, meet Graham. Graham, this is Ali. Now, I'll join my wife and leave you two to your private discussions."

"No, Donovan, that won't do. You can't leave us alone," Ali retorted. "You should be a witness to our discussions. Otherwise, my government may think that I will be recruited as an agent of the Americans. That won't do."

"I agree," opined Graham. "Stay, Donovan."

"But, you promised..."

Both looked like spoiled children who had just had a toy taken away.

Donovan silently sat down in his chair at his desk and swiveled it around to face the other two who, tea in hand, settled themselves into two overstuffed American-built chairs.

Ali opened the discussion. "Graham, Donovan has told you about my rather unique perspective with regard to the Indian effort to build an atomic bomb. I must provide my government an accurate assessment of India's nuclear weapons progress. We are very concerned that India is moving rapidly to a nuclear bomb test. I would like your help and that of your government to determine more precisely what progress they have made. We'd like to have an assessment of how much time they may take before they assemble and test a nuclear weapon."

"I can understand your concern."

"Pakistan is not interested in competing in a nuclear arms race with India, but neither can we allow India to obtain a bomb and thus change the current military equilibrium in their favor. We have two choices. We can destroy their nuclear weapons development sites by attacking them with our airplanes. That would lead to another Indian-Pakistani war. On the other hand, we could start a new crash program of our own to match the Indian bomb. Neither is very appealing to us."

Always the professional, Graham's mind raced at Ali's words. He quickly realized that he was having tea with a Pakistani spy. He decided to get as much information from Ali as possible even if it turned out to be...hogwash. Graham told himself that Ali would have to be very convincing.

Graham retorted, "Ali, I am happy to meet you but I have no information about India building or testing a nuclear weapon. I am very dubious that India would develop a bomb and thus upset the military balance between India and your country. You will have to provide me with details, hard intelligence, more than just general speculation.

"Look, Ali. Why would India, now, of all times, want to make and test a bomb? That would be very disruptive to India's way of peace and harmony with certain other nations of the Third World Movement. Also, India and the Soviets are closer than ever. The

Soviets already have the bomb. We detect no Soviet interest in giving India a nuclear weapon. You will have to be very convincing for me to pay any attention to this issue beyond this meeting."

Ali responded, "OK. Let's review a bit of history here. You undoubtedly know that your President Eisenhower established the Atoms for Peace Program in 1953 as a means of providing nuclear power for peaceful uses to other interested countries. Both India and Pakistan benefited from that program. The idea then was a good one. Allow non-nuclear nations to obtain nuclear technology and nuclear materials to provide much-needed electricity. The problem is that once a country has the capability to use nuclear power for peaceful purposes, that technology can all too readily be turned into nuclear weapons. That is what is happening here in India, now!

"Developing nuclear power takes years, not months. Our analysts have been following India's nuclear development since the mid-1950's. They have concluded that the Indian scientists are driving the weapons program just as they have been driving the peaceful uses of nuclear power. These scientists, not the Indian politicians nor the Indian military, have pushed bomb development. The politicians have over the years acquiesced to the nuclear weapons plans of their scientists."

Ali stopped long enough to savor a mouthful of tea.

"Graham, Homi Bhabha was the acknowledged father of India's nuclear program. In 1948 India's first premier, Jawaharlal Nehru appointed Bhabha as the first director of India's new Atomic Energy Commission and separately and quietly instructed him to develop nuclear weapons. Bhabha received his doctorate in nuclear physics in 1933 at Cambridge University in England. His first love was conducting experiments about particles which emitted large amounts of radiation."

Graham sat back in his chair and blurted out, "So what?"

"The bomb is the natural result of Bhabha's lifelong work. He realized that India would have to use local supplies for its nuclear programs so he proposed a three stage program based on India's large thorium reserves. Without my going into detail about this three-step process, just know that it is more complicated than starting with a known design for a uranium or plutonium bomb. A thorium program takes more time to develop. When Bhabha died in a plane crash in 1966, the thorium alternative died with him."

Ali paused and glanced at Donovan, then back at Graham. He continued.

"As you know, Indira Ghandi became India's Prime Minister in 1966. Our sources told us that under her sponsorship India started work on a nuclear weapon as early as 1969 or 1970. Just two years ago we fought another war with India, this time along the Indian-East Pakistani border. As a result, the former East Pakistan became a new country, Bangladesh. My uncle, the air marshal, was not pleased at the ease with which Indian troops put down our Pakistani military. He and his staff are highly upset at even the thought of an India with atomic weapons. They will do almost anything to stop that from happening, even if it means another war."

Graham swallowed his ire and forced an even-tempered response. "Thank you for the history lesson. You have stated generalities about Mrs. Gandhi's interest to develop a bomb but let's not dwell on generalities. How about some specifics? Who is in charge of this project? Where is the bomb being designed? Where will it be built? What progress has been made so far? When will detonation happen? I have more questions should you be able to answer these."

"All right, Graham. We have information that the bomb is being developed at India's Atomic Research Institute in Trombay, near Bombay. Once the design is complete, the components will be built in three or four separate locations. The bomb will be assembled at the Trombay Lab and will be detonated somewhere in the Rajasthan desert. Is that enough to get your attention?"

Graham, frowning, said, "Assuming that is true, what would you have *me* do about this? Why do you want to involve me?"

Ali straightened in his chair.

"I'd like to share my information about this with you without revealing my sources. In return, I'd like you to share whatever information you may be able to provide to me, realizing that I will transmit both your and my information to my uncle, the ISI, and our Prime Minister Bhutto. If I can convince you that India truly is building a nuclear weapon, perhaps you can advise your Ambassador Moynihan to intervene with Mrs. Gandhi before she approves the bomb's detonation."

Graham grimaced at the mention of Ambassador Moynihan. "You are asking me to share our classified information with you, a foreign spy. This is highly unusual."

Ali pressed on. "Graham, you are a professional in the collection of secret information. Do you have any assets at the Trombay Lab? Can you determine the current status of the Trombay bomb project?"

Graham put his glass of iced tea on the side table and smoothed the part on the side of his head.

"To answer your questions, we have no information to indicate that Trombay is developing a bomb. If India is, indeed, building a nuclear bomb, my government would like to know about it before a nuclear test happens. Yes, we may be able to exert some pressure on the Indian government to prevent a test *if* we have concrete information that a bomb is in the works. We will, however, need specific, concrete information... I mean, specific and irrefutable details. My government is certainly not interested in standing by while India and Pakistan start a nuclear arms race. I will work with you as long as I see some benefit to my government and as long as I do not have to reveal my secrets, which in my sole opinion, I should not have to give you. Is that acceptable?"

"Yes! Please take another look at the Trombay facility. The International Atomic Energy Agency last inspected it about two years ago. Can you get your government to request IAEA again to make an inspection? That would be very helpful. If I can tell my uncle that IAEA was there for an inspection and found nothing suspicious that may cause our hothead generals to reduce their concern."

"I will follow up on the IAEA request through the usual government channels. That may take some time as I am not aware of what is involved."

"Here's another possible lead for you, Graham. In 1963 both India and Pakistan signed a partial test ban treaty banning all nuclear weapons tests except those conducted underground. India will test the bomb underground. Please get your spy satellites to go over the Rajasthan desert to look for an underground atomic bomb test site. You will surely find the site and then call out Mrs. Gandhi on it."

"The desert is huge and growing. That's like searching for a needle in a haystack, Ali, but I will see what we may find there."

"Please tell me what you find out at our next meeting. I will also try to get new information. I assume that you *do* want another meeting?"

"Yes. Let's take this one meeting at a time. We may decide later to end our conversation. I suggest that tea after dark at Donovan's is a good place to meet for now...I'm out of the country for the next ten days. My wife has been insisting for months that we vacation in Ceylon with some British friends whom we knew from a previous tour."

Graham sighed, indicating that he did not want to take the time away from work. As explanation he said, "We are scheduled for beach walks and a trip upcountry to the spice gardens at Peradeniya, the ancient capital at Kandy and the tea plantations...How about meeting one month from tonight, here?"

Ali said, "If Donovan agrees. Yes? Then, done! Thank you both."

Ali, showing a big grin, got up, shook hands enthusiastically, and left through the separate direct door to the front verandah. Graham and Donovan sat alone for a few seconds, each reflecting on what had just been said.

Donovan commented first. "Graham, you and Ali both have government security concerns that are way beyond anything I can help with or can contribute to. I am just an American sales representative trying to make a living in a difficult country. By meeting here in my house and getting me involved, you are placing me and my family in jeopardy. I ask you to find another place to meet Ali. Don't you have a place somewhere you can use?"

"Yes, I realize that nuclear power and nuclear weapons are not your specialty but Ali trusts you and wants you to at least witness our discussions. You cannot appreciate how much *trust* is required between a spy and his case officer. I'm not saying that you fit that description but for some reason, Ali is comfortable with you, as am I. Maybe it's your unassuming way or smiling, thoughtful face. Whatever it is, you represent a place where we can both come in secret confidence and, again, in full trust.

"You obviously realize that we are discussing possible events that could trigger another war between these two countries. No one wants that, not the Indians, not the Pakistanis, certainly not the Americans. Not Ali, not you, not me."

Graham finished his tea in one gulp.

"Yes, I do have places where Ali and I could meet but I do not wish to divulge my secrets to him, at least not yet."

Both men stood.

Graham reflected. "Ali is a very affable and fine man. He is knowledgeable about his subject and well-spoken with a good American accent. I have to remind myself that he is a spy for a foreign country and resist the temptation to recruit him. I know that he is working here to protect his family and country, as am I. He is the best kind of spy. He is morally motivated to do the right thing. Money, or status, or guilt, or even blackmail will not cause him to be an agent for us, or anyone else. He's just not motivated by those things."

Graham chuckled. "I gave some thought to turning in this Pakistani spy to the Indian Intelligence Bureau, India's counterspy organization, as a goodwill gesture. You know the old adage that if I do you a favor, then you do one for me. I have decided as a result of this meeting tonight that this subject deserves more conversation with Ali and a lot more research on my part. We do *not* want India to develop a bomb.

"Besides, Donovan, it is providence which brought the two of you together. Both taking tennis lessons at the same time at the same place. Both living on the same street in a town of millions. Both with sons in the same Delhi Day School class. I do not believe in such coincidences. Let's take advantage of the providential hand we have been dealt."

Graham took Donovan's hand and shook it warmly. "Now, I have some work and a little catching up on nuclear history before our next meeting. Thanks for the tea."

With that, he followed Ali's footsteps out the front door to the veranda and vanished quietly into the darkness.

A scowling Donovan turned off the lights and punka fan. As he found his way through the darkened house to the bedrooms, he wondered what to say to Emily.

An expectant Emily sat up in their bed and greeted him, "Well, dear, did you get rid of these two so we can get on with our lives?"

Donovan, perplexed, looked sheepishly at his lovely wife. "Not exactly. They want another meeting here. They said that this is the safest place for them to meet."

"Dear, you promised to withdraw from this international intrigue. You are not a diplomat with immunity. You could wind up in an Indian jail. Then, what would Matt and I do? Please think of us, dear, and the danger you are facing by facilitating these two men."

"I agreed to one more meeting here in one month's time."

"Dear, I have tolerated a lot over the months that we have been here. Yes, you did finally get the electricity company to increase the house wattage so we could run two of our three air conditioners in the summer on *low* without blowing fuses. Yes, you hauled five gallon cans of drinking water from the Embassy until we convinced our landlord to install a water well. You made a sand box for Matt to play in on the side yard and put up my clothesline on the roof. You pay the servants. May I remind you, dear, that you are gone on business half of the time. I have the full time job of keeping ourselves and our servants healthy, buying food, managing our servants every day, buying them uniforms, even enduring the dhobi's slapping our already washed clothes in the bathtub like the women who wash clothes on the rocks at the river's edge...All in the hottest, dustiest place on earth...Surely you can convince these two guys to meet somewhere else...for my sake?"

"Yes, love, I will do my best."

"I reluctantly agreed to help you organize this first meeting, assuming it would also be the last. I am truly fearful for you. My friendship with Ambika is my only plus from this arrangement."

SHIREE MEETS ALI

June, 1973
Oberoi Hotel
Dr. Zakir Hussain Marg
New Delhi

Ali tapped on Diana's door on the seventh floor of the Oberoi Hotel. He had not met Diana. What would she look like? Not that it mattered.

Diana opened the door. As trained by the ISI, he quickly made a mental note to himself. A statuesque blond, perhaps 5 feet 8 inches tall, almost as tall as Ali, perhaps 130 pounds, a full figure.

She wore a tight fitting Western red dress, subtle makeup, and matching red shoes. She exuded elegance.

"You're Ali. I'm Diana. Please come in. I will have you meet Shiree in about fifteen minutes. We have time before she arrives to get our stories straight."

They moved past the two double beds, TV stand, dresser drawers and writing table. They settled into two low reclining chairs adjacent to wide windows that overlooked the parking lot and nearby park where evening strollers meandered.

Ali told Diana what name she should use for him with Shiree and showed her his new business card. She told him what information he could expect from her at their future meetings and suggested that at each meeting Ali give Shiree a list of required information, a date, time and place for the next meeting.

Ali smiled. He was pleased at the businesslike attitude of this lovely woman.

A knock at the door. Shiree presented herself. She wore a Punjabi outfit which revealed her fine figure. Her long black hair was pulled back in a braid which nearly reached her waist. Ali thought of how jealous Ambika would be if she knew he was working with such a beautiful woman.

Diana introduced Ali as a local Indian working for the non-government organization called Feed the Poor. Ali gave Shiree his fake business card which showed his alias, New Delhi phone number (an extra High Commission number not now in use), and headquarters address in New York City. Diana confirmed that she would no longer be able to visit Shiree in New Delhi.

She explained, "My American Embassy contact in London thought it best, Shiree, that you have more frequent contact from now on with someone who is here in New Delhi. Our friend here will act as the middleman with the American Embassy in town. He will pass on any information you give him to his CIA contact here at the American Embassy. In that way, you are protected. The CIA Embassy person expects that our friend will give him the information from you but the CIA person does not know who you are and cannot contact you directly. That is for your security. Do you understand why we are doing this?"

Shiree thought for a moment. "Yes, I do. Thank you for protecting me. I can never thank you enough for what you have done in my life."

With that, Shiree broke into tears. Diana hugged her.

Diana said, "I am leaving you in good hands, Shiree. I am now going for a walk in the park while you two get to know one another. Shiree, I trust that you have some information to share. You will also want to decide how and when to meet next. Of course, Shiree, I am always available at my London address."

Diana closed the door softly behind her.

Ali and Shiree got down to business.

A KGB DEFECTOR?

July, 1973
Smith's House
Diplomatic Enclave
New Delhi

Graham and Melanie were just finishing a quiet, late and most peaceful chicken curry dinner at home when they heard a loud knock on the front door.

"Who can that be at this time of night?" Melanie asked. "Are you expecting someone from the Embassy tonight, dear?"

"I definitely am not. Prakash will get it," Graham replied.

The cook-butler appeared at the dining room doorway to announce only to Sahib Smith that there is another American at the door asking for him.

"Please see him into the study," Graham advised.

"Please go to bed, dear. I will catch up with you in 5 minutes... or fifty." He kissed her hard on the lips and left the dining room.

As he approached the man standing in the middle of the study, Graham, by habit, quickly looked him over. Long blond hair, eyeglasses, about 5 feet 9 inches, perhaps 175 pounds, muscular, tan slacks and a light blue short sleeved shirt, no apparent physical handicaps. About 35 years old.

"Do I know you? What do you want?" Graham asked politely.

"I am Peter Ilich Penkovsky. I work for the KGB at the Soviet Embassy. I want to leave the Soviets. I want you to help me to go to America."

Graham was astonished. Several thoughts simultaneously ran through his mind. He noted Penkovsky's American accent and wondered if this was a dream come true. He'd always hoped for a Soviet defector, but this man dropped into his lap too easily. He must be cautious. What if Penkovsky was a double agent intending to spy on America?

Graham held out his hand and smiled.

"I am glad to meet you. I am Graham Smith, the Third Secretary at the American Embassy. Perhaps I can help you."

"Yes, I know that you are Mr. Smith, a fine American family name for the boss CIA man here. I have studied your dossier on file at our Embassy. That is how I know where you live."

Graham stepped back, more to assess his possible catch.

"Before I can help you, I must be sure that you are who you say you are. Do you have any documentation with you?"

The Russian put his hand in his pocket and pulled out his photo identity card.

"Here is my national diplomatic identity card which shows that I am attached to the Soviet Embassy here."

Graham scrutinized the photo which definitely matched the man standing before him.

"Yes, but this does not state that you are KGB. If you are not KGB, then I cannot help you. I suggest that you come to our Embassy tomorrow morning. Bring documents with you that prove you are KGB, and I can help you. Can you do that?"

"No, I will not come to your Embassy because it is watched all the time by the Indian IB and by local people KGB employs. That is not safe for me. I will bring documents to you here, to your house, tomorrow night at this time. You will then know that I am telling the truth. Be prepared to get me out of this Indian hell hole."

Without a further word, he strode around Graham and let himself out the front door, to disappear in the surrounding darkness.

Graham turned off all of the remaining lights in the living area, contemplating how he might protect this man. He found his wife in bed reading a novel.

"Well, dear, what did that American want?"

"Oh, just another newspaper man wanting a special insider's story. I sent him away. I have nothing to tell him."

Before his Indian assignment Graham had plied his secret trade in three other countries. He and Melanie were well versed in special meanings, making their own small talk, just in case someone was listening in on them, even in bed. Still, they realized that India was not as difficult a place for an American spy as Indonesia had been at the time of Suharto.

Melanie read for a few moments before she put her book down on her lap. That was her sign to Graham that she wanted to talk.

Graham sat, facing Melanie, on his side of the bed.

Melanie opened the conversation. "I'm concerned, darling, that you are again spending so much time away from home. It's not just the extra hours at the office, but also your trips out of town. Can't you slow down a bit? Let others do? You are fit as a fiddle, but I need you beside me for many more years."

"Dear, you knew that I would have greater responsibilities here. I am responsible to our ambassador on intelligence matters. I am in charge of all of our Company in-country efforts. I must decide what targets to go after and how and where to look for information. Of course, I have target priorities from my boss back home. He gave me a list of generalities that I must translate into plans to be implemented by my team. He told me to keep India out of the Soviets' clutches, to get intelligence on their activities here, to try to understand what the closer Soviet-Indian relationship means to us. (1) I am rather good at that, if I say so myself."

"Yes, I know you thrive on this work. Please, darling, you have good people working with you. Surely your team can take up some of the load you're now carrying. I'm concerned that you are getting too stressed out."

"Yes, dear, we have a meeting about that very issue next Tuesday to balance our overall workload. Truth is, we are all going flat out right now. I promise we'll slow down at the Christmas holidays."

"Darling, you are such a romanticist. Christmas holidays in a Hindu nation. Indeed! Anyway, it's only July. Christmas, even if we celebrated it here, is still six months away."

"Well, dear, we did have a wonderful time with Jack and Sally in Ceylon. That was a good respite for me."

"Yes, we both enjoyed their fine hospitality, but you came back to your usual hectic pace here. That is not good for you. Please slow down!"

Graham, rather subdued, promised to slow down. He also reminded Melanie that, as COS, he had an obligation to run three very highly placed agents who would not accept working with someone else. Unfortunately, secret meetings with them took him out of town on a regular basis.

"By the way, have you any recent news about Christopher?"

"Nothing new, dear. I know from my associate in Vientiane that he was fine as of two months ago."

Melanie adjusted the pillows behind her head.

"Graham, I truly do not know what I would do if we lost him. Of course, he had to follow in your footsteps. I say that from pride, not resentment. First, Harvard. That was good. I'm sorry that his girlfriend flaked out when he told her he wanted to live and work overseas. She was a lovely girl and it's too bad that she's missing the fun and excitement of living in a faraway place. So, now, Chris is working for the Company in Laos feeding food and weapons to the Hmong tribesmen. I worry about him."

Now standing, Graham said, "My dear." He held out his hand.

Melanie recognized his signal and immediately got out of bed. Holding hands, Graham led her through the darkened house to the study. He turned on a few lights and his Akai tape recorder. Tchaikovsky's Fifth Symphony filled their surroundings.

The two stood, facing each other in the middle of the room.

Graham whispered in her ear, "The so-called American says he is a KGB agent wanting to defect. He will return tomorrow night with documentation to prove it. Please, no last minute socializing tomorrow night."

Melanie hugged him and kissed him lovingly, then led him back to bed.

"Tomorrow's another opportunity, my dear."

"Darling, you've said that to me every night since we got married. That is, whenever you were home. I love you, dearest Harvard man."

(1) Clarridge, Duane. *A Spy for all Seasons: My Life in the CIA*. New York: Simon & Schuster, 1997. Print, page 76.

A KGB Defector

July, 1973
Smith's House
Diplomatic Enclave
New Delhi

Graham toyed with his dinner as Melanie, correctly judging her husband's growing internal stress, talked rather casually about her day's happenings. Groceries at the PX, a quiet lunch with the wife of the American International School principal, and a noisy six table bridge party of gossiping Ford and Rockefeller Foundation and diplomatic American, Australian, English, and German women.

She thought, *Here I am going on and on while he muses. He is so far away, distant. I don't mind. I know he is focusing on something important. This has happened so many times before...*

My dear Graham, you always were one for adventure. You wanted badly to get into the war. You graduated Harvard and immediately enlisted in the Army. You found yourself assigned to the Army Engineers. That was too tame for you so you volunteered for a more reckless assignment. You wound up with the local resistance in Singapore, spotting and reporting on Japanese troop ship movements through the Straits of Malacca and avoiding Japanese soldiers who wanted to kill you. After the war you attended Georgetown for a Master's Degree. That's where we met. We both wanted to join the State Department but State would not have either of us. You found the CIA by a fluke. One of your Army buddies from Singapore suggested you join the new CIA. You did, and here we are in India.

You are so good at what you do. I am truly proud of you, darling.

What makes you a true professional in this spy racket? You are driven to achieve your own set goals, focused, and hard-nosed when necessary. You excel at recruiting and motivating agents to break

116

the law of their own country. You actually seek the personal excitement of a meeting with your agent. As you once told me, that gives you an emotional high almost as good as sex.

Most important, you consistently exhibit that most required characteristic for a professional spy... integrity. (1) Yes, a sense of integrity is also essential, especially when the case officer must deal with agents who are the scum of the earth. Those agents sometimes have access to the most sensitive secrets. My guess is that Langley recruits those who have a high IQ and who also want the excitement of living overseas AND who have integrity. How does one measure that?

A case officer must report the unvarnished truth back to headquarters. Else, why send him out in the first place?

You treat everyone around you but especially your agents with respect. You strive first and always to protect them. You are honorable in your dealings with them, always fair. They, in turn, respect and honor you.

You are the most ethical person I know. Yet, you willingly break the local law for the good of your own country. You have a quiet faith that what you do is for the greater good.

"What a racket our talking made over bridge!" she concluded aloud to the air around her.

Graham was lost in meditation, wondering whether his potential agent would appear and if it would be possible to get him out of the country. His reverie was interrupted by one loud knock at the front door. He raced Prakash to the door.

"I'll get it, Prakash. You may leave us now. We will close up the house."

"Very good, Sahib." The servant pushed his bike from the alcove at the back door and pedaled down the darkened street to his home.

Graham found Penkovsky at the door, dressed as an Indian street person and furtively surveying his surroundings. Penkovsky wore a hat over his almost bald, short, black crew cut hair.

"Please come in. Follow me to the study."

Graham asked Penkovsky to sit but he declined. He remained standing in the middle of the room with his back to the wall of bookcases. His eyes darted from side to side as though he was expecting some muscled goons to come in to subdue him at any minute.

"Here are some secret documents from my Embassy. These will prove to you that I am KGB."

Graham looked them over, and understood enough Russian to know that they were authentic secret documents.

"Good. You have proven yourself. Here are some instructions to get to..."

Penkovsky cut Graham short with a wave of his hand.

"I will not stay with you here in New Delhi. It is too dangerous. I can too easily be caught by my former associates. I give you eight days to make a plan to get me out of the country. I will meet your representative in exactly eight days at the date, time and place on this card. You must by then have a plan ready to get me out of the country. Until then, I disappear. I am invisible. Do we agree?"

"Yes, but you cannot simply disappear from the people who will try to find you..."

"You are incorrect. I have spent many days in a similar situation in Tashkent. I will meet your people as on the card. Thank you."

Penkovsky once again strode past Graham, opened the front door and walked out into the night. As Graham closed the door he held only the documents and Penkovsky's card on which he read a date, time and street address in Bombay.

Graham had to arrange things quickly. He would need to get a debriefing team to Bombay to interview Penkovsky before he left India. Penkovsky would need a disguise, documentation and a number of other things to leave the country safely. Graham called Jay Jay at home and asked him to meet at the Embassy in half an hour. Jay Jay, always available, agreed. Graham kissed Melanie and drove to the Embassy. On the way he considered how he would draft the FLASH message to Langley about his Soviet defector.

(1) Paseman, Floyd. *A Spy's Journey: A CIA Memoir*. St. Paul: Zenith Press, 2004. Print. Paseman's Ten Axioms of Spying, page 282. "Axiom 4: Integrity is one of the most important traits of a good spy."

Graham's FLASH Message

July, 1973
Late Evening
American Embassy
Shantipath
Chanyakapuri
New Delhi

The Marine guard quickly recognized both Graham and Jay Jay who proceeded through the main entrance.

"Thanks for coming in so quickly, Jay Jay. I have a FLASH message to send to Langley tonight. It is very important. May I write it out in the conference room, and pass it to you to send NOW?"

"Sure, Boss."

As he gave Jay Jay the message to forward to Langley, Graham explained that he had just met a possible Soviet KGB defector. Both men knew that Langley had to act swiftly on this or lose the defector.

"Boss, this is great work," enthused Jay Jay.

WHERE'S PENKOVSKY?

July, 1973
American Embassy
Shantipath
Chanayakapuri
New Delhi

Graham sat in his cushioned, high-backed chair anxiously awaiting a phone call. His eyes moved to the artifacts from other parts of the world he had displayed in his office. His gaze lingered on a framed picture of the Taj Mahal, personally and affectionately autographed to him by the current American Secretary of State.

Graham read the lengthy message about Penkovsky for the umpteenth time. It stated that Penkovsky moved to Washington with his "uncle" who was assigned to the Soviet Embassy there. Evidently, uncle was not the Rezident but a senior KGB member. Penkovsky attended two years of high school in Chevy Chase, Maryland where he readily made high school acquaintances. A natural linguist, he easily polished his American English. He then attended Georgetown University in Oriental Studies for two further years where he concentrated on Urdu. When uncle was transferred, Penkovsky also left. Uncle disappeared into the web of KGB bureaucracy on Lubyanka Street in Moscow. Penkovsky also disappeared for a number of years, until now.

Penkovsky told the debriefing team that he had received his engineering degree at the Moscow Institute. He recruited and managed agents for the KGB in Karachi and Islamabad before moving to the Soviet Embassy in New Delhi. He ran three local agents in New Delhi. He used forged Indian national identity papers to conceal himself from the local and Russian authorities during the week before the meeting in Bombay.

Penkovsky came from a family of that name from Georgia. Unusual, as Penkovsky is not a typical Georgian name. According to

Penkovsky, the family was very close to Stalin in Georgia before he rose to fame and power in the Communist movement. As Stalin gained more power, so did the Penkovskys.

Penkovsky identified his three Indian agents. He identified the other KGB members he knew in India and in his prior assignments. He gave detailed information on the KGB's activities in India, Afghanistan, and Pakistan. He also provided a summary of the KGB training program for new spies similar to that which the CIA held at the Farm in Virginia. He was an information treasure.

Graham turned to the newspaper clippings that Jenny had cut out. The local papers had a field day guessing about the missing Soviet diplomat. Was he kidnapped by another country? Killed? Did he run away with his mistress to Nepal? Where was he? At the American Embassy, British High Commission? More and more speculation. On and on. That sold many newspapers.

Graham's phone rang. Graham jumped instinctively. He had already instructed Jenny not to pick it up.

"Hello," he said.

"The goods have been shipped." The line went dead.

Graham went through his open office door to Jenny sitting just outside.

"I'm going to be with Jay Jay for a few minutes. I'm not expecting any appointments for the rest of the morning. I just might sneak away to take some personal time off this afternoon."

"Yes, sir," she cheerfully replied.

"Jay Jay, I have an IMMEDIATE to send to Langley. We got the Soviet defector out of the country. He's on his way to his new home."

"Good work, Boss."

THE REZIDENT'S QUESTION

July, 1973
Indian Intelligence Bureau (IB)
Undisclosed Location
New Delhi

As was often the case, Colonel Bhandari happened to be alone in his office when the phone rang. He set aside the most intriguing report from Four about possible foreign espionage penetrations in the Indian Air Force. Several Indian Air Force officers were recruited by the KGB while in Russia training on the latest MIG and Sukhoi jet fighters now used by the IAF.

The Colonel contemplated how he might turn those men to spy on the Russians for India.

"This is Colonel Bhandari."

"Hello, Colonel Bhandari. This is Vladimir Yankovich. I am the Rezident at the Soviet Embassy here. May I have a minute of your time?"

Yes, Mr. Yankovich, I know who you are. How may I help you?"

"It seems that one of my Embassy staff has gone missing. I wonder if you know of his whereabouts."

The Colonel could not help himself. He noticed a clear English accent in the Russian Rezident's speech.

He replied, "Mr. Yankovich, I do not know where he is. I know only what has been stated in the local newspapers. Bold front page headlines, I believe, for several days running, including a fine picture of the young man, a Mr. Penkovsky. Surely you do not suspect what we may call foul play?"

"We do suspect that he has been, as you say, kidnapped by some foreign agency. Please call me immediately, Colonel Bhandari, if you find information about my missing staff member. We are already working with the Customs and Immigration Authorities and the Police to try to find him."

"I will contact you at your Embassy, should I acquire any information."

"Thank you, Colonel. By the way, I should make an appointment to visit you one of these days. I have been here in New Delhi only for a few months, and have not had a chance to meet too many people."

"I would welcome meeting you, Rezident Yankovich. In fact, I did try twice to meet you some months back but unfortunately, you were too busy. Perhaps, another time."

"I truly appreciate anything you can do to help us find this young man. Surely, you realize that I must account to my superiors in Moscow. I must find him!"

"Again, Mr. Yankovich, I will notify you in the event that we learn where he is. Goodbye."

Colonel Bhandari hung up. He doodled as his feelings about his just concluded conversation boiled up within him. He meditated with his own thoughts for a few minutes.

Amazing, just amazing!

I know you, Mr Rezident. You are in charge of the ten KGB agents in New Delhi we have so far identified. Mr. KGB, you are in a pickle, as the English say. Through no fault of your own, you will tell your masters in Moscow. The KGB bosses get angry when one of their own defects, especially to the Americans.

Mr. Rezident, I am aware of your many devious machinations since you arrived here ten months ago. I can count the number of local Indian newspaper reporters on your payroll. I know which Indian politicians you are bankrolling. You are financing that rag if a paper, the Communist Party of India's mouthpiece. I suspect one in the P.M.'s cabinet is in your pocket. Unfortunately, she would not believe it even should I show her proof. Not just because she once was given a mink coat by your Premier, but because she is too unworldly, too idealistic, to understand despots and their nasty ways.

Well, I understand your despotic ways, and I do not like them. It is simply not fitting for such a powerful country to feast on us in the hinterland, the third world. You so easily take advantage of our leaders' quiet desires to amass great amounts of money. Yes, we are aware of the corruption around us. That does not mean you should take advantage of it.

Oh, yes, you took over the East European countries, not with the ballot but with your tanks. You brutally put down local insurrections in Czechoslovakia, Hungary and another country, I forget which. What does it matter? You are brutal.

Yes, the Indian IB is just like the American CIA and the Russian KGB. We each have our different values and methods. Rather, I say that the CIA and the IB have values that reflect their own country's values. The KGB? I see no values there.

Just like its predecessor, the Cheka, or the NKVD. Or, is it NVKD? I cannot remember.

Oh, well.

I am intrigued that Graham Smith came to this office within the first month of his tour here. Not like you, Mr. Rezident. He showed me his Embassy credentials. He did not state it outright, but, by inference, said that he is the head of the CIA here, and hoped that we could find a way to work together for our mutual benefit. (1) He said that he is not interested in stealing Indian secrets, but very interested to know what the Russians are stealing here.

You Russians are stealing our country, that's what!

I found Mr. Smith's approach to be very refreshing. Indeed, we have collaborated a few times over the months he has been here.

Of course, I will never tell Mr. Smith that we have him at work and his house from time to time under observation. That's just not how we play the game. As he is a professional spy, he knows that we are watching him and his staff. True, we pay much more attention to the more threatening Russian, Chinese and Pakistani spies than we do to the Americans.

Fortunately for the IB, most of the diplomats on our surveillance list live in the Diplomatic Enclave. It is easy to position one surveillance team to look after several diplomats' houses. That was not the original purpose of developing a Diplomatic Enclave but it helps us keep track of numerous comings and goings. That American spy masquerading as a polo player lives in the adjacent house to the Smiths. How convenient for us.

Let's see. Where is that surveillance report? Here it is under another stack. Yes, just about ten days ago. A man of European description visited the Smith home two nights running. It was unusual as the Smiths were not throwing one of their rather subdued parties at the time. What caught the attention of our surveillance team was not the clothes the man was wearing but his shoes and his hair. The team stated that the shoes were definitely Russian made. His hair the first night was long and blond. The second night he had a cap pulled over his head which was almost bald. He lost his hair overnight. The man's description matches that of the KGB agent Penkovsky.

Mr. Rezident, do you think that I would tell you that we observed your Mr. Penkovsky at the CIA man's home, not once but twice? I think not. Quiet congratulations to you, Mr. Smith. Your secret is safe with me.

(1) The CIA has liaison arrangements with numerous foreign partners as stated by Crumpton, Henry. *The Art of Intelligence, Lessons from a Life in the CIA's Clandestine Services.* New York: Penguin Books, 2012. Print, pages 83-98.

ALI'S ANXIETY

July, 1973
Juhu Beach Hotel
Near Bombay, India

An accelerated heart rate and apprehension arose in equal parts as Ali fought indigestion from his just completed dinner. He signed his name and room number on the bill, rose from the table, nodded to the elderly couple nearest him, and left the dining room. He walked through the reception area, noting that it was empty of guests. He nodded to the hotel clerk as he passed the sign-in counter.

No one interested in me.

He opened the large glass swinging hotel door and descended the front steps. Lingering moisture from the recent monsoon rain hit him in the face. The sun cast a red glow on the low clouds as it disappeared over the Arabian Sea. A slight breeze blew in from the seaside.

Dusk quickly fell as Ali strode away from the beach and to his car, parked around the corner just a few hundred yards down the street. He looked around, pulled the key from his pocket, unlocked the door, and slid into the driver's seat. He glanced up and down the street one more time but saw no one. He listened intently for a noise but heard only the surf pounding on the nearby beach. He smelled the salt air and a whiff from the nearby open nallah ditch. He started the car and drove off to meet his agent.

Ever cautious, Ali had carefully planned the 13 miles to pick up his agent. He knew exactly how many minutes the drive to the train station would take and he'd planned to be in the immediate vicinity a few minutes before the train arrived. He had previously agreed on an alternative place and time to meet Dutta, should they miss the first rendezvous.

Ali's thoughts turned for a moment to Ambika, waiting nervously at home for his return.

As he drove, Ali reviewed his meeting plan again in his head. He had reviewed it many times in the days before this meeting. He knew what he had to execute down to the minute. He again mentally went through the ISI checklist:

What did we discuss at our last meeting?

What requires my follow up?

What are my objectives for this meeting?

What personal issues does my agent have?

Does he have workplace problems?

What cover story to tell, should we both be in the car and have an accident?

Set a date, time and place for the next meeting.

Ali's mind wandered as he wove through the local traffic. Cars, buses, bicycles, and a few trucks flowed as one body around him in the accelerating darkness. Ali slowed and honked at a Vespa scooter overtaking him and cutting him off. A sari-clad lady on the back of the scooter turned and scowled at him.

Ali turned on the running lights of his black four-door car. He tried, somewhat unsuccessfully, to distance himself from the vehicles around him. Ali felt that he was in a tube, fluid and full of jostling things, all moving at the same speed in the same direction, and he was thankful for the darkness that surrounded him.

The closer Ali got to his rendezvous, the more nervous he became, checking repeatedly in his rear view mirror. If he detected surveillance before he picked up Dutta, he would have to abort his meeting. He was glad they had arranged for an alternative rendezvous for later that night.

Ali's lower jaw tightened as he approached the GTB Nagar Station. He felt cold sweat on his hands as he downshifted the car.

He found a space on a side street to hover for a few seconds as he awaited the train. His reverie was interrupted by a roar on the overhead track. The train appeared, an electrified grey-green monster with unruly open windows. As it came to a full stop, hundreds of passengers flowed down the steps to the street level like lava out of a volcano.

Ali scanned the crowd for Dutta but did not see him. His heart pounded like a hammer under his cotton shirt.

Once he recognized Dutta standing under a street lamp, he drove up to him.

"Welcome, brother. Please get in."

"Thank you for picking me up!" Dutta exclaimed rather loudly to anyone nearby.

He got in and closed the passenger door.

Ali drove away from the Station.

"Ram Lal, I am glad to meet you. How are you?"

"I am well," he replied, moving his head from side to side as only an Indian can do.

"Do you have any concerns, or need anything that I can provide?"

"No. I am fine. Thank you for asking."

"Do you have a new list of visitors? That information is very helpful to us."

"Yes, I do. You know, we operate the nuclear reactors 24 hours a day, seven days a week. I regularly volunteer for the third shift. That shift always has the fewest staff. I sometimes have the place to myself for hours so it is easy for me to access the latest names on the visitor logs. Of course, I have gotten very familiar with some of their names, as they have been regular visitors for several months. I usually do not actually meet them as I am only involved in operations and maintenance."

Ali checked his rear view mirror again for surveillance and found none. He started to relax a bit as the initial stress of picking up Dutta was over.

Dutta continued. "This month we have seen new names from the Ballistics Research Lab in Chandigarh. Their names are in my report. They huddled for a whole week in one of our conference rooms with our own scientists. As you know, over the last several months we have regularly had visits from what I will call the old list of Chandigarh scientists. I suspect that the old list is the development team. The four men who were at the Lab two weeks ago are new to us. I believe that these scientists are part of a build team. I can only conclude that the design phase for whatever part of the nuclear bomb Chandigarh is responsible for is over. Here are the new names."

Ram Lal shifted in his seat sufficiently to pull a piece of paper from his pants pocket. He placed the paper on the edge of his seat nearest Ali.

"This is very interesting, Ram Lal. You told me in May that a new group of scientists from the Pune Lab visited, perhaps part of a build team, and that the Pune design part may be over. You did not have any new names to report when we met last month. What do you think, now?"

Ali drove past the turnoff for the Chunabhati Station, swerving to miss a stray cow.

"First, Pune. Now, Chandigarh. I think that the total bomb design has been finalized. Based on the new scientist names on the visitor sign-in list I believe the build process has truly begun. As I told you in May, I believe that the Trombay Lab has assigned other labs to design and build various parts of the bomb. I don't know which labs have been assigned to build which parts. I believe the bomb will be assembled at my Lab before taking it to the Rajasthan Desert for explosion. That is why the builders must first visit Trombay, to confirm their part and to schedule the final assembly. The various components have to be assembled in a precise sequence for the bomb to detonate."

Ali piloted the car down a narrow side street. "Can you tell me what other sites may also be designing and building the bomb components?"

"Well, I can guess that the Kalpakkam Lab may also be involved. I do not know of any others."

"So, we can conclude that the build process has begun and that it involves Pune, Kalpakkam and Chandigarh. The critical question, then, is how long will it take to complete the build and assemble the bomb? Can you estimate that?"

Ram Lal pondered the question for a moment then stated, "I think that the build process will take about a year. So, assume that the bomb will be ready for detonation in May or June of next year."

Concentrating on the traffic flow ahead, and with both hands in a steel grip on the steering wheel, Ali said, "That is a valuable estimate, Ram Lal. Do you notice anything else that's not routine at your Trombay Lab? Anything we might also be interested in?"

"Last week our top three scientists were out of the Lab for three days. They left together and returned together on the same day. It is against Lab policy for all three of them to be away at the same time. I asked one of their assistants where they went. He said that they had appointments in New Delhi. He did not know why or with whom. I believe they were conferring with some of the politicians, perhaps even the Prime Minister herself, about the bomb's progress."

Ali moved back to the main road. He slowed behind a five tonne truck crabbing in the same direction. He dared not pass it.

"That is good information, Ram Lal. Please also note such future travel activity in your next reports. How is your work going otherwise?"

"Oh, we are having some difficulty with the CIRUS nuclear reactor. Nothing of great danger, mind you. The heat shield is cracking and we cannot control the core temperature as precisely as we should. I am looking into a fix for that."

"I did not ask you last month about the proposal you received to marry. Do you have news?"

Embarrassed, Ram Lal shifted in his seat. "I told the match maker that I was not interested. He did not like my answer but he persisted. I finally had to tell him that I was interested in someone else, not the lady in question. He then offered his services to me to arrange a marriage with the lady I was interested in. I told him to wait a week for me to decide. After a week I told him that my lady already had an arranged marriage offer. That turned him off. I am just not willing to get married now."

Showing relief in his voice, Ali replied, "Well, there will be a right time for you to get married. You will know when that is. By the way, here are some rupees for your work. They are but a token of our appreciation." Ali handed Ram Lal an envelope from his shirt pocket. Ram Lal folded it once and deposited the envelope in his pants pocket.

Ali continued, "You know that you are doing us a great service by telling us about Trombay's involvement in designing and building a nuclear weapon. With your facts we may be able to stop Prime Minister Gandhi from approving a nuclear explosion. Your parents would be justifiably proud..."

"I gladly provide this information. I know you will make good use of it."

"You know that our car meetings at night are the best way to protect us both from being discovered...I will drop you at the main Kurla Station. You can find your way home from there."

The two agreed on arrangements for their next meeting one month later.

As he stopped before the Station to let Dutta out, Ali said, "Ram Lal, you are very much appreciated by those in Pakistan who receive this information. At some time in the future, you will be well received there. For now, remember, should you be compromised because of your work with us, I will immediately send you our secret signal to leave the country. When you receive it, you must immediately leave. That is for your own protection."

"I understand. I will do so. Thank you. I wish you many blessings."

Dutta got out of the car and joined the flow of humanity up the stairs to the overhead platform. Ali's adrenalin slowed as he put the car in gear and drove back toward his hotel with a broad grin and twinkles in his eyes.

Ambika's Relief

July, 1973
J Block
Green Park
New Delhi

The sun was starting to set behind dark rain clouds as the taxi from Palam Airport dropped Ali and his overnight bag and briefcase in front of his house in Green Park. He sauntered through the front gate, eager for the embraces of his family.

"Ambika! Kumar! I am home!"

Ambika and Kumar met him halfway up the short driveway. He hugged both, then picked up Kumar and carried him into the house. Ambika quietly followed with the bag and briefcase.

"I missed you, Dad. Did you bring me anything from Bombay?"

"Yes, son. Look in my bag."

Kumar pulled out a toy MIG-21 jet fighter with Indian insignia on the wings and tail. He ran around the living room, bombing everything in sight.

"Ambika, you look lovely. I missed you. It's nice to come home to a loving family and tidy house," Ali gushed. "Oh, I see you bought a new standing lamp for the living room. It looks nice there."

"How was your business trip?" Ambika queried in a rather halting voice.

"It was very successful. Both you and Akbar should be pleased at my results. You know, I can do this work...I see the silverware and dishes on the table for dinner. What are we having? I am starved."

"I am relieved that you are home. I promise not to get upset again until you have to visit Bombay to do Akbar's work."

GRAHAM NO LONGER DUBIOUS

July, 1973
J Block
Green Park
New Delhi

Emily graciously poured cold tea for the three men as they settled into their regular places in Donovan's office. She put the iced tea bottle down and passed sugar to Ali and Graham. Fortunately, neither required milk, because there was none to offer that evening. Emily gave Donovan one last, penetrating glare as she closed the door to the rest of the house.

The heat and moisture of the day filled the room. The oppressive monsoon effect on temperature and moisture was evident everywhere. The punka fan slowly turned overhead pushing the hot, wet air around. A moment of silence lengthened as the three looked at each other, sipping their respective drinks. Who would start? Graham or Ali? Certainly not Donovan.

Graham broke the silence. "Ali, you asked about the Trombay Lab. We have no information that Trombay is developing a nuclear bomb. As you well know, neither India nor Pakistan has signed the Nuclear Non-Proliferation Treaty. So the Trombay authorities are under no compulsion to open their doors to the IAEA. They allowed the IAEA access two years ago not because they had to, but to show the world that the Trombay nuclear work was totally peaceful in nature. If your information is correct, I doubt that the Indian authorities will allow the IAEA to inspect now. Trying to get the IAEA involved now will only produce a dead end."

"Have your satellites detected any bomb preparation in the desert?"

"No, we have not. Have you any new information for me?"

"Yes, I do. I told you that P.M. Ghandi had approved the development of a nuclear weapon and that she had assigned the

Trombay Lab to oversee it. Our source at Trombay now believes that the bomb development phase has been completed. He says that bomb components are now being built at various unknown locations. Trombay will put the bomb together before it is sent to the Rajasthan desert for the test. Since Bhabha died, the Indian scientists have switched their work to a plutonium implosion device. We suspect that the nuclear test will be held with plutonium. We have another confidential source who is aware of this project but does not have access to any details about it. He tells us that this project is top, top secret. Only a few in the Indian government know about it. Even some of the top military leaders are not aware of this secret project."

"You have a second, confirming source for this bomb project?"

"Yes, another agent, in Indore."

Graham made a few notes on his slim pocket notepad. Ali paused to allow this information to sink in.

Graham replied, "Thank you for this information. Are you sure that the nuclear device will be using plutonium? Where is Trombay getting the plutonium?"

"Our scientists back home believe that the plutonium is coming from the CIRUS reactor at Trombay, the Canadian-Indian Reactor with U.S.-supplied heavy water. It was installed at the Trombay site in 1956 before the IAEA was formed. CIRUS became operational in 1960. It burns natural U-238 uranium fuel and can produce seven to ten kilograms of spent plutonium per year. That plutonium, of course, has to be reprocessed to a much higher purity before it can be used in a bomb.

"Your 'Fat Man' atomic bomb dropped on Nagasaki in 1945 took about 6 kilos of highly reprocessed plutonium to produce an explosion equal to 20,000 tons of TNT, totally destroying Nagasaki. By the way, the plutonium used in nuclear weapons is a man-made substance. The Manhattan Project engineers in 1943 named it after the planet Pluto and gave it an atomic number of 94.

"Graham, in 1958 Prime Minister Nehru authorized a plutonium reprocessing plant. The reprocessing project, known appropriately as the Phoenix, became operational in 1961. The Phoenix is providing the enriched plutonium for the bomb.

"Here is another item to add to your list of suspicions. Your scientists in America will tell you that the plutonium must be properly placed in the core to obtain an explosive chain reaction, not a dud. The Indian scientists built the Purnima research reactor to determine how to place the plutonium. That reactor came on line last year.

"I told you that the Indian scientists have been driving this nuclear bomb program for years. Please write down these dates:

1956 Apsara nuclear research reactor came on line.

1960 CIRUS 40 megawatt reactor came on line.

1961 Phoenix plutonium reprocessing plant came on line.

1972 Purnima research reactor for plutonium bomb design came on line.

1974 India's expected first nuclear bomb explosion.

Does that get your attention?"

Now visibly agitated, Graham stated, "Obviously, Ali, I will have to alert my government about this supposed development. Just so you know, I will send a message to my American headquarters about your information. I will explain that the original source is an Indian government official, not known but that the intermediary source is a reliable foreign national. I will state that this information cannot be confirmed. Is that OK with you?"

"Yes. Please do not tell your headquarters about my nationality or situation here in New Delhi."

"You indicated that the bomb may go off sometime next year. When? What is your source for that estimate?"

"My agent at the Trombay Lab estimated by May or June of next year. Of course, P.M. Gandhi must give the final approval to explode the bomb. We hope your Ambassador may be able to convince her not to detonate it before she gives the approval."

"Ali, I am still dubious about this information. Is your Trombay agent making this up? You know, some agents have large imaginations especially when they think their information, false information, may get them more money, or prevent their termination as an agent."

"No, this information is absolutely correct. It comes from a highly reliable agent who has the highest motivation, not money."

"Still, I cannot believe that Prime Minister Gandhi would be so foolish as to approve the development and detonation of a nuclear bomb. Since we met, I've done research about this issue. For your information the American government told the Indian authorities in 1970 that using the spent plutonium from the CIRUS reactor for a bomb would be a breach of the U.S.-Indian nuclear cooperation agreement. There would be dire consequences. Canada in 1971 also told Mrs. Gandhi that India's development of nuclear weapons would cause Canada to withdraw its support for their nuclear reactors used for peaceful purposes. I just cannot believe she would be so reckless."

"Graham, I can assure you that this information is true and not fabricated."

Graham paused for a few seconds, collecting his thoughts.

"Ali, you have given me a short history about India's development of the atomic bomb. Let me give you an assessment of India which you can send back to your ISI headquarters in Islamabad. Tell your bosses that this comes directly from the head of the CIA in New Delhi."

Ali crossed his arms on his chest.

"You know that Indira Gandhi along with Nasser in Egypt and Marshall Tito in Yugoslavia are the leaders of the non-aligned Third World Movement. All three leaders preach socialism by their own yet different definitions. The three talk a good talk about peace and love thy neighbor. The Third World Movement by last count constituted more than 35 countries. It already is a rather large and growing block in the United Nations. It has gained some international importance because of its moral statements.

"Ali, an India, once having exploded a nuclear device, loses all pretense of moral leadership with these other nations. Once she approves a nuclear explosion, Mrs. Gandhi risks giving up her moral voice, her moral influence. She totally loses credibility. Why would she do that? You have no answer, do you? Furthermore, India has a vibrant history of non-violence going back to Mahatma Gandhi. A nuclear weapon is not in India's psyche. I cannot believe Mrs. Gandhi is willing to forgo her worldly influence for a bomb."

"Well, Graham, perhaps these other countries might quietly compliment Mrs. Gandhi for not bowing to the wishes of the world powers."

"OK, consider this. Of the three leading countries, India is the most open society because it is a democracy. The other two are not. So, India is more susceptible to outside manipulation by another country."

Graham paused. Ali crossed his legs and sipped his tea.

"Now, what is of great interest to me and to the American government is that the Soviet Union is focusing on India, this more open society, in order to sway India and all of the Third World towards the Soviet Bloc. The Soviets, and especially the KGB, are more active here than in any other third world country...

"Just two years ago the Soviets signed a friendship treaty with the Indian government. The two countries agreed to a closer relationship of equals. They agreed to increased economic and political ties.

"The Soviet KGB over the last five years has totally penetrated all aspects of Indian life. These KGB officers have recruited as their agents some members of Parliament and top officials in the defense, foreign affairs, police and agricultural departments. We suspect that one of Mrs. Gandhi's cabinet members is also on the KGB payroll. Of course, corruption in this country is nothing new. It has just come to a higher level because the KGB is taking advantage of the numerous wide open opportunities which this democracy presents. We have evidence that the KGB is secretly funding the Communist Party of India and has on at least two occasions also funded Mrs. Gandhi's Congress Party elections. There is little that I or my government can do about this. The Indian government is responsible for stopping this corruption.

"Ali, I compete with the KGB for the influence of the Indian politicians or government officials on the basis of recommending the ethical thing to do, not in a bidding war where the highest paymaster wins. My job here is first to track the local activities of the Soviets, and then to deflect their influence. Mind you, my resources are nowhere near those of the KGB.

"Mrs. Gandhi is paranoid about the CIA. She has publicly stated that we want to assassinate her. That is farthest from the truth. I would willingly show her proof about massive KGB infiltrations into her government but unfortunately, she would not believe me."

Graham concluded, "Why am I telling you this now? For only one reason. The Russians have their own nuclear bomb technology. The Russians have deeply penetrated all aspects of Indian life. I know for a fact that they have not detected any bomb-building here. You can be sure that they would not tolerate an India building a nuclear bomb. The Russians have shown no interest in helping the Indian scientists develop a nuclear bomb. None! We think that if the

Russians knew of India's bomb development, they would quickly and quietly advise against it."

Ali immediately replied with a chuckle, "Well, then, Graham. Perhaps you should call the KGB head here in New Delhi and tell him India is developing a bomb."

"He also would not believe me. There is no love lost between the KGB and the CIA. Remember, we two are locked in a secret global war to influence other peoples toward our very different ways of life."

Both Graham and Ali reflected on their conversation before continuing.

"Let's not schedule another meeting now," Graham suggested. "We should meet when one of us has more information. Let's agree to contact Donovan when we're ready to meet, after either you or I have more information."

"Agreed."

They stood up as one and shook hands. Ali left first, again out the direct door to the verandah. Graham, practicing good tradecraft, waited 15 minutes before leaving.

Graham confessed, "Well, that was a rather intense meeting. I hardly finished my tea. This is a very serious development. Ali has been very convincing. I must devote more time to it."

He left without a further word. Donovan took ten deep, meditative breaths to calm his nerves before joining Emily to tell her what happened.

SHIREE MEETS ALI

August, 1973
English Book Store
Connaught Circus
New Delhi

Ali perused the Indian history section in the front of the bookstore until Shiree glided into the store. He was impressed at the quality of her embroidered silk sari, the red color usually worn by brides.

Shiree moved to the back of the book store where some of the older English novels were shelved. Ali walked slowly after her. No one else in the store paid any attention to them. The bookstore's young clerk was on the telephone in animated excitement with, undoubtedly, her boyfriend. The few other patrons were just browsing. Ali detected nothing suspicious.

"I just love Conan Doyle. Don't you?" She said softly, passing one of the Sherlock Holmes books to him. He took the book and saw that the edge of an envelope protruded from inside the back cover.

"Why, yes, this is a very interesting story," he replied, removing her envelope and putting his own into the book. "I'm sorry that I just do not have time to read such light material."

He passed the book back to her. She removed his envelope, put it into her purse, and replaced the book on the shelf.

"Is all well with you?" he whispered.

As she turned away, she replied, "As good as can be expected."

With that, she left the store. Ali examined a few more books before leaving.

THE PARSI

September, 1973
Taj Mahal Hotel
Bombay

Graham was tormented about the turn of events caused by his second conversation with Ali Khan. He gave a lot of thought, sometimes at 3 A.M., about some way to confirm what Ali had said about India's bomb project.

He considered all of the imponderables, the unknown pieces of the puzzle. As always, he distrusted the information from an unknown agent. How reliable was Ali's agent? Was Ali himself making up this story to embarrass Ambassador Moynihan with the Prime Minister?

He had the overwhelming and chilling thought that Pakistan might just start a new war by bombing the Trombay Lab. He knew that if the bomb did go off, and he had not already warned Langley, that he would not be well received back home.

Ali's agent indicated that the bomb would not be ready for detonation until May or June next year. That gave Graham some time to dig deeper. He decided to pursue other possibilities.

He reserved a table for two at his favorite Taj Hotel restaurant. He stayed at the Taj when he had to overnight in Bombay. Just not this time. The majestic six story building at Apollo Bunder faced west overlooking the Arabian Sea. He knew that the India Gate in front of the hotel had been built for King George V's visit in 1911. How ironic that the last of the British soldiers departed the newly independent India in 1948 through the same gate.

Graham always had the taxi driver deposit him at the side entrance of the hotel. He surmised that the front entrance was under surveillance of one kind or another. Besides, he liked to give a handful of rupees to the disfigured beggar who, Graham suspected, was assigned there by the beggar lords of Bombay.

He awaited his guest for a delicate lunch and a business discussion. He enjoyed delicious meals served on fine china with linen table cloths and fresh cut flowers in ornate vases, one perk of his current frustrating situation.

B.K. Mehta entered the dining room. A ramrod, handsome Parsi in his sixties with greying hair and a clean shaven face, Mehta always looked forward to a meeting with Graham. At each meeting Graham gave the Parsi a unique and challenging task. As usual, the Parsi wore a western business suit despite the humid Bombay weather. He noticed Graham sitting at the usual corner table, and as he stood, they shook hands.

"Graham, how nice to see you again! You find the best spot of the best restaurant in town. I can see the India Gate through that window."

"Welcome, B.K. I trust that you and your family have been well. Let's see, I last met you about six months ago. The information you gave me then was invaluable. Thank you."

"Always at your service, as long as you pay for lunch," B.K. jested.

As was their custom, the two chose from many delicious dishes on the menu. B.K. ordered Parsi dhansaak, Graham lamb kebob and lentils.

"This restaurant serves the very best meat with curried lentils and rice. Of course, being a Parsi, I can eat meat. I must confess that I have meat two or three times a week. I must blame my faith and that of my family on Zoroaster."

Having ordered, the two turned to business.

"As you know, B.K., we Americans are straightforward and direct when it comes to business matters. We do not waste a lot of time in non-essential talk. Your family has been operating your export-import business here in Bombay since before the British times. Your clan is well connected here and you know everyone of any importance. I have a list of equipment, items which are not manufactured in India. They have to be imported and I would like to know if you, or another company you may know, have imported them. Please know that the items on this list are not illegal. However, they are all components to manufacture an atomic bomb."

The Parsi grimaced and held his hands up, palms open. He narrowly missed spilling the water glasses. "Graham, are you telling me that the Indian government, my government, may be developing an atomic bomb? God forbid!"

"Yes, I am. Obviously, this is very confidential information. Should you find that some of this equipment has been imported, it most likely has been shipped to the nearby Trombay Atomic Research Lab."

Graham gave the Parsi a list of items, single spaced on one page.

Graham continued, "If this equipment has, indeed, been imported, it is very serious. My government will be deeply concerned. I'd like to come back to you in two months' time to obtain what results you have found. But for now, let's enjoy our lunch."

THE IB AND WONG

September, 1973
Indian Intelligence Bureau (IB)
Undisclosed Location
New Delhi

It was almost four P.M. and he was nodding off when Colonel Bhandari heard a knock at his door.

"Enter," he bellowed.

One and Three stepped into the spacious office.

"Well, Gentlemen, you have asked for a special meeting to discuss Mr. Wong, the Chinese trade representative. I have some cold tea or nimbu pani still on the side table. Please help yourselves and have a seat."

They both did so.

The Colonel poured a cool glass of ice water and lime juice for himself and joined them.

"Three, I understand that you had a surveillance team look after Mr. Wong when he was last in Calcutta. Please tell us what your team found out."

"Colonel, Wong spent the morning visiting trinket shops and art galleries. He purchased a number of more expensive items to send to Hong Kong. He had a bit of lunch in one of the street noodle stands. I would not recommend that, but he is, after all, a Chinaman familiar with noodle stands in his own country. I am sure that his stomach can take Indian noodles."

"Enough of noodles, Three. Just tell us what Wong was really up to."

"As I suspected, Colonel, Wong spent that afternoon visiting people that I would call cutouts for the Naxalites. He was seen going into back rooms of three different restaurants to give large bags of rupees to three different local men. We did manage to follow each of the three after they left Wong. They each first took some of the money for themselves and gave the rest to known troublemakers, Marxist insurgents. Wong is funding the CPI Marxist insurgency in West Bengal."

"Well, Three, that is a good but incomplete report. Please tell us, is Wong doing this as a true agent of the Chinese Communist government, or is he a rogue working for himself or some powerful taipan in Hong Kong?"

"We can only confirm that Wong is giving money to the local CPIM people. We do not know who his backers are or what his source of money is. We do know that he is receiving much more money from Hong Kong into his trade account than he needs to purchase the goods he buys. He is using that excess money to fund the CPIM insurgency."

"Are the vendors who sell their goods to Wong also giving him a cash discount that he could give to the CPIM?"

"We have asked them and they say that they are not giving any cash back to Wong."

The Colonel summarized the situation as was his habit.

"Let us then review. We have concrete information that Mr. Wong is providing rupees to the insurgents. What he is doing is against our law. He is an accredited Chinese official with a diplomatic passport. What should we do with him? Expel him? Turn him? Trail him to learn who his local accomplices are? What is your recommendation, One? You have been uncharacteristically silent through all of this."

One joined in. "Thank you, Colonel. My first impulse is to declare him *persona non grata* and kick him out of the country. That may be short-sighted. We know that he is paying the insurgents. Perhaps we could better track his movements and his contacts to learn more about the leaders in their network. Forcing him to leave India may have some small political repercussions with the Chinese government but that should not be the reason to let him stay here. If we do tell him to leave, we can also be sure that some other Chinese will replace him. It is clear to me that someone in China is now funding the Marxists and will in the future continue to do so."

"Well, One, what do you recommend?"

"I recommend that we allow him to continue with his purchasing farce, and learn more about those to whom he is giving money."

"Three, what do you say about this?"

"Sir, I heartily agree. We can gain measurably more by learning who the insurgent leaders truly are. As you know, those who take the lead in the public protests are not the true organizers, the true planners. The lead demonstrators are cannon fodder, so to speak. We want to know who the true planners are, so we can apprehend them."

"Well, then, we have a consensus. Three, it is up to your organization to follow Wong, and report on his contacts. Agreed?"

"Yes, Colonel. I shall give both you and One regular reports about our progress. As usual, I ask both of you for your continuing recommendations as we go forward. Perhaps we should meet again about this in a month's time."

The Colonel made a few notes on his notepad.

"Gentlemen, there is yet a further avenue to pursue here." That comment drew One and Three back to their seats.

The Colonel continued, "One, I would like you to contact the bank here in New Delhi receiving Wong's money from Hong Kong. You may simply state that you are pursuing a drug ring or give the top bank official some other vague story. After all, you are responsible for providing our state security against all kinds of local groups trying to subvert our society. Please obtain what information you can about the Hong Kong bank which sends the money to Wong. Then, once you know the name of that bank, please get our economic counselor at our Hong Kong Consulate to ask discreetly about the Chinese sources of these funds. We may then be a bit closer to knowing who is behind this project to cause unrest and insurrection in West Bengal. Can you do that, One and advise us the results?"

"Yes, surely, Colonel."

"There is one other matter before I release you. Three, please give me any new information about the Pakistani professor, Mr. Khan."

Three straightened up in his comfortable chair and pulled a folder from his briefcase.

"Yes, Sir, I was hoping to have time to give you an update. We had promised to place surveillance on him again in November. As it turned out, one of our surveillance teams was available to follow him for a full day late last month. As is our practice, we started at his home in the early morning. He did not leave his bungalow until about 10:00 A.M. then drove to the IIT campus in Haus Khas. We watched him interviewing students in front of the campus dining hall until about 11:30 A.M. He took notes on a clipboard as the students answered his questions. He then walked to the professors' office building, picked up two professors, and escorted them to his car."

Three looked at his notes.

"The three ate lunch at the Haus Khas Sweet Shoppe at the nearby market. They laughed a lot over lunch. We did not get close enough to them to learn what they were having fun about. Khan paid the bill and escorted the two professors back to the campus. Khan visited the campus book store and was seen carrying two engineering texts back to his car. He drove directly home, arriving at his house in Green Park by about 2:20 P.M. He did not go out for the rest of the day.

"I should also mention, Sir, that we did observe the American lady from down the street drive by the Khan's home to pick up the Khan's young boy. It was just before 9:00 A.M. She drove off with her own son and Khan's son in her car. About 2:40 P.M. Mrs. Khan drove off, and returned some thirty minutes later with her son in the car. We surmise that the two ladies have a car pool to take their boys to the same school. Of course, we just noted those comings and goings on the file. We were there to follow Khan, not the ladies."

"Remember, Three, I expect Mr. Khan to leave India by November when his one-year tour should be up. Please note that on his file. If he has not left by then, we will need to find out why."

Three consulted Khan's file.

"Yes, I noted on his file that he should leave us by this November. I will follow up on that in two months' time. I still give Khan a C rating. He seems to be doing a legitimate job. Still, he is a Pakistani. We should be wary. I will definitely track Khan again in November as we initially planned. I will keep you advised."

"Well done, gentlemen, and thank you," Colonel Bhandari said, sipping the last of his nimbu pani. The two men bowed and left quietly.

GRAHAM'S SURPRISE MESSAGE

September, 1973
American Embassy
Shantipath
Chanyakapuri
New Delhi

The Chief, Middle East Division (C/MED) of the Clandestine Services (CS) was responsible for the Arab Desks at CIA Headquarters in Langley, Virginia. The C/MED oversaw the countries from Egypt to Pakistan. Many of the best CIA spies operated in these countries which gave them familiarity with the considerably different cultures. They obtained over time an excellent understanding about a totally different way of looking at the world. Both the C/MED and the intelligence his group collected were held in high esteem at the Agency. After all, that part of the world was the second most inscrutable to American intelligence. The first was the Soviet Union which had its own CIA Division.

Graham, the CS Chief of Station in India, was responsible to two people. His first duty was to his Ambassador, his local and immediate boss. His equal duty was to the Chief, South East Asia (C/SEA). His boss at Langley Headquarters ruled the Agency's secret intelligence operations from India and China to the Koreas, Japan and Indonesia.

Graham knew that each geographical division was an independent entity, sacrosanct to itself. He was surprised and shocked, then, to receive a special "eyes only" message from the Indian Desk about Pakistan's decision to develop a nuclear weapon. First, the information had to come from the Pakistan Desk to the Indian Desk. He knew that it could come only through the coordination of the chiefs of the two divisions. Second, he was shocked at the contents of the message. It stated that Pakistan's Prime Minister Bhutto in January, 1972 assembled a group of scientists and engineers to develop a nuclear weapons program—21 months ago!

That information infuriated Graham. He had to confront Ali. He called Donovan to arrange for an emergency meeting that night.

The same message stated that the analysts on the other side of the house thought that India did, indeed, possess sufficient technical knowledge to develop and build an atomic bomb. They confirmed that India's nuclear scientists since the early 1950's had consistently pushed to obtain approval from the Indian politicians for bomb development. The analysts estimated that once a political decision to do so had been made, it would take the Indian scientists about two years to complete the bomb project. Graham remembered that those same analysts said in June that India's actual development of a nuclear weapon would be "highly unlikely" because the Indian politicians would not approve it.

GRAHAM CONFRONTS ALI

September, 1973
J Block
Green Park
New Delhi

Graham arrived at Donovan's first. Hands clenched at his sides, he stood in the center of the small office, refusing to sit down.

"Donovan, I have called this meeting because I have new information. I want to confront Ali with it. He has been playing both of us for fools. I can tolerate a lot in this God-forsaken place, but not to be taken for a fool."

"What do you mean?"

"I have just learned that the Pakistani Prime Minister approved the development of a nuclear bomb over a year ago. Here, we both have been under the great illusion that Pakistan did not want to develop a bomb, but wanted the Americans to stop India from having one. Now, I find that Pakistan is just as two-faced as India!"

"Graham, I am shocked. How can your CIA have learned about such a secret and sensitive decision? Surely, only a few even in the highest Pakistani government circles can know about this decision!"

Before Graham could answer, Ali appeared in the door from the verandah. He smiled.

"Donovan said that you wanted to meet me tonight. Do you have some new information?" Ali asked.

Seeing Ali, Graham's temper got the better of him.

"You've been lying to me!" Graham stormed. "Your Prime Minister approved the development of your own nuclear bomb twenty-one months ago!"

Still standing, Ali backed away as though he expected Graham to hit him. He said nothing.

Donovan stood between the two men, frowning, arms folded.

Graham continued, "You cannot deny it. We have the evidence. The Multan meeting in January, 1972. You must have known about it all along!"

Ali replied, defensively, "We have known for some time that India is developing a nuclear weapon. We have learned from bitter experience that we cannot rely on other friendly countries for help when it comes to our own defense. Pakistan must do everything possible to defend ourselves when India does explode a bomb. This means we, too, must have the bomb. We consider our own bomb to be a necessary deterrent against a neighbor with whom we have fought three wars in the last 26 years!"

Graham retorted, "So, now you acknowledge that your government is in a race with India to develop and test your first nuclear weapon!"

"What did you expect, Graham? We were not going to wait until India already had a bomb and could hold nuclear terror over our heads. We will always be prepared to defend ourselves against such a hostile neighbor!"

Donovan interrupted them. "OK guys. Your loud voices are carrying back to my family and our servant's quarters. Stop yelling, sit down, now, or out you both go!"

Both men sat down in their usual chairs, glowering at each other.

Ali sighed as he sat back in his chair. He resumed in a less belligerent, quieter voice. "Graham, you must understand that my government made this decision only after great deliberation. We knew India was developing a bomb. We had two choices. We could bomb India's nuclear bomb-making facilities and thus start another war on the subcontinent. That is what my uncle, the air marshal, is so anxious to do. Or, we could build our own bomb. Yes, we have chosen to build the bomb so both countries will have a nuclear deterrent. Neither India nor Pakistan will have a military advantage. The military stalemate will continue, just at a higher level."

"This is nonsense! Yes, at a higher level of insecurity and danger to both countries! It takes only one Pakistani general like your uncle, hell-bent on destroying a major Indian city, to start a conflagration not seen since America dropped atomic bombs on Japan in World War Two."

"Yes, Graham. But, look at your country and the Soviets, enemies since the end of World War Two. America and the Soviets can annihilate each other with nuclear destruction many times over. Consequently, neither uses nuclear weapons. Your two countries have come to the brink of mutual destruction only once, during the Cuban Missile Crisis in 1962. It can be the same for India and Pakistan. Because both have nuclear weapons, neither will use them."

"That greater danger and, indeed, temptation, is now there, Ali. It was not there before."

Graham shifted in his chair and frowned, "So, if your country was so intent on building the bomb why did you involve me in this issue? You certainly do not need the Americans to exert pressure on the Indian government. Just proceed with your own bomb-making!"

"Getting you involved was my idea. It was approved by my boss here and my government in Islamabad. Remember, I am a university professor and not a professional spy. I am not a diplomat who can form foreign policy but I still believe that your Ambassador Moynihan may be able to stop India from testing its first nuclear weapon. Besides, Graham, as you are in the espionage business, surely you want to know what India is doing to build and test a bomb!"

Donovan, still standing, interrupted their intense dialogue. "OK, gentlemen. This is the end of my involvement with you. You are both adults. If you want to harangue each other, or fight, you will have to do it somewhere else. When you want to meet each other, find another place. I'm done with this. I am going to bed. Leave when you are finished. Good night."

With that, Donovan left them to argue further.

As he entered the bedroom, Emily asked, "What is all of the yelling about? Are they going away, finally?"

"Yes, love. I told them to leave, and not to come back. They can find another place where they can meet secretly without me. I am done with this intrigue."

She sighed. "Thankfully, at last. Now I can sleep at night." She closed her paperback about India's long history and gave him a big hug and kiss.

The Parsi's Report

November, 1973
Taj Mahal Hotel
Bombay

Graham was running late. His plane to New Delhi was departing in just two hours. He hoped that his Parsi friend was already waiting for him at their favorite restaurant at the Taj.

He greeted the maître d' and saw with relief that B.K. had, indeed, preceded him to the usual corner table. B.K. waived and gestured for Graham to join him.

Shaking hands, Graham puffed, "I'm sorry to be late. I just have time for some tea before I have to catch a plane. Thank you for coming."

"My pleasure, always, to meet you here. We will not be disturbed as this is a dead time for the restaurant. I have already taken the liberty of ordering for both of us. Here, let me pour you some tea."

"Old friend, have you any information about the list I gave you in September?"

"Yes, I do. Perhaps you will not be surprised at my findings. I give you back your list with my notes about those items that have been imported either by me or by one of my associates. Of course, I have retained confidentiality about my enquiries. That is one of the great benefits of belonging to the strong Parsi business community here in Bombay. We look after each other in business as well as spiritual matters."

B.K. pulled a folder out of his briefcase and gave it to Graham. The folder contained Graham's original one-page list plus several additional pages of B.K.'s notes.

Graham scanned the pages.

"You've found some imports going back to 1966! Most of them seem to have been sent to the Trombay Lab. I see that you list a few as going directly to Pune or Chandigarh. This is valuable

152

information. I cannot thank you enough for this, B.K. I owe you a great debt. How can I ever repay you?"

"You are welcome. I hope this in some small way can help you prevent India from taking the foolish step to build a nuclear bomb. How can you repay me? Simply by thinking of me when I am laid out on the Towers of Silence on Malabar Hill."

Graham got up, pocketed the notes, nodded and left to hail a taxi to the airport, his tea untouched.

BOMB-MAKING DETAILS

December, 1973
Pakistan High Commission
"The Palace"
Shantipath
Chanakyapuri
New Delhi

Ali carefully pulled a folded piece of paper from his pants pocket.

"Here, Akbar, is the list of important nuclear research centers where the Indian scientists are now building bomb components. When ready, the parts will be put together at the Trombay Lab. From there the completed bomb will be transported to the Rajasthan Desert site for detonation."

"Ali, this is great intelligence. We both can be very proud of your lovely Shiree for getting this vital information from her Committee."

Akbar took the single sheet of plain white paper and read the small typewritten note on it.

Trombay has enough high grade plutonium for an implosion nuclear bomb.

Trombay will assemble the bomb and transport it to the Pokhran test site for detonation. The electrical system is being made at The Centre for Advanced Technology, Indore. The reprocessed plutonium and the neutron initiator at the Atomic Research Centre, Kalpakkam. The conventional high explosive system at Terminal Ballistics Research Lab, Chandigarh. The diagnostics equipment and instruments at the High Energy Materials Lab, Pune.

"Of course, Ali, it is one thing for the bomb to be ready, and quite another for P.M. Gandhi to issue the order to detonate it. I believe that only she has that authority, not some Indian general hell-bent on getting his fifteen minutes of fame."

Akbar reflected for a moment.

"So, the most important aspect about this information is still missing. We do not know whether or when P.M. Gandhi will make the decision to detonate the bomb. And our source, however good, cannot tell us the P.M.'s *intentions*! We are still guessing about her possible decision and the timing of the detonation."

"Yes, you are correct, Akbar. At least we now have concrete information that the bomb is being built. I will now share this information with Graham Smith. He must get his Ambassador Moynihan to convince the P.M. not to detonate the bomb before she gives her approval."

"Please do so, but I doubt that the P.M. will either acknowledge the bomb or be influenced by the Americans if she has already decided to give her approval when the time comes. The critical issue now is whether the American Ambassador will confront the P.M. *before* she gives instructions to set off the bomb. Yes, please, go ahead, contact Mr. Smith. I must immediately inform the ISI in Islamabad. This is irrefutable proof that India is well on its way to assembling and exploding a nuclear bomb. Frankly, I cannot predict what our generals including your uncle will do when they receive this information. Perhaps they will send our fighter jets to destroy the four Labs and the bomb making equipment. That would start another war!"

Ali started to leave the room. Akbar's parting comment caused him to stop and turn around.

"Ali. A quick reminder. You remember how disappointed and disgusted you were with Shiree last month. She gave you information about India's nuclear progress in reactor development, information that had nothing to do with bomb development. For us, it was useless information which we simply discarded. I told you then not to chastise her, as both you and I have been taught to do when our women disappoint. No, always, always treat your agents with the dignity they deserve. Do not belittle their efforts, even when their results are way off target. It is they who are putting their lives on the line for us. If we are caught, we leave the country. If they are caught, they rot away in a local jail cell, forgotten by everyone involved. Please remember always to respect and protect your agent."

"Yes. Thank you, Akbar."

AKBAR'S CRITICAL MESSAGE

INTEL
CRITICAL
20 December, 1973
To: ISI, Islamabad
Attention: Head, India

Case Officer BAKRA obtained the following information from Agent BOKARO on 19 December by brush contact.

Trombay has enough high grade plutonium for an implosion nuclear bomb. Trombay will assemble the bomb and transport it to the Pokhran test site for detonation. The electrical system is being made at The Centre for Advanced Technology, Indore. The reprocessed plutonium and the neutron initiator at the Atomic Research Centre, Kalpakkam. The conventional high explosive system at the Terminal Ballistics Research Lab, Chandigarh. The diagnostics equipment and instruments at the High Energy Materials Lab, Pune.

This Agent did not have a timetable for the assembly. Agent BALOO told us earlier that it would take only months for the bomb components to be built and assembled. Given when Agent BALOO said that, we can predict that the bomb will be ready for detonation by May or June of next year.

The actual detonation must have the final approval of P.M. Gandhi. We cannot determine if or when she may give the approval.

C.O. BAKRA stated that this intel can be treated as very reliable.

Although Agent BOKARO is new, this Agent has access to highly classified information and has no reason to fabricate such a detailed and disturbing report.

Signed,
India Control

HAS KHAN LEFT INDIA?

December, 1973
Indian Intelligence Bureau (IB)
Undisclosed Location
New Delhi

Colonel Bhandari flipped through his ever-growing notes. He finally found what he was looking for, chastising himself for his disorganization. He wondered if it might be time to retire.

He picked up his internal phone and called Three.

"Three, this is the Colonel. I have a quick question. Did the Pakistani Khan already leave India? His one year stay here was over last month."

"Colonel, we did put a surveillance team on Khan again last month... per schedule. He was clean, again. But, he is still here. I cannot explain why."

"Well, Three, perhaps we are not casting a wide enough net for Khan. As you know, his work takes him to all of the IIT campuses. Perhaps he is clean in New Delhi but doing nefarious work in other places. The next time he makes a plane reservation to another city, please have one of our surveillance teams track him there and report back."

"As good as done, Sir." Three grinned. He congratulated himself on continuing to fulfil his promises to the Colonel.

Three softly placed the phone back on its cradle and called an associate to implement the Colonel's instructions.

GRAHAM REFUSES ALI'S REQUEST

December, 1973
Oberoi Hotel
Dr. Zakir Hussain Marg
New Delhi

"Thank you, Graham, for reserving this room so we could meet." Ali said as Graham opened the door and ushered him into the fifth floor hotel room. The two men stood adjacent to the bed and desk.

"As I said to you on the phone, I have some very interesting information for you. Here is a handwritten list of the sites where the nuclear bomb components are being manufactured." Ali passed a slip of paper to him.

"Thank you, Ali. I see that the Labs in Chandigarh, Indore, Pune and Kalpakkam are being used. Do you have a way to confirm this information? I do not have any assets at these places."

"Only the separate information from our asset at the Trombay Lab who told us in May that the build has begun in at least three or four different places. He did not know where, though."

"Well, then, is this information accurate? Can we trust your agent who gave this to you?"

"Yes, this agent is well placed to get this sensitive information. I cannot divulge more."

"I still have a hard time believing that India would be so reckless as to develop and set off an atomic bomb."

"Well, believe it! It is going to happen! Will you *now* get your Ambassador to tell Prime Minister Gandhi that you know she has approved the bomb, and convince her to stop this madness?"

"No, Ali, I will not. If the information is not correct, and he does complain to the P.M., Ambassador Moynihan will be seen as a fool of foreign intrigue. I cannot let that happen."

It was now Ali's turn to be upset. "Graham, you now have irrefutable proof that the bomb is now being built. I am keenly disappointed that you will not ask Ambassador Moynihan to talk to the P.M. about this bomb making. After all, I got you involved in this only so you could convince him to intervene before the bomb goes off!"

"I will do this, Ali. I will send this information back to CIA headquarters. I will request that the appropriate CIA person tell the American State Department representative about India's building a nuclear weapon. I will ask State to tell Ambassador Moynihan what to do about this. This is now a policy decision, not a matter of intelligence gathering."

"At least, you can get your satellites to spy on the Pokhran test site in the Rajasthan desert. That is where the bomb will be set off. Perhaps then you will believe me."

"I believe you, Ali. I am convinced that India will test a nuclear weapon. Again, it is not my place to decide what to do about this information."

Graham, now the cool head, arranged for another meeting with Ali on the assumption that he would learn of a decision from State before then.

The two spies departed, both rather dejected.

Graham Advises Langley

Late December, 1973
American Embassy
Shantipath
Chanakyapuri
New Delhi

Graham meditated quietly in his high-backed chair at his office. He doodled as he considered various options to resolve the issue of India's bomb.

He was convinced that India would, indeed, set off a nuclear bomb. He saw no outside force strong enough to stop it short of Pakistan starting another war.

Try as he might, he could find no effective solution beyond what he had already told Ali.

Graham had been in the intelligence business long enough to know that his bosses back home preferred two separate and reliable sources to validate both the information and the source. For a spy master to take unilateral action on only one "reliable source" sometimes caused one to have egg on his face, or worse.

Graham composed another message to CIA Headquarters. He referred to the previous alert of the same heading which detailed information about the bomb component imports from a known and reliable American agent, the Parsi in Bombay.

Using Ali's list, he wrote down the nuclear research sites where the bomb components were supposedly being produced. He was careful to note that the second list could not be confirmed as it had been given to him by a known Pakistani ISI spy. The Pakistani's information source was not known. He requested that Langley confer with State to determine what action to take.

He hoped that his message would receive immediate attention and cause a quick response.

THE AIR MARSHAL'S WAR PLAN

January, 1974
Eastern Air Command
Pakistani Air Force Base
Chaklala
Rawalpindi
Pakistan

Two Star Air Vice-Marshall Ahmed Anwar Khan held up a piece of paper to his close-knit assembled staff in the headquarters arena. All were standing for his one-minute instructions.

"This paper is irrefutable proof that India is not only designing a nuclear warhead but is now starting to build its components. This firm intelligence from one of our agents in India says that the components are now being assembled in Chandigarh, Pune, Indore, and Kalpakkam. These four places are prime targets for us to destroy before India can put together its first atomic bomb.

"Your immediate task is to plan for air strikes on two of these targets. I have chosen the Terminal Ballistics Research Lab in Chandigarh and the High Energy Materials Lab in Pune for our aircraft to strike. The two cities are just minutes away by jet. Our air squadron from Lahore will target Chandigarh. Our air squadron from Hyderabad will target Pune. Pune is still well within reach of our Hyderabad-based aircraft. You already have the coordinates for the Indian government's labs at Chandigarh and Pune.

"You will develop a detailed plan of attack including covering air support and air rescue operations for any of our downed pilots. You will present this well-thought-out, detailed plan to me by 1600 tomorrow. After my review with you I will take that plan first to our Air Marshal then to the General Staff and finally to Prime Minister Bhutto for final approval."

"Is that clear?"

In unison, "Yes, sir!"

"Are there any questions?"
There were none.

THE REPUBLIC DAY PARADE

January 26, 1974
Republic Day Parade
Rajpath
New Delhi

Donovan had promised Matt to take him to the big Republic Day Parade. They battled the crowds to find a standing place along the broad Rajpath near the historic India Gate. To their left they could see in the distance the imposing red sandstone government buildings.

The Republic Day Parade was New Delhi's way of celebrating the adoption of India's Constitution on January 26, 1950. According to the English *Times of India* newspaper, this day was one of three national holidays. The paper had featured a story about the Parade including who would be marching. Donovan took a copy of the article with him so he could identify each group to Matt as it passed.

The excitement was intoxicating. First, Prime Minister Gandhi laid a wreath at the tomb of the unknown soldiers at the nearby India Gate. Everyone waved as she passed in her car on her way to the official reviewing platform further up the Rajpath.

The crowd was startled by a 21-gun salute then heard a band playing the Indian National Anthem. The crowd around Donovan and Matt waited patiently for the marchers to get to them. A ripple of excitement ran through the crowd as they spotted the first marchers coming down the Rajpath toward them.

Military units passed by one by one. Matt jumped up and down and waved as the Punjab Regiment of Sikhs passed in their colorful dress. All applauded The President's Body Guard on horseback. The Border Security Force Band on their camels brought a roar of approval from the crowd as they played their instruments atop their plodding steeds. Matt loved the sounds the tanks made as they clattered past. Donovan reminded him that the tank tracks were like those of the TEC bulldozers. Matt also loved the elephants although Donovan could not determine which military unit they came with. Each elephant had a soldier sitting on top with a 'mahout' walking alongside guiding the elephant with a long stick. They lost count of the different military units dressed in bright-colored uniforms.

Toward the end the crowd was surprised by a formation of jet fighters careening overhead followed by a squadron of helicopters in formation.

As they walked back to their car, Donovan bought Matt a balloon on a stick, pointing out that the balloon colors were those of India's flag. Donovan knew Matt would never forget this day.

A few days later Venkey, Donovan's distributor sales manager, phoned at his Old Delhi office. Since he hardly ever phoned, Donovan wondered what he wanted.

He first told Donovan to sit down.

"I'm already sitting down. What's up?" Donovan asked.

He said, "We just lost the Ladakh loader order to the Yugo."

"What!!!"

Venkey explained.

"Every year our government invites another government leader to attend Republic Day. This year Marshal Tito from Yugoslavia and the Prime Minister of Ceylon were the honored guests. They were celebrated at the Republic Day dinner given by P.M. Gandhi that evening. Marshall Tito sat next to Mrs. Gandhi. He asked her over dessert to give the Ladakh loader business to the machine from Yugoslavia. She agreed."

"I can't believe this!"

"You recall that my Army Border Roads contact advised me last month that we had won the Ladakh order because our TEC machine outperformed the Yugo in the three-month cold weather trials. He expected to give us the order for 45 machines next week. He called me just now to tell me he has been instructed to give the order to the Yugo instead. He can do nothing about the decision because it comes from the head of our government. He also said that he managed to order not 45 but 60 Yugo loaders. He feels that he will use the additional 15 machines for spare parts when he puts the 45 to work. As consolation, my contact said that he would buy the TEC loader which has done so well in the Ladakh trials. We do not have to ship it back to Japan."

"Wait a minute. Surely, the fact that our loader worked at Ladakh's high elevations in cold weather while the Yugo broke down several times must have some bearing on the order outcome. Can you get your contact to award the 45 machines to the Yugo, but also give an order for, say, 15 machines to us?"

"No, that is not possible. The Indian government will pay for the Yugo in soft currency, not the hard currency U.S. dollars that TEC required. That is another point in favor of the Yugo."

"What do you mean, soft currency?"

"The Indian government has economic agreements with certain Socialist governments like the Soviets, Yugoslavia and the Eastern Bloc Countries. These are government-to-government agreements for exported products. India exports goods to Yugoslavia and in return gets the Yugo loaders. Payment is not made immediately. Every six months the two countries add up their total trade balances and net out. Only the balance owed either by India or Yugoslavia will be paid in hard currency. Each country negotiates pricing for the goods once a year. India always inflates the price of its goods over what it would obtain in the West for hard currency."

"Why does India play games with the pricing of its goods?"

"India realizes that Yugoslavia, for example, may buy Indian goods for which it has no internal market. Instead of consuming locally the Yugo government may sell those goods for hard currency at a discount in the West in direct competition with India. By inflating the price of India's goods, India hopes to deter Yugo and others from selling them further in the West for hard currency."

Donovan cleared his throat and found his voice. "This is too much for me to understand. You know, the order I just received from the River Valleys Development Board in Ceylon is less than my sales quota for this year. My friend, we will have to find some other business in order for TEC to keep me here in India."

"I just now have a telex from our Madras branch sales manager stating that the Minerals and Metals Trading Company is looking for four to six large rubber-tire loaders for ore handling at the Madras Port. He asks for your visit to offer TEC's loaders."

"By coincidence, I plan to travel through there next week on my return from Colombo. Give me his telex when I see you tomorrow so I can reply to him."

A dejected Donovan hung up. He telexed his boss in Singapore and the TEC joint venture in Japan that Marshall Tito had convinced Mrs. Gandhi to give the Ladakh loader order to the Yugo—over dinner! He also wrote that the TEC trial machine which did so well would be bought by the Border Roads organization.

AT THE RED FORT

February, 1974
Lahore Gate
Red Fort
Old Delhi

The sun was a great red ball setting through the haze from the dung fires when, as arranged, Graham and Ali met at the Lahore Gate of the Red Fort. They strolled together down the Chatta Chowk toward the main courtyard amid many others out for a walk in the late afternoon inside the vastness of the Fort.

As they walked, Ali explained that he had toured the Fort with a group from the Pakistan High Commission. He advised that the massive red walls were of sandstone, and that at the time Shah Jahan built the Fort in the 1640's the Yumna River flowed around it, providing a moat. The Fort itself occupied about 250 acres divided into military and palace sections. He pointed to the Public Audience Hall now facing them down the path where the Shah heard the grievances of his people.

Their unnamed concern loomed over them like a ghost of past Mogul kings.

"Ali, I arranged this meeting in advance because I expected to have an answer from Washington by now. Unfortunately, I have not received a response."

"I understand."

They walked in glum silence.

Graham said, "When I sent headquarters your list detailing where the bomb components are being built, I also recommended to share this information with our State Department. State should be the one to make a formal protest through Ambassador Moynihan. I have heard nothing since about this subject, not from the Agency, not from the State Department."

Ali just nodded his head.

Graham had decided to share his suspicions about the confusion at CIA Headquarters, but not the confirming information from the Parsi.

"I am convinced that the information your agent gave us is correct. I am sure that India is proceeding to build and detonate a bomb. My message about this issue should have raised a lot of concern at CIA headquarters. I can only surmise that headquarters has two opposing views about India's intentions. The first view is that developing a bomb is not in the gentle nature of the Indian psyche. Undoubtedly, CIA's analysts also doubt that Madam Gandhi has the determination or will to make such a drastic decision. It just is not in her peaceful make-up. Actually exploding a bomb would destroy the Indian government's credibility as a leader of the non-aligned Third World Movement. Therefore, some say that India in principle will not develop and not set off a bomb. Others at headquarters say that your intelligence supports what we already know about India's push to develop a bomb. Those analysts traced the Indian bomb development back to Prime Minister Nehru, the first leader of independent India, also Mrs. Gandhi's father. As there is no agreement, even after the information which I have given Langley, we have a stalemate at the CIA."

"There seems nothing more that we can do," Ali replied.

The two turned and walked toward the Delhi Gate.

"Ali, I will ask for another meeting as and when I have more information from Washington."

"Agreed."

Graham motioned to Ali that he would continue toward the Delhi Gate. Ali nodded, turned and strode back to the Lahore Gate.

The Friends of Freedom

February, 1974
American Embassy
Shantipath
Chanakyapuri
New Delhi

"Shamus, please join me in our conference room."

"Sure, Graham."

Graham closed the door and sat across the table from Shamus. "What's up?"

"I have a favor to ask of you. You are the most gregarious and affable American in New Delhi. You have extensive contacts beyond your agents and have developed what you call your local Friends of Freedom. They are not agents but your good Indian friends who either already know of or at least suspect your work for the Company. They have previously agreed from time to time to give you valuable information about specific situations. This is another one of those times.

"I would like you to contact each of them personally to ask what they know, if anything, about India's developing and building a nuclear bomb. I specifically would like you to reach out to your friend in the Foreign Ministry, your polo buddy who is on the P.M.'s staff, and the Indian Army buddy you play poker with. We know that the bomb project exists. Let's see if your friends can give you any confidential information about it, and I'd like you to share your results with me one way or the other in two weeks. Can you do it, along with all of the other things on your plate right now?"

"Sure, Boss. You can count on me."

Graham Visits Calcutta

February, 1974
Grand Hotel
Calcutta

Graham hated visiting Calcutta. He hated Calcutta, period and traveled there as infrequently as possible. He was relieved to let Pete develop contacts for the Agency there. Graham knew that if Pete could survive Calcutta, he would have a great future.

Sadly, this trip was unavoidable. Here he was, checking into the Grand Hotel on a Sunday afternoon. It took him half of his usual one day per week off just to get here. He was not in a happy mood.

He knew he needed to generate some inward enthusiasm before meeting Raj that evening. Raj was one of the highly placed agents whose sensitive intelligence required the COS—Graham—to meet him regularly. Raj had indicated that his bag of "goodies" included more information about how the Russian military was penetrating and exploiting the Indian military.

He reached his room, while ruminating over the quiet battle between the KGB and the CIA in this so-called neutral, third world country...both vying to get India to take "our side" on whatever issue...the Indian politicians saying one thing and doing another...Graham thought that it's in their character, their DNA.

As Graham unpacked his few overnight clothes, his thoughts turned to Raj. He'd recruited Raj when Raj was in America taking one of those sometimes boring advanced military staff courses given by the U.S. military for officers from other countries. Graham had played on Raj's sense of indestructibility and disdain for all things Russian. Graham knew that Raj wanted eventually to migrate to the U.S. with his wife, a totally witting accomplice in the espionage work that Raj did for the CIA. Graham pledged to help Raj settle in the U.S. when the time was right, just not yet. When Graham recruited Raj he was a major in the Indian Air Force. Since then Raj had distinguished himself in the recent 1971 war with Pakistan. He'd flown several missions in his Indian-assembled Russian jet fighter as the Indian and Pakistani forces fought along India's eastern border. Raj was delighted that his efforts helped Bangladesh to be born as a new nation. He also grudgingly admitted that the Russians do design good fighter jets.

Because Raj was currently flying a desk in New Delhi, he preferred to spend long weekends away from Delhi when he needed to meet Graham. He felt more secure away from prying eyes, and he enjoyed the opportunity to see another part of the country. He often brought his beautiful wife with him. Graham was relieved that she was not coming along this time. Calcutta was no place for a supposed romantic get-away.

Graham found Calcutta crowded and dirty, with too many people in too little space. On his previous visits he had witnessed many street demonstrations. At least the Calcutta protesters were mostly peaceful, unlike the university students in Madras. He had once watched Madras college students burning a number of already well-used London double-decker buses to protest the removal of the English language from their curriculum.

Graham and Raj had agreed to meet at 7:00 P.M. at Chowdri's Restaurant in downtown Calcutta. They would not eat there, but walk to another place where they would have more privacy.

Graham had stayed at the Grand before on Agency business. It had the elegance and age of 19th century British India. He did appreciate its majestic four-story façade, palm trees, numerous arches and balconies. He was delighted to sleep in a four-poster bed that night. At least the food was acceptable, the water and ice boiled, and sheets changed after each guest.

Graham remembered the last time he'd stayed at the Grand. Before breakfast he'd taken a brief walk around the block, stepping over a number of sleeping souls on the sidewalk. As he passed, he prayed that none of them had died during the night.

He tried to do some non-secret paperwork in his hotel room but grew agitated and distracted as the meeting time grew closer. He spent minutes looking out the window of his room from which he could see part of the bustling side street and the back of the hotel, a spot where he knew hundreds would assemble in the early morning hours to get kitchen leftovers from the previous night.

Restless at 5:30 P.M., he decided to take a stroll around the immediate area of the hotel. He traversed the front door of the hotel and walked aimlessly down the sidewalk. A bicycle rickshaw driver hailed him as he strolled around the corner from the hotel's front entrance.

"Sahib, can I give you a ride?" the rickshaw driver asked in good English, pedaling abreast of Graham. Graham explored the driver's saucy black eyes and noticed his well-manicured goatee and sinewy legs. Graham had experienced rickshaw rides in Hong Kong but not in India. This rickshaw had the usual three large wheels and a platform with cushions for two riders on the back. It sported a large red and white overhead canopy for shade or against rain.

Graham scrutinized the rather old but well maintained rickshaw.

"How much to drive me around the block of the hotel?"

"Only 50 paisa, Sahib." That was half of one rupee.

"Done."

Graham stepped up and took a seat on the soft fabric cushion behind the driver. Off the driver flew, merging into traffic, clanging his bicycle bell at the trucks, cars and other bicyclists on the road. It was a scene of high congestion, yet not one vehicle hit another, a miracle in motion.

The driver did not exert a lot of energy. He showed years of experience, his sinewy legs pumping like Graham's grandfather's steam locomotive.

He piloted Graham in silence around the block and back to the main entrance of the hotel. As Graham stepped out, he turned to thank him and give him a whole rupee.

Anticipating payment, the driver stated, "That will be four rupees, Sahib."

"What!" Graham retorted in a louder than usual voice. "You promised to carry me for only 50 paisa."

"Oh, but, Sahib. You have so much and I have so little. Surely you can afford such a small sum."

Shaking his head silently, Graham paid him the four rupees and walked back into the hotel.

It was 5:40 P.M.

The Grand Hotel bar loomed ahead. Large and ornate, with the longest bar in India (Rudyard Kipling had actually measured it), and with punka fans turning slowly from the ceiling, it remained as though transfixed in time. One might expect a British officer in full uniform to breeze in at any moment. Graham turned and strode through the bar's two swinging doors as in the old American western movies.

He looked around the vast cavern only to note that it was empty except for the bartender. He sauntered up to the bar and ordered a nimbu pani, lime and water. The bartender filled the glass with ice, put in the nimbu, and added water. Graham paid him, and carried his drink to a table nearby where he could watch the door.

Graham had almost finished his drink when he saw two Indian ladies enter the bar.

They were not dressed in saris but wore western dress, if one dared call it that. The first, more aggressive one was darker and pudgy. She tried but failed to walk gracefully on red stiletto high heels. She wore a short skirt and halter which revealed the spongy flesh of her belly, and a large purse with long straps slung over her shoulder like a rifle.

The other one was just as short but slender and lighter with fine facial features. She was similarly dressed.

Both women wore too much makeup.

They nodded to the bartender and approached Graham. The bartender nodded back, obviously aware that they were not hotel guests.

Graham's danger sensors immediately went on red alert.

"Aren't you going to invite us to sit down for a drink?" asked the heavier one in passable English.

She came closer. Face flushed, Graham turned around, hoping that someone else might answer that opening question. No other takers in sight. The bartender, Graham noticed, moved to the far end of the bar, miles away.

"Yeah, I mean you!" she rasped.

Graham knew better than to be rude. "Why, certainly. Please have a seat."

He counted his options. Leave immediately, report both of them to the management, just sit here and laugh, engage in conversation for a few minutes while they finish their drinks...

Both ordered, and their "regulars" magically appeared immediately from the bartender. With much fuss they sat down, one on either side of Graham, facing him across the round table. They introduced themselves as Sarah and Michelle.

"Who are you? Where are you from?" demanded Michelle, the heavier one.

"My name is Thomas. I'm from America."

"Thomas, we're out for a good time. Do you want to have a good time with us tonight?"

She was certainly not making any small talk but getting right to the purpose. She took a large gulp of her drink.

"I cannot do that, but thank you for the invitation. I'll be happy to pay for your drinks…Tell me about yourselves."

"Oh, I have three lit-tle ones at home and no dad-dy for them. I hav't' work two jobs to keep scraps on th' table," Michelle slurred.

For the first time Sarah opened her mouth.

"My daddy beat me when he first learned I was out on the streets. I haven't seen him in three years. My friend, here, helped me to learn what to do."

Graham couldn't help but wonder how she could call Michelle her friend for introducing her to prostitution.

Michelle turned the conversation to a more immediate interest. "Thomas, you may be concerned that both of us may be too much for you. Why, I can make you hap-py by myself. I'm more ex-per-ie-nced. My friend here can jus'go n' get 'nother cus-to-mer."

Sarah interrupted, "Thomas, be careful. She is not as clean as she should be."

"Well, ladies this is not the time to argue over me. You see, I cannot go with either of you tonight, or ever."

They both looked surprised.

Graham continued, "You probably noticed that I am wearing a wedding ring. My wife would not be pleased to have me do anything with you. Also, you should know that I am an Episcopal priest, a man of God. In India my church is called the Anglican Church. My people call me Father Thomas. I usually wear a white collar around my neck to show that I am a priest of the Church. I'm here in Calcutta for a conference of 'The Brotherhood' this week."

Michelle scowled, not knowing what to say. Clearly, she was at a loss for words and feeling very uncomfortable about it.

Sarah's eyes sparkled. She asked, "Please tell me Father Thomas, what should I do?"

"Do you still love your father?"

"Yes. Very much."

"He must also still love you very much. Why don't you go to him and ask him to forgive you and to take you back into his family?"

"I will consider that. Do you really think he will take me back?"

"Yes, I do."

Michelle scowled at Graham even more, suddenly realizing that she might lose her companion as a result of a few minutes' conversation.

Michelle faced Sarah, and said gruffly, "Let's get out-ta here."

Both got up without finishing their drinks. Michelle burst through the doors of the bar, followed meekly by Sarah, who turned and waved to Graham as she exited. He waved back.

Graham walked over to the bartender and paid for the ladies' drinks, then looked at his watch. 6:05 P.M. He made sure that the ladies had definitely left the lobby area before returning to his room, alone, to clear his head and to review his plans for the 7 P.M. rendezvous.

Dusk fell as he arrived punctually at Chowdri's. He had not been there before. It was a large, low restaurant with long tables and bench seats. It was crowded and very noisy and smelled of exotic Indian spices. He saw both Indians and foreigners seated at the tables. The waiters literally had to force themselves through the seated crowd to bring the food trays to the tables. It reminded Graham of Moti Mahal in Old Delhi, one of his favorite spots to experience India's traditional culture and food.

Graham lingered in the doorway, waiting for the receptionist. She asked for the number in the party and he told her he would just sit and wait in the entrance hallway for the others before making a reservation. She smiled and walked away.

He plunked himself down on one of the small, uncomfortable rattan chairs in the waiting area. He had just gotten settled in the saddle of the chair when he noticed three large, obviously American men coming down the path to the door of the restaurant. He could always tell Americans by their shoes and loud voices.

The first American coming toward the restaurant, only about 20 feet away, was Bob, the Economics Counselor at the American Embassy in New Delhi. They knew each other well, and Graham did not want these Americans to see him meet Raj.

Graham jumped up and strode over to Bob as he opened the restaurant's door. The other two were excitedly talking, still outside, about fifteen feet behind Bob. Bob recognized Graham immediately. Surprise showed on his face. Graham shook Bob's hand vigorously, stopping him in the doorway.

"Bob! Glad to see you in pleasant Calcutta." He leaned forward to whisper, "Bob, I have to meet someone here, confidentially, in a few minutes. I would really appreciate your taking your friends elsewhere for dinner."

Bob gave Graham a knowing smile and replied, "I understand."

He turned to the two men now approaching the door, and said, "Sorry, guys. This place is full. We'll go somewhere else." The three turned around and left without another word.

Minutes later, Raj entered the restaurant. Graham got up and shook his hand.

"Let's go," Raj said. The two walked down the street together, chatting about wives and kids as old friends do. It had turned dark rather quickly.

Raj gestured, "Let's cross over and walk through the park. I have some 'chocolates' for you."

They walked along the edge of a vast park right in the middle of the city.

"This is just like our Central Park in New York City, Raj. You'd enjoy all of the different things you can do and see there. It's a great place. hope you and your family will visit us when Melanie and I are back there."

"I will visit America again. As you know, I dream of it often. I think I would like it. My wife loves to talk to your wife about all of the gadgets you use in your homes."

They were now crossing the park on a diagonal. This area of the park was wide open as though it was used for soccer or cricket fields. Graham knew that they would come out somewhere at the park's other end near his hotel.

Raj continued to walk briskly, "Here, let me give you these 'chocolates'. Please be very careful with them. I took many back-breaking hours to make them. There are eight rolls of them, and they have not yet been developed."

He passed a wrapped package to Graham, rectangular in shape and heavy. Graham immediately put in into the inside pocket of his blue blazer.

They walked a few more steps. Suddenly, they heard the rumble of a Jeep's engine. Coming closer, the Jeep turned on its headlights. They found themselves directly in the Jeep's light beams. The Jeep was not more than 60 feet away and coming at a high speed directly at them across the open lawn of the park. Both men froze in the headlights, silenced.

The Jeep stopped before them, keeping them in its glare. It was a military vehicle with an open top. An Indian man in a tan brown police uniform stood up in the passenger seat. He towered over them from a distance of perhaps twenty feet.

"It is very risky for you to walk out here in the dark," he admonished them in perfect Oxford English. "We have had a few recent cases of theft and even one killing here. Please go back to the well-lit area of the streets."

For once, Graham's voice box did not respond. Always the calm one under pressure, Raj raised himself up to his full military stature and replied in equally good King's English, "Thank you for your concern, SIR! We shall immediately return to the street."

Raj pointed Graham away from the Jeep's lights. He did not have to prod. They slowly walked over to the better lighting of the street. The Jeep roared off into the dark of the park, again without lights. Graham paused until his racing heartbeat returned to normal. What if they'd been searched? What if he'd been caught with the films of Russian military documents in his pocket? He'd be declared *p n g* and have to leave India, his work unfinished.

As the two walked away, Graham thanked Raj for his coolness. They decided where and when to meet next, agreed on two alternate dates and times, shook hands and parted before they got much into the lights of the busy street.

Relieved, Graham made his way back to the Grand Hotel. He was already discussing with himself how he would present this new Soviet military information to Langley headquarters.

He knew it included yet another agreement between the Russians and Indian Air Force about stationing more Russian military advisors at India's military bases. Hopefully, it also included a new list of names of Russian officers and where they were stationed in India. The Agency's Soviet Division would try to cold recruit a few of them while they were still in India to spy for the U.S. The Agency was especially interested in the GRU members, the Soviet military intelligence officers. Once recruited, they would become invaluable after their return to the Soviet Union. They always did. Their stay in India gave the Agency easier access to them.

The Yumna River Walk

March, 1974
Yumna River Walk
Red Fort
Old Delhi

Graham and Ali were two among many walking in the early morning on the foot path near the Red Fort. The river was on one side, the Fort on the other. It was pleasant to walk before the sun burned too high in the eastern sky.

Suddenly, Graham's sensors went on red alert. The hair on the back of his neck tingled.

"Ali, we are being followed," Graham advised Ali, casually.

"Not a problem, Graham. The surveillance team is mine."

Graham silently congratulated himself on his ability to recognize a foreign surveillance team.

"I wanted to tell you that my headquarters have finally decided to advise our State Department about India's bomb project. State now has enough information to tell Ambassador Moynihan to call out Prime Minister Gandhi before the bomb is exploded. It is now up to the State Department to give the Ambassador instructions."

"Well, Graham, that is progress but you well know that time is running out for a protest before the blast occurs. Can you somehow get your State Department to recognize the urgency of this situation and make an immediate decision? Better yet, can you now go directly to your Ambassador with the information which State already has, and ask him to intervene with P.M. Gandhi?"

"No, Ali, I told you that I will not be the one to get the Ambassador involved."

Graham said that he had worked to prepare a list of consequences from America should India actually set off the bomb. The list would be presented to the P.M. by the Ambassador after the test has actually taken place.

They parted after only a few minutes.

Shamus' Reply

March, 1974
American Embassy
Shantipath
Chanakyapuri
New Delhi

"Boss, I have the results of my discussions with my Friends of Freedom."

"Ok, Shamus, let's go into the conference room for a cup of coffee."

The men poured coffee and did not bother to settle into the blue Embassy swivel chairs. They stood. Graham waited for Shamus to say something.

"This makes for a short report, Boss. I talked to all three on a one to one confidential basis. None of my Indian friends knows anything about an Indian nuclear bomb. This project has to be *very* deep."

"Thank you, Shamus for running those traps. You are the best!"

P.M. Bhutto's Response

March, 1974
Eastern Air Command
Pakistani Air Force Base
Chaklala
Rawalpindi
Pakistan

Two Star Air Vice-Marshal Ahmed Anwar Khan stormed back into his headquarters inner office. A heavyset, rather muscular man with a powerful ego, he tossed his hat and coat carelessly on the first vacant desk he came to. He paid no attention to his two staff assistants, a Group Captain (GC) and a Chief Warrant Officer (CWO), who had immediately jumped to attention on his entry. They were still standing, rigid, at attention.

Marshal Khan moved to the operations table, cussing under his breath. He stood the two assistants at ease. Then, in one large motion of his arm brought his huge fist down on the map of India which lay on it. Both aides jumped at the sound of his blow.

After some moments of total silence, the GC screwed up his courage. "Sir, how was your meeting with Prime Minister Bhutto? Did he give approval for us to bomb the Indian nuclear bomb-making sites?"

Suddenly exhausted from the stress of a meeting with Pakistan's Prime Minister, Marshal Khan eased into a nearby chair.

"The meeting itself went well but I did not get the decision I wanted from the P.M. He listened attentively while I explained our very detailed and well thought out plan to dispatch our warplanes to two of the nearest Indian sites. I specifically mentioned the ease with which we could overcome the Indian defenses and hit precise targets at Chandigarh and Pune. These two sites are well known to us and easy targets. I gave him the list we had prepared showing which squadron would be employed to target which site. I told him that we had one hundred percent certainty to hit and destroy the bomb-making facilities at the two locations. I told him that the two strikes would be focused only on the two target buildings. We do not believe many civilians would be hurt. I gave him our minute by minute schedule of attack. I told him that our attack would be such a surprise to the Indian defenses that all of our aircraft would return home safely.

"He asked why we were not targeting all four sites. I told him that we did not need to destroy all four. If we destroy two buildings with all of the equipment inside, that would sufficiently set back the Indian bomb-making effort, perhaps permanently.

"He asked me if this plan was my way to start yet another war with India. I told him that such a lightning strike, suitably backed up by considerable follow-up publicity by justifying the strikes to the world, would likely not cause India to retaliate in a full scale war. I told him that the ISI agreed with me on that.

"He asked me if this plan had the backing of our General Staff. I explained that the Head, ISI for India and I had briefed the General Staff and that they approved the plan. The General Staff agreed that we cannot allow India to test its first atomic bomb.

"The P.M. appreciated all of the work we did to put our plan together and to get appropriate approvals. He thanked us but he disagreed with me and the ISI about the consequences of bombing the two facilities. He said that our air strikes would surely start another, larger war with unknown consequences. His decision was that we will under no circumstances start another war with India. He said that he had received over the last several months some of the same ISI intelligence that I have been receiving. He said that we can agree that India is, indeed, building a bomb. He said that we have only a small chance of stopping it from happening short of war. He hinted that by the time India explodes its first nuclear bomb, we will also have developed one. So, we will have a military stalemate between India and Pakistan at a higher level. We both will have nuclear weapons."

"But, sir," the CWO piped up. "We have not been told anything about our side developing a nuclear bomb. Surely, we in the Air Force would have to devise one or more means of delivering it in order for it to be an effective counterforce."

"Yes, CWO, you are correct. You know that we have been working on missiles to launch space probes and spy satellites. A small bomb could easily be fitted to any of our existing short-range missiles. After all, India is just a few kilometers away.

"Well, gentlemen, what is important for today is that our P.M. spent considerable time listening to my plan. He rejected it for a better one known to him, and only a few others, I am sure. He did say that he gave Munir Khan the assignment some months ago to develop our own bomb suitable to fit on a missile.

"He also said that he wanted to avoid any confrontation with India at this time. He has already told the ISI not to organize demonstrations in Kashmir when the snows melt this coming spring. He was visibly upset about President Nixon's first visit to China last year. He is afraid that a new American-Chinese relationship will dampen China's enthusiasm to support us against India. He said that a reckless act on our part might cause the Chinese to stop or lessen their support. He did not want that to happen."

"Sir, did the P.M. comment on the good work your nephew has been doing in New Delhi under difficult circumstances?" The GC asked.

"Good that you asked. Yes, the P.M. was very complimentary about Ali's spying for the ISI in New Delhi. I, of course, told the P.M. that I had pulled strings with the ISI to get him assigned there."

The General inflated his chest, showing his many ribbons, "After my presentation, and after the P.M. told me to pound sand with my plan, he invited me to a cup of tea. Rather unusual, I would say. I was delighted at his hospitality. He was most cordial."

SHIREE PONDERS

March, 1974
Shiree's apartment
Greater Kailash Colony
New Delhi

Shiree heated water for a cup of tea as she contemplated her enjoyable dates with Ravi since they first met at the Polo Club. Fortunately, she kept a diary. She thumbed through its pages, recalling how they often laughed together even at the smallest thing.

They had hardly gotten to know each other before Ravi had to travel to Canada for a six-month training program with his equipment supplier. At last, he had come back home.

October 12. Met Ravi again at the Lotus Blossom Tea House for a cup of tea and cakes. He said that he had missed me while in Canada but that his training was worth it. He suggested we take up our relationship by visiting some of the well-known Delhi historical places, just to explore. I agreed. That gave us an opportunity to get to know one another better while keeping within the bounds of the family values we were taught.

October 19. Ravi and I walked the Red Fort grounds. We agreed to meet at the Lahore Gate entrance where a lot of craft stores are located. He regaled me about how Shah Jahan, the same Mogul leader who built the Taj Mahal for his wife, built the Red Fort from red sandstone. Ravi pointed out the moat around the Fort used water supplied from the nearby Yamuna River. I reminded him that the Fort was part of the seventh city of Delhi, the current one being the eighth. Before we left the Fort he bought me a flower bouquet from one of the shops. No one had done that before! He told me that I will have to nominate the next place where we meet.

November 2. I brought a picnic lunch to share with Ravi today. We met at the Lodi Gardens and Tombs on Rabindra Nagar. This was my favorite place to visit with my uncle when I was growing up. Uncle had regaled me time and again about the history of the tombs. I showed Ravi Mohammed Shah's tomb, the first tomb, built about 1444. Then, we walked to Sikander Lodi's tomb. According to my uncle, it was built about 1517. Sikander's son, Ibrahim Lodi, was defeated by Babur in the first battle of Panipat in 1526. Babur became the first Mogul King. Shah Jahan was the fifth. We enjoyed a lovely picnic on the grass in front of Mohammed Shah's tomb. Ravi was impressed at my sense of history.

November 16. Ravi suggested we celebrate Diwali tonight by joining the crowds milling about at Connaught Place. Many lights, fireworks! We walked arm in arm. I felt totally safe.

December 2. It's my turn. Where to meet Ravi this time? I called him again on my mobile phone. We arranged to meet at Humayun's Tomb near Nizamuddin East. This lovely edifice, the first to use large blocks of red sandstone, was completed in 1572 some years after the Emperor actually died. I mentioned that Humayun's wife was the motivating force to build the tomb, waterfalls and gardens. We took a lovely walk together on a sunny, rather cool day!

December 18. Ravi suggested we meet at the India Gate at dusk. He wanted to show it when it was already lighted. Of course, I had driven around the Gate numerous times over the years. I knew all about it, or so I thought. It was getting colder! I wore a wrap. Ravi reminded me that the British constructed the Gate in 1921 as a memorial to the 90,000 soldiers who died in World War I. We walked under the gate itself. I had not done that before. He showed me the eternal flame burning day and night to the immortal warrior.

He explained that he was a fighter pilot in the Air Force during the 1965 War with Pakistan, and how he lost friends in combat flying over the Rajasthan Desert. He had not told me about such heart-rending times. I guess I always assumed we live in a perfect and safe world. Tears came to my eyes and I kissed him. He kissed me back!

January 5. My turn again. Ravi and I met at the Qutab Minar. I regaled him about how it was started in 1192 by the first Sultan of Delhi and not completed until sometime in the late 1330's. He challenged me to climb the circular steps up to the top and fifth story. We both climbed to the top, me first. What a view of Delhi! He counted 379 steps, I counted 377. We debated whose count was correct. We decided not to go back just to recount the steps, but to go back at some future time to remember today. I was glad I wore a Punjabi outfit and not a sari!

January 20. Ravi suggested we met at the Spice Market near the Red Fort. We walked to a nearby rickshaw station. We climbed in and had a wild ride from one end of Chandni Chowk to the other. We decided not to get off at the Fort's Lahore Gate but rode back to where we began. It was such fun!

February 9. I invited Ravi to join me for the Sound and Light Show at the Red Fort tonight. As always, it was lovely. We noticed a lot of European tourists.

February 23 Ravi invited me to a one-hour golf lesson at the Delhi Golf Club on Dr. Zakir Hussein Marg. Not fair! He played golf with his father when he was growing up. I hit a more accurate shot, but not as far as he could.

Shiree noticed the diary notation of her secret meeting in just two days. She closed her diary. She felt a sudden and tremendous ache in her stomach.

She was having serious misgivings about her involvement with the Food for the Poor agent. She consoled herself by saying that she was doing the greater good by telling the Americans about her country's bomb development because she did *not* want India to develop a bomb. She worried that she could be caught for treason, tried and put in jail forever. If so, she would not see Ravi again, a thought that disturbed her beyond words. What to do?

She wondered who she might ask to help her end the relationship with the Food for the Poor man. Uncle Sena? No, she cannot ask him. He would be terrified at what she had done and afraid for her. Her treason would reflect badly on him, the most honorable Rajya Sabha representative. No. Not Uncle.

She ran the list of her friends in her mind, rejecting each one in turn. She finally recognized her desperation. She *had* to ask Ravi for help. She weighed the possible outcomes. He might willingly forgive her treason and help her. Or, he might be so shocked at her betrayal that he leaves her. Whatever the outcome, she decided she must rely on Ravi.

With that thought, she called Ravi on his mobile phone and asked him to come to her apartment. She said she urgently needed his advice.

Once he was inside her apartment, Shiree confessed to giving the NGO man secrets about India's nuclear bomb program. She did not want India to develop a bomb. She blurted out her story about being recruited by Diana, then being turned over to the Food for the Poor man in New Delhi. She explained that she gave him a summary of the notes she made from her job as the Nuclear Power Commission secretary. She understood that he passed on that information to his American Embassy contact in New Delhi. Diana had promised her that the Americans would stop the bomb project.

"Ravi, I am supposed to meet him in two days! I do not want to do this anymore. What should I do?"

"How many times have you met this man?"

"Several times before. I have lost count."

"How do you transfer the notes to him?"

"Each time we met, I passed him a paper in an envelope. That is my report about our nuclear developments but not all of our nuclear developments. He only wants to know about our progress in making a nuclear bomb. He passes me another paper in the same kind of envelope. That gives me instructions for the next report I should write, and places and times to meet next. The transfer takes seconds. We do not talk to each other, just pass by. No one around us notices."

"My dear Shiree, you understand that what you are doing is treason against India?"

"Yes, but Diana said that I was doing what my conscience dictated. She said that is morally correct."

Ravi refrained from arguing with her. He knew better than to browbeat her for her foolishness. He did not want to make her even more fearful for her situation.

"You are in a very serious situation. We must get you out of this arrangement. This is like a wedding that you do not want to go through, but much more serious."

Ravi thought for a few seconds.

"I can think of two or three ways for you to end this. First, does the Food for the Poor man know who you are, where you work, where you live?"

"I am sure he does although I have not told him anything about my personal life, nor has he asked. He just wants the information I give him."

"OK. Here's one possibility. You do not meet him in two days. Let's wait and see what happens then."

"Yes, but then he will expect me to meet him at the second designated place in five days. I want to be totally rid of him!"

"Then, you will type a paper to give him. On it you will tell him only that you cannot meet him anymore. It is not important that you give him a reason. You will not give him any more information about the Commission's discussions. Tell me where and when you will meet him in two days. I will be in the immediate area, watching you. After you give him the paper, he will walk away from you. I will see who he is and follow him to the American Embassy to be sure that he does go there. The Americans will read your paper and know that you will no longer work for them. They will accept that. Please write it now and put it in that envelope."

Shiree got out her typewriter and typed a very curt message. She took the paper out of the typewriter and showed it to Ravi.

"Very good. Now, where in two days will you meet him?"

"I am instructed to buy a cup of tea and sweet promptly at 3 P.M. at the Amber Restaurant at number 19 on the N ring at Connaught Circus. He will be waiting for me outside the restaurant. We will exchange envelopes as we pass each other on the street."

"In that case, I should easily see him and be able to follow him. Are we agreed?"

She replied, "Yes, oh yes! Please, Ravi, help me to get out of this mess."

Two days later Shiree met Ali as arranged. They passed envelopes as planned while Ravi watched. He followed the Food for the Poor man.

Some minutes later, Ravi called her on his mobile car phone. "I must meet with you, now! I'm coming to your apartment to tell you what happened after you exchanged envelopes."

Shiree answered her door a second after Ravi knocked. She closed it and they stood close in the living room.

"What did you find out by following him?"

"I watched as he dropped his envelope on the sidewalk right in front of you. You bent over to pick it up, and in the process gave him your envelope. That was very smooth. I followed him to the corner. I did not see anyone watching you, him or me. At the corner he stopped, turned around once, looked back towards me, and ripped open the envelope you had given him. He read the typewritten words, became quite visibly agitated, and literally ran to the nearest taxi cab stand. I got into another taxi and instructed the driver to follow his cab at a reasonable distance. His cab, as I expected, drove down Shantipath towards the American Embassy. I was surprised to watch it *pass* the American Embassy. The cab drove a bit further on Shantipath into the Pakistan High Commission. The NGO man got out of the cab and went into the High Commission."

Shocked, Shiree cradled her hands around her face. She asked, rather dejectedly, "Does that mean he's...?"

Ravi put his hands on his hips. "Yes, Shiree, Diana fooled you. I believe you have been giving our Indian nuclear secrets to the Pakistanis, not the Americans. In either case, you could be charged with treason and put away. I certainly do not want that to happen. I care too much about you."

"What can I do? Confess to my uncle? He'll be very upset!"

"No, Shiree. The only people who know about what you have done are the NGO man, possibly one or two others at the Pakistan High Commission, Diana, you, and me. We will keep it that way. We will not tell anyone else. You have now told them that you quit. They may accept that, or they may try to contact you here at your apartment or at work."

Ravi thought for a second, his brows furrowed, then continued. "Please be wary of any strangers approaching you, day or night. Our best action now is to do nothing and wait to see what develops. The Pakistanis do not want this to leak out. They would also be compromised if it does. Hopefully, your identity and these secrets will stay secret. You will not be harmed.

"Now, I must go. But, let's stay in mobile phone contact. If you get a visit or call from the agent, call me immediately. Whatever you do, do not agree to meet him."

"I'm so relieved. Ravi, thank you. Please help me get this behind me. Please forgive me for my foolishness." Saying that, she hugged him so hard he thought his ribs would break.

She's Quitting!

March, 1974
Pakistan High Commission
"The Palace"
Shantipath
Chanakyapuri
New Delhi

Ali presented his credentials to the guard at the entrance of the building and walked hurriedly through the lobby to the stairs. He mounted them two at a time and sailed all the way down the hall to the back of the building. The carpeted floor softened his steps but not his pace. He literally blew past Akbar Choudry's secretary. He entered Choudry's private office, Shiree's paper still in his hand.

"Do come in, now that you have established the immediate need to see me," Akbar greeted him with a smile.

Akbar stood up, shook Ali's hand and motioned him to a nearby comfortable chair. Ali did not sit down.

"She's quitting!" an exasperated Ali roared. He pushed Shiree's paper in Akbar's face.

"Calm down. You are a professional, you do not scream at your superior. Now, sit down! Tell me everything, and I mean everything, that happened."

Ali, somewhat calmer now, sat down. He related how the brush contact had gone well. He met Shiree as arranged in front of the restaurant, exchanged envelopes, and quickly left the scene. He reached the corner only to open the sealed envelope to read that she is quitting. He immediately got into a cab and came here.

"She cannot do that! We must get her back!" Ali stated in his most forceful voice.

"What if she is not willing to give us any more information? What would you do to her? Would you tell the *Hindustan Times* that she has committed treason? What would be your part in this? As an accomplice? As a professional Pakistani spy? I do not think you will betray her. If you betray her, you betray us as well. Consider that!"

Ali settled in his chair, grimacing. Akbar continued.

"You know that an agent is only as good as her commitment to turn over state secrets to us. If she is no longer willing, we do not have a lot of choices. As a matter of fact, she has very likely already given us all of the information we need about India's nuclear bomb development. We know that the bomb is being put together, and where. We know that it will be moved to the detonation site. We do not know if or when the P.M. will give the approval to detonate. That, at any rate, is a political decision and not within the purview of the Commission she is secretary to."

Ali, exasperated, "But we cannot just let her quit without some repercussions, some punishment! That makes a bad precedent."

Akbar in his most rebuking tone as though he were explaining a rule to a child, "Ali, you are acting like a college professor who wants to flunk his student! You should by now know that there is no such thing as precedent in this spy business. There is only the target information, the target agent, and the enemy. Yes, we can let her go, now, and note on her dossier that she may become useful to us at a later date. We could possibly force her to continue to work for us by blackmailing her but I see no need to blackmail her at this point.

"Look at the bright side, Ali. We have already told ISI headquarters about the ongoing bomb assembly in Trombay, thanks to your good work. You may look forward to a certain ISI promotion."

"But, Akbar..."

"Now, Ali, I will write to ISI saying that the girl is no longer useful. We, note we, have decided to end our association for now, as we have already obtained all of the information from her that we need. Agreed?"

Ali forced a smile but his slumped shoulders betrayed his disappointment.

"Yes, agreed."

"Let me remind you, Ali, that you still have to meet your agent in Trombay. He should be giving us very useful information about the actual bomb assembly at his lab. When do you see him next?"

"Early April."

Just then, Akbar's private phone rang. He picked it up and listened for a few minutes. He put the receiver back on its stand.

"That was our surveillance team that was looking after you when you met Shiree. Yes, the exchange went well, as you said. After the exchange she went one way, you went another. But, when you stopped at the corner to open her envelope, the team noticed an Indian man very interested in you. On opening the envelope, you become very agitated. Unfortunately, you did not follow the ISI rules for disengaging with an agent. You made the big mistake of letting your anger get the better of you. No, you impulsively ran to a taxi and came straight here. That's a big mistake, Ali. The other man got into another taxi and followed you. He saw you come here into the High Commission. He continued in his taxi back to Connaught Circus. He got out and the team lost him in the crowd...

"So, Ali, someone followed you to us here. He now knows that you are giving Shiree's notes to us, not to the Americans. That's an interesting development. What can you make of that? Can you guess who he is?"

Ali shook his head. "No."

"You must be more careful. Please keep your head. Do not act on anger or impulse. You know too well that your agent's life is at stake."

Suitably chastened, head down, a mute Ali gave Shiree's paper to Akbar and quietly left the room.

Akbar reflected on what had just happened with Shiree and Ali's work over the past year. Ali had been effective in meeting his two agents but, as Akbar had predicted, he would make a mistake at some point.

Akbar could cover for Ali's mistake this time simply by saying that he has decided to terminate the Saksena woman. She has already given all of the valuable intelligence she has access to. Akbar knew that it is difficult to terminate an agent who has worked well in the past but is no longer producing good intelligence. There is no proper way. Yet, it must be done. Akbar vigorously reviewed the agents' production every six months and did not tolerate a non-performer, even for a minute.

Akbar confessed to himself that Ali had found a determination, a focus, and discipline in performing his spy duties. Perhaps, even a certain deviousness which a spy must first have in order to violate the local government's laws against treason. Perhaps he had also found a sense of excitement for playing "The Great Game". Still, he doubted that spy work would be Ali's lifelong calling.

Why? Ali will fail the successful spy's prerequisite:

Recruiting agents of value.

No. Ali did not have the resourcefulness, the thoughtfulness, the thoroughness to spot, evaluate and assess, then recruit agents. He was a poor judge of what motivates another person. In this spy business one is evaluated on how many agents one recruits. The better the intelligence from the agent, the better the case officer's evaluation. Ali was managing two already recruited agents. He did not recruit them but was simply servicing already motivated and recruited agents.

Akbar still believed that after this assignment Ali will have had enough of this stressful experience and will willingly return to the safety and comfort of the University.

Akbar reminded himself that a professional spy thrives outside his own country. He works best with diplomatic cover in his own country's foreign embassy or consulate. He strives to learn the local language, enjoys meeting people of the host country, and learns about their local history and culture. He *hates* being assigned to headquarters. (1)

With that thought, and a chuckle, Akbar turned to write the memo advising of the termination of the Saksena woman.

(1) Kessler, Ronald. *Inside the CIA: Revealing the Secrets of the World's Most Powerful Spy Agency*. New York: Simon & Schuster, 1992. Print, page 41-42. "The most prized officers are those who can recruit almost anyone, yet they are not necessarily good managers. Many of the best spies do not want to work in headquarters."

THE P.M. CALLS

March, 1974
Indian Intelligence Bureau (IB)
Undisclosed Location
New Delhi

The phone rang. Colonel Bhandari picked it up and stated, pleasantly, "This is Colonel Bhandari."

The reply, obviously from a secretary, "Please hold for the P.M."

Colonel Bhandari scribbled on his scribble pad. He decided some time ago to have a second notepad on which he could scribble while waiting for some highly placed government official to come to the phone.

Prime Minister Gandhi came on the line. The Colonel straightened in his chair and smoothed his shirt.

"Colonel, I am pleased to talk to you. I trust that you are well. I thank you for your regular reports about threats to our country. I do so rely on them."

"Madam Prime Minister, it is my pleasure to serve you and our country. What can I do for you?"

"I have a special request which I know you will perform with your usual efficiency and in total secrecy. For the next two weeks I would like you to target your surveillance teams on the Pakistanis on your list, even to the neglect of the Chinese or other diplomats. Find out what they are up to, where they go, who they contact. Can you do that and give me a report of your findings?"

"Yes, certainly."

"Without going into details, I can assure you that this is a matter of top national security."

"I understand. Consider it as good as done. You will receive my complete report in two weeks' time."

"Thank you." She rang off.

The Colonel sat back in his chair for a moment, contemplating. He then called Three on the internal phone and asked him to come immediately to his office. A matter of utmost urgency.

Surveillance!

1 April, 1974
Monday
Juhu Beach
Bombay

Ali's Indian Airlines plane was on time. He deplaned with his overnight bag and briefcase and took a taxi to his hotel on Juhu Beach. It was another hot Monday afternoon. He was thankful for the slight breeze off the Arabian Sea to cool things off a bit. He smiled as he anticipated his morning walk on the beach, both for the exercise and to notice the bikini-clad airline hostesses sunbathing along his path.

He checked into his hotel. As the sun set, he walked to his designated car, always in wait a few hundred yards from the hotel. As he walked, he thought about Ambika.

He knew that his IIT work would not last forever.

He started the car, put it in gear, and drove to the Kurla Train Station to pick up Dutta.

It was easy for Dutta to travel by train from Trombay which was on the rail line to Bombay Center. Dutta got off at the prearranged connection station and just waited a few minutes for Ali to come by and pick him up. For all appearances, Dutta was being picked up by a family member or friend. The two would talk while Ali drove around for a few minutes before dropping Dutta off at another station on the same line. The same meetings sequence had worked for a year.

This time Ali saw immediately that Dutta was more than usually excited.

"Here is the list of all of the scientists who visited the Lab recently. It is three times as long as the usual list I give you each month. Something *big* is happening! In these past three weeks I have seen many more scientists from at least three different locations. There has been a lot of coming and goings with many extra hours spent in closed door conference rooms. I believe these scientists are now planning their part of the actual bomb assembly. As I told you, the various bomb components have to be assembled in a very specific sequence. I can say for sure that we are not far from the actual detonation."

They talked for a few more minutes. Ali slowed as he approached the next train station. As always, Ali's last words were a warning.

"Remember, Ram Lal, should we be found out, I will give you the emergency signal that you must immediately leave the country. It is very important that you use your pre-planned escape route. Do not hesitate. A better life awaits you elsewhere. Go in peace."

Dutta got out and blended into the crowd at the station waiting the next train.

Ali started back to the Juhu Hotel.

He noticed another car behind him. When he turned, it followed. He turned again, and it followed. He made two more turns just to be sure. The same car continued to follow him. He cursed quietly. He was being followed, but for how long? Had they been behind him as he drove to meet Dutta? He did not notice them then. Had Dutta been able to lose himself in the crowded station? Ali was thankful that they always met during a rush hour on a weekday, always the heaviest passenger use.

He reminded himself to keep calm, to continue with his plan to return to New Delhi the next day. He would have to admit to Akbar that he had been followed and that Dutta may have been compromised. He chided himself for not paying closer attention. He must warn Dutta as soon as possible.

Ali parked his car and returned to the hotel for a restless night.

ALI IS BLOWN!

2 April, 1974
Tuesday
Pakistan High Commission
"The Palace"
Shantipath
Chanakyapuri
New Delhi

"Akbar, I am blown! I did not notice the car following me until after I dropped Dutta off at the railway station. I can only hope that he was lost in the station, that no one was able to find him in the crowds. I had arranged for him to be dropped off just as two trains were picking up passengers, one train south to Bombay, one east to Trombay."

"Are you *sure*, Ali?"

"Yes, I am certain. What should I do now?"

Akbar rubbed his nose and chin for a moment.

"First, send the emergency message to Dutta. Get him out of the country immediately. He is much more useful to us in Pakistan, not rotting away in an Indian jail. Remember, he does not have diplomatic immunity as you and I do."

Akbar thought for a few more seconds.

"Second, please go home and tell Ambika that you have been called back to Lahore University. Tell her that you are urgently needed there to plan the next phase of the higher education improvement program. Your tour here is over. Make preparations now to return to Lahore. You may have up to ten days to stay, no more.

"Ali, I see the puzzlement on your face. Of course, you are not versed in the pleasantries of making a foreign diplomat *persona non grata*. This is what will happen. The IB headquarters in New Delhi will in a few days receive the report of your surveillance from the IB branch in Bombay. It will recommend expelling you. The IB, based on whatever evidence they have, will notify the Ministry of Foreign Affairs to withdraw your credentials. That may take another week or so. Once you are officially told to leave, you will be given only two or three days to pack up and leave."

Akbar continued, now carefully selecting his words.

"So, you have maybe ten to twelve days from now to get out. That is why I am saying you should tell Ambika, now, that you are being called back to Lahore. It is better that she thinks your cover work is over than to be told the real reason for your leaving. Do you understand what I am saying?"

"Yes, Akbar. I am still shocked at my own mistake. I should have seen my surveillance and not met Dutta. I will immediately signal him to leave the country. He will know why. I will tell Ambika now that I am being called back to Lahore. She has a few days to say good bye to her friends and to her father. That will be the hardest for her. We will plan to be out within a week."

Now, more like a father scolding a naughty son, Akbar continued. "Look at the situation this way. You are not a professional spy. You made a mistake. Fortunately, you realized you were being followed, so we can correct in time to avoid sacrificing Dutta to the Indian authorities and a jail cell. Now, go!"

"Thank you, Akbar, for your understanding."

After Ali left the room Akbar fumed at Ali's mistake, one which Akbar cannot cover for him. Ali must immediately leave India. He will not suffer bad consequences for his blunder. He just will no longer be welcomed at ISI.

GOODBYE, GRAHAM

4 April, 1974
Thursday
Raj Ghat Park
Old Delhi

The sun set as an orange ball as Ali and Graham strolled together toward the Gandhi Darshan, the place where Mahatma Gandi was cremated following his assassination in 1948. Neither had been followed.

Ali told Graham that his cover has been blown and that he and his family would leave India by the following Monday. Ali explained that he had told his agent in New Delhi to break off contact that his agent at the Trombay Lab would have to leave the country.

Ali silently hoped that Dutta was already on a plane.

"My work here is finished. I have told Ambika that we will be leaving on Monday. She will say goodbye to her father on Sunday," Ali stated.

"I do have one last favor, Graham. Please tell Donovan that I am leaving India and thank him for me. I know he will be relieved not to have me as a neighbor anymore but I know that Ambika will miss Emily. They have become good friends."

The two continued walking in silence. Ali stopped and faced Graham.

"I want to thank you, Graham for your patience in listening to my cause."

"Ali, I wish you and your family all the best for the future. You have many talents. Please understand that not everyone is cut out to be a spy. I do suggest that you spend your time from now on as an outstanding university professor. Please use this experience to improve higher education in your country. After all, that is what you were sent here to learn about. As for your spying, please do not mention a word to anybody. Total silence in our world of spies is the rule. Never, ever, tell others what you did. Besides, no one would believe your story, anyway."

"Thank you for the kind words."

"One more thing. We both can put on a knowing smile when India sets off its first atomic bomb. We know we don't have to wait much longer for that to happen. We both know that we can do nothing to stop it. We may be consoled that the anticipated explosion will not start a war between your country and India."

The two men shook hands and parted, one last time.

Graham mused at how he had developed a respect and fondness for Ali.

He thought to himself as he walked, *I am the professional spy, saying goodbye to a very fine and capable Pakistani. I must admit that I respect Ali for what he has tried to do. I have never had this kind of experience before. I am more accustomed to treating all foreign spies as enemies. Not this one.*

Graham turned and went his separate way.

AKBAR'S CRITICAL MESSAGE

ADMIN
CRITICAL
4 April, 1974
TO: ISI, Islamabad
Attention: Head, India
Ref: Case Officer BAKRA

IB agents trailed C.O. BAKRA by car as C.O. met with Agent BALOO on 1 April. BAKRA is sure that he has been blown by the IB. Consequently, I have advised him to prepare immediately to leave the country.

BAKRA committed the unpardonable sin of exposing himself and one of his valuable agents to the IB. C.O. has diplomatic immunity so will be asked to leave the country. I cannot recommend him for another ISI assignment.

We do not know whether BAKRA's careless actions also compromised Agent BALOO. We have immediately taken steps to get Agent BALOO out of the country and to safety. Agent BALOO has consistently received Distinguished ratings for his excellent intelligence. Please welcome him accordingly.

Now, perhaps, you will accede to my original request to assign a true ISI professional to this important office in such a hostile environment.

Signed,
India Control

WE'VE GOT HIM!

5 April, 1974
Thursday
Indian Intelligence Bureau
Undisclosed Location
New Delhi

Three knocks on Colonel Bhandari's solid door identified the visitor.

"Enter," the Colonel bellowed.

Three appeared, smiling, though he did not often smile. He said that his job was too demanding to smile.

"Colonel, we have him! Well, we do not have Khan in custody, because he is a diplomat. But, we have enough against him to force him to leave the country."

"Please sit down, Three, and tell me the full story."

Three related how the Bombay IB surveillance team had followed Khan from the airport as he took a taxi to the Juhu Beach hotel, how Khan stayed at the hotel until after sunset, then walked to a car conveniently parked nearby, and drove off. The team suspected Khan would be alert for anyone following him as he drove. He would likely notice the usual surveillance team in one car so the IB Bombay director had decided to use six men in three cars, actually two cars and a taxi, to fool the Pakistani. And it worked. The team switched lead cars as Khan drove through traffic. The team believed he was not aware they were following him. He drove to one of the local train stations where he picked up a man. They drove for a few minutes to the next train station where the man got out. The lead team lost the man in the crowd at the station. The man must have taken one of the two trains that stopped at the station, one to Bombay and the other to Trombay.

"Well, this is not the usual performance of our university professor, is it?" posited Colonel Bhandari. "But, no matter how unusual, we cannot tell him to leave India after his erratic behavior on just one night. He may be doing suspicious things not related to national security. He may be dealing drugs, or running a prostitute ring. As the surveillance team did not apprehend his pick-up, we can only surmise that he was doing something against our country. That may not be good enough. What else do we have to implicate him on national security grounds?"

Three spoke slowly, referring to the dossier on his lap.

"Colonel, as usual, you are correct. One night's activities are not enough to send him home. As you know, he is here ostensibly to learn about our IIT education system. We know that he has visited all eight of our IIT campuses at least once. Per your previous instruction we did follow him to the IIT locations in Madras and Kanpur. He was clean on both trips.

"We then checked his recent flights to Bombay against his known visits to the IIT Bombay campus. He has flown to Bombay from New Delhi once a month for the last eight months. His travel is always on a Monday when there is no full moon. He visited the IIT Bombay campus only four times in the last eight months. What else was he doing in Bombay?"

Three closed his dossier and folded his hands over it.

"May I suggest that you yourself told me that Professor Khan should finish all of his work at the IIT Universities within one year from the date of his arrival. After all, he has only eight locations to visit. He has been here 17 months, surely more than enough time. He should have finished his official work before now."

He concluded. "We also know that Khan and his family have developed a relationship with an American family living on the same street in Green Park. We have also checked the American. He is a sales representative for one of the American-based international companies. We have confirmed that he is legitimate by talking to two Indian managers with whom he works at his distributor.

"There is one other, perhaps unrelated item. We received a phone call today from the IB Bombay director. He said that the Trombay Lab reported that one of their engineers has not shown up for work for the last few days. He did not report sick. The Lab tried to contact him at his apartment. No one was home. The Lab does not know where the engineer is. Is the missing engineer the same man Khan met?"

"Let's not jump to conclusions, Three. What do you recommend we do about Khan?"

Three replied with enthusiasm, "Khan has showed activity incompatible with his diplomatic status. I recommend we tell the Foreign Ministry to cancel his *bona fides* and send him back to Pakistan. I also recommend we send home one Akbar Chaudry. We have evidence that he is the ISI boss at the Pakistan High Commission. We have a lot more evidence against Chaudry than we do against Khan. Let's send both of them packing!"

"Three, your exuberance about this is overwhelming. I shall today put the wheels in motion to send them both back home. As you know, we thankfully do not have to give a reason to the Foreign Ministry. They know well enough that when we ask them, politely, to withdraw credentials, we have good reasons which shall remain secret. That is the only way we can work. No one dares second guess us."

The Colonel wrote a few lines on his notepad.

"So, we are sending Khan back home solely on the basis that he has been here long enough to finish his work. Please so note on his file, of course, along with our suspicions. Remember, they are only suspicions. As we did not apprehend the man that Khan met, we may only surmise that he was doing something against our national interests.

"I will convey my personal thanks to the IB Bombay director. By the way, the Prime Minister called to thank you for your excellent surveillance report about the Pakistani diplomats' activities. A job well done, she said to tell you. Thank you, Three, for your excellent service to our country."

"My pleasure, Colonel." Three left, promising himself to relay the P.M.'s comments to his surveillance teams.

T.R.'s Question

April, 1974
Indian Intelligence Bureau
Undisclosed Location
New Delhi

Colonel Bhandari's telephone rang. He had a number which was not listed in any phone book. He did not get that many calls, and did not need anyone to screen them. He expected each call to be an important one. After all, he was the head of the Intelligence Bureau for all of India.

He picked up the receiver and said pleasantly, "This is Colonel Bhandari."

"Colonel Bhandari, this is Nair, a representative from Kerala to the Lok Sabha. I am inquiring about my son-in-law, Asaf Ali Khan. He has been here in New Delhi for some months doing a research project for the Lahore University. He and my daughter, his wife, have now left India. I want one question answered.

"Did you rescind his credentials with the Indian government? You may know that he is a Pakistani citizen here on diplomatic status."

Colonel Bhandari was used to these kinds of calls. He wisely deflected all of them without divulging any information about the person in question.

"Shri Nair, thank you for the telephone call. Yes, I remember you from my presentations to the Lok Sabha Money Committee. It is kind of you to call about your son-in-law. You are obviously concerned. No, I did not instigate any order for him to leave India. In all honesty, the IB did create a file on him, Shri Nair, as he is after all a Pakistani. We found nothing over these several months that would indicate any national security concern on our part. If he has been recalled, it has been by the University which surely misses his talent. We wish him and your daughter a safe and speedy trip to their destination. I would hope that you, sir, may be able to visit them in the future wherever they are in this small world.

"By the way, Shri Nair, I do appreciate your helpful work on our annual intelligence budgets. We at the IB realize the good you do for our country. Thank you."

"Thank you, Colonel, for all you do to keep this country safe." Nair hung up.

P.M. Gandhi is Exuberant

Early May, 1974
Prime Minister's Residence
Rashtrapati Bhavan
New Delhi

Prime Minister Gandhi and her chief of staff conferred together over tea and cakes. Resplendent in a lovely pink and purple sari with gold threads running through it, she was not in a happy mood.

She was concerned about the close Congress by-election win in Uttar Pradesh and the riots in Gujarat. She knew that J.P. Narayan was preaching revolution in Bihar. Worse, his cries were gaining traction. Inflation was again on the rise. That hurt the poor the most. India was also facing a severe drought. No one could control the rains. Worst of all, the railway workers were on strike. Negotiations with them to get back to work had totally broken down.

The country was generally unhappy with the way it was being run. She was being blamed even for the lack of rain!

P.N. Dhar gave her the usual verbal and written reports. He explained that all is under control, but just barely. He reported that her personal approval has nosedived to the lowest since she took office. She was at her height of popularity just after India fought and won the 1971 border war that begot a new country, Bangladesh. Much to her delight, newspapers then had called her "The Empress of India."

She told him that the next few weeks would both improve her popularity and catapult India to the center of the world stage. She had confirmation just yesterday from her personal astrologer. Dhar knew that she sometimes made government decisions after hearing what her astrologer had told her. She confided to Dhar that the astrologer had told her that India would be seen as a very powerful nation, that her personal reputation would soar, and that she would see a great sense of enormous pride throughout the country.

Little did he know that she was thinking about the upcoming nuclear explosion.

She thought, *I need something spectacular to cheer up our people. This nuclear explosion will, indeed, give every Indian, from the poorest farmers to the big city dwellers, a great sense of pride in this country. And, it will give me a big boost in my ratings. I need that!*

I know that some of the Third World Movement leaders will not be happy. But, I believe that most of them will silently cheer me for secretly developing and testing a nuclear weapon. By so doing, India is saying that this country will not be pushed around by the so-called world powers. No, we will not be forced to sign a Non-Proliferation Treaty. Yes, we are a country to be reckoned with!

He wondered why her long, thoughtful pause had made her suddenly exuberant.

THE SMILING BUDDHA (1)

May, 1974
Pokhran Test Site
Rajistan Desert
India

13 May
Dr. Rajagopala Chidambaram was worried. Not about the bomb itself and not about his safety or that of those around him. He, Iyengar, P.R.Roy and the rest of his team prepared the bomb perfectly today. Just as planned.

No, he was afraid that some spy satellite roaming overhead would discover their work here in the middle of the desert. That another country, perhaps America, would, at the last minute, pressure the P.M. to stop the explosion. Yes, all had been told that the Indian Army was digging a deep tunnel to find water. Some even speculated, oil. A mere question about why *the Army* would do such a thing came to his mind. Would that come to the minds of others?

He knew that they had camouflaged everything from spying eyes and felt confident that nothing could be seen from the air. Let them come!

15 May
The team placed the bomb deep into the shaft 350 feet below the surface. They sealed the shaft with sand and cement to prevent venting of toxic fumes. They were ready for the final decision by Prime Minister Gandhi.

18 May
8:05 AM. P.R. Dastidar pushes the red button. A small mountain of sand rises from the desert surface before collapsing. No fumes escape. The team succeeded! India has just become a nuclear weapons power! Mrs. Gandhi receives word that "the Buddha is smiling."

8:35 AM. American Ambassador Daniel Patrick Moynihan is informed of a nuclear detonation "for peaceful purposes."

9:00 AM. All-India Radio announces an "underground nuclear explosion for peaceful purposes."

This "peaceful" nuclear explosion would be forever known as "The Smiling Buddha."

(1) Richelson, Jeffrey. *Spying on the Bomb: American Nuclear Intelligence from Nazi Germany to Iran and North Korea*. New York: Norton, 2006. Print, pages 195-235.

AFTERWARD

Asaf Ali Khan and his family returned to Lahore University where Professor Khan became noted for implementing many improvements to the University's curriculum and the way it selected its students. These same changes were copied by the other engineering universities in Pakistan. Professor Khan attributed many of his reforms to his "learning experience" at the IIT Universities in India. He did no further work for Pakistan's ISI.

To the delight of their families, Shiree and Ravi became engaged and married a year later. Neither ever disclosed Shiree's relationship with the Pakistani spy.

Graham Smith's excellent work in India was appreciated by the CIA heads at Langley headquarters. He left India with Melanie in 1975 to become the CIA's chief of station at the U.S. Embassy in Bonn, West Germany.

Donovan and Emily Griffin moved to Düsseldorf, West Germany with their two children where he was assigned to The Earthmoving Corporation's sales operations there. Donovan and Graham Smith would cross paths again in Germany. But, that is another story.

POSTSCRIPT

Both India and Pakistan continued their secret nuclear bomb development through the 1990's. American spy satellites from time to time looked in at India's Pokhran test site. In 1995 and 1996 the spy satellites detected new construction. The Indians were building two new tunnels and adding additional infrastructure.

On April 6, 1998 Pakistan tested its Ghauri missile.

On April 8, 1998 India's Prime Minister Vajpayee approved new nuclear weapons tests. On May 11, 1998 India successfully exploded three nuclear devices including a fission-fusion 45 kiloton hydrogen bomb. India tested two more devices on May 13. The tests were called Operation Shatki.

Not to be outdone by India, Pakistan immediately finalized its own testing. American satellites over the Pakistani test site detected preparation for tests on May 14, 1998. On May 27 Pakistan's President, Nawaz Sharif, admitted to President Clinton that he would proceed with the tests.

On May 28 Pakistan successfully conducted one large and four small nuclear tests, and one more on May 30. A.Q. Khan was quoted as saying that the one big explosion was from enriched uranium, not plutonium. Pakistan's tests were conducted at Chagai, Baluchistan in an underground tunnel constructed in the 1980's. Pakistan became the 7th country to develop and successfully test nuclear weapons.

The Stockholm International Peace Research Institute in 2014 listed nine countries with nuclear weapons. Included were India with an estimated 90-110 warheads and Pakistan with an estimated 100-120 warheads. www.sipri.org.

Other nations have tried to develop nuclear weapons. Israel reportedly has nuclear weapons but has not tested any. South Africa, Libya, Iraq, North Korea and Iran at one time or another have pursued nuclear weapons development.

ACKNOWLEDGEMENTS

I am deeply grateful to those who critiqued my many drafts: Kelli Glenn, Matt Glenn and *Wayfarer*, an author in her own right who has published four books (www.wayfaringtraveler.com). I should also mention the thoughtful review by Carol De Marinis and the St. James Writer's Group. They were most helpful in making recommendations for a more interesting novel.

Thanks and gratitude to Ann Marie Mershon of Mershon Writing, my editor, who improved my plot and corrected numerous grammatical mistakes. She encouraged me to continue to write, write, and write some more. She made me realize that my writing will forever remain incomplete and can always be improved upon. She may be reached at www.annmariemershon.com.

Thanks, too, to Debora Lewis who masterfully formatted the manuscript and designed the covers. She saved me a world of headaches. She may be reached at www.arenapublishing.org.

I must mention the CIA spymasters whose careers I followed via their autobiographies: Duane Clarridge, Tom Gilligan, Ted Shackley, Floyd Paseman, Henry Crumpton and Antonio Mendez. They showed through their writings the characteristics of a professional American spy: integrity, perseverance, deeply held patriotism, dedication to their work, substantial emotional involvement sometimes to the detriment of their personal lives, quiet successes, and the excitement of living elsewhere. Their true life stories inspired me. I digested their experiences and added my unbounded imagination to develop and refine this historical spy novel. I respect their substantial accomplishments.

To the CIA professionals whose secret, untold work keep our country safe: Thank you for your service.

Most of all, I am thankful for my wife, Gwen, whose lifelong love, forbearance and wisdom brought me to this page.

Appendix

Indian-Pakistani Nuclear Power Time Line to 2004
India = (IND)
Pakistan = (PAK)

30 October 1909

Homi Jehangir Bhabha born in Bombay, British India into a wealthy Parsi family. Homi in Persian means "conqueror of the world". His uncle was Dorab Tata.

19 November 1917

Indira Gandhi born as only child of Jawaharlal Nehru in Allahabad, Uttar Pradesh, British India.

20 May 1926

Munir Ahmad Khan born in Kasur, Punjab British India.

5 January 1928

Zulfikar Ali (Z.A.) Bhutto born in a Rajput landowning family, Sind, British India.

1935

Homi Bhabha obtains doctorate in physics from University of Cambridge, U.K. He obtains several scholarships to continue his basic research on particles which release a great amount of radiation.

1 April 1936

Abdul Quadeer (A.Q.) Khan born in Bhopal, British India.

1939

War in Europe. Homi Bhabha, on vacation, is stranded in India.

1943-44

Nuclear scientist Homi Bhabha convinces Jawaharlal Nehru to start India's ambitious nuclear program.

1944

Bhabha establishes the Cosmic Ray Research Unit at the Indian Institute of Science. Bhabha independently conducts research on nuclear weapons.

6 August 1945

U.S. drops Uranium U-235 "Little Boy" atomic bomb on Hiroshima, Japan during World War II.

9 August 1945

U.S. drops 22 kiloton plutonium "Fat Man" atomic bomb on Nagasaki.

1945

Bhabha establishes the Tata Institute of Fundamental Research.

1946

Atomic Energy Research Committee formed with Bhabha as head.

14 August 1947

India obtains independence from Britain. East and West Pakistan established separate from India. Millions of Muslims move to Pakistan, millions of Hindus and Sikhs move to India causing communal riots and mass murder in the process.

15 August 1947

(IND) Jawaharlal Nehru becomes India's first Prime Minister. He supports peaceful uses of nuclear energy.

October 1947

First Indo-Pakistani war. Pakistan starts war over disputed Kashmir. UN Resolution 47 calls for cease-fire. Line of Control splits Kashmir between India and Pakistan.

30 January 1948

(IND) Mahatma Gandhi, Hindu leader of the peaceful resistance to British rule, assassinated.

1948

(IND) Prime Minister Nehru establishes the Atomic Energy Commission. Bhabha serves as its first chairman.

1949

(PAK) Munir Ahmad Khan earns Bachelor's in Electrical Engineering from Punjab University.

1950

(PAK) Z.A. Bhutto earns B.A. in political science, University of California, Berkeley.

1951

(IND) India signs nuclear cooperation agreement with France.

1951-52

(PAK) Munir Ahmad Khan earns M.S. in Electrical Engineering from North Carolina State University.

1952

(IND) Prime Minister Nehru details a plan to begin to build India's nuclear infrastructure.

1953

President Eisenhower announces the Atoms for Peace program.

1953

(PAK) Z.A. Bhutto earns LLB and LLM degrees from University of Oxford, England.

1954

(IND) The Department of Atomic Energy created as the successor to the Atomic Energy Commission.

1 March 1954

U.S. detonates first Hydrogen Bomb at Bikini Atoll. Fifteen megatons, 1,000 times more powerful than each of the bombs dropped on Japan during World War II.

September 1954

(PAK) Pakistan joins the U.S.-led Southeast Asia Treaty Organization (SEATO)

March 1956

(PAK) Atomic Energy Commission established to take advantage of the Atoms for Peace program. (PAEC).

1956

(IND) Apsara research reactor becomes operational with uranium supplied by the U.K.

April 1956

(IND) Canada supplies India with uranium fuel and the U.S. provides heavy water for the CIRUS (Canada-India-U.S.) nuclear reactor at Trombay near Bombay. CIRUS burns natural U-238 uranium and gives plutonium as a byproduct. CIRUS installed before the IAEA formed. CIRUS can produce 7-10 kg of low grade plutonium per year.

1956

(PAK) Munir Ahmad Khan earns M. Sc. in Nuclear Engineering from the N.C. State University.

1958

(PAK) Z.A. Bhutto appointed as Pakistani Minister of Water and Power by Field Marshall Ayub Khan.

1958-1972

(PAK) Munir Ahmad Khan works on various nuclear energy programs for the International Atomic Energy Agency (IAEA).

10 March 1959

Tibetan Uprising. India grants asylum to Dali Lama.

1960

(IND) CIRUS reactor becomes operational.

1960

(PAK) Z.A. Bhutto promoted to Minister for Commerce, Communications and Industry under Ayub Khan.

1960

(PAK) A.Q. Khan receives BSc in metallurgy from Karachi University.

1960-61

(PAK) Pakistan Institute of Nuclear Science and Technology (PINSTECH) established in Rawalpindi.

April 1961

(IND) Approved by Nehru, India constructs reprocessing plant to extract plutonium from spent nuclear fuel. The plant was sized to process one year's supply of plutonium from the CIRUS reactor. Program called the Phoenix.

September 1962

(IND) The Atomic Energy Act mandates government control over atomic energy development.

1962

Sino-Indian Border War along 3,225 km in Ladakh. (20 October-20 November)

1963

(IND) Bhabha publicly calls for India to develop nuclear weapons.

1963

(PAK) Five MW light water reactor installed in Rawalpindi.

1963

(PAK) Z.A. Bhutto appointed as Pakistan's Foreign Minister. A socialist, he develops close relations with the neighboring People's Republic of China.

May 1964

(IND) P.M. Nehru dies, Lal Bahadur Shastri becomes new P.M. Shastri appoints Sarabhai as head of the nuclear program. Because of his beliefs Sarabhai pushes for peaceful purposes rather than weapons development.

16 October 1964

The Peoples Republic of China detonates its first atomic bomb estimated at 20 kilotons.

27 November 1964

(IND) Jana Sangh offers Parliament resolution to develop a nuclear bomb. P.M. Shastri says he will never approve a bomb, but will use nuclear power only for peaceful purposes.

1965

Second Indo-Pakistani War. Pakistan attacks Kashmir. Pakistani forces repelled by Indian forces. Indian forces attack Punjab and along Rajasthan border. Peace treaty and cease fire agreed at Tashkent. (5 August-23 September)

October 1965

(PAK) Munir Ahmad Khan of IAEA meets Z. A. Bhutto in Vienna to reveal information about India's nuclear program and weapon facility in Trombay.

1966

(PAK) Munir Ahmad Khan becomes Chairman of the PAEC.

10 January 1966

(IND) Prime Minister Lal Badadur Shastri dies of a heart attack.

24 January 1966

(IND) Homi Bhabha dies in Air India crash near Mont Blanc France.

24 January 1966

(IND) Indira Gandhi becomes P.M. replacing Shastri. She allows Sethna to develop weapons grade plutonium.

June 1966

(PAK) Z.A. Bhutto resigns from Ayub Khan government over strategy about Indian-Pakistani war.

1 August 1966

In order to try to stop India from developing its own bomb, President Johnson approves sharing U.S. intelligence with India about China's ongoing difficulties and limitations to develop nuclear weapons.

1966

First U.S. Special Forces group arrives in South Vietnam.

1968

Over 500,000 U.S. combat troops in South Vietnam.

March 1969

(IND) Secret plutonium plant known as Purnima constructed. Work on nuclear weapons at Trombay started.

25 March 1971

Pakistan Army launches military operation to keep E. Pakistan. Pakistan's Air Force attacks Indian military bases causing the Third Indo-Pakistani War. Pakistan split in two, Bangladesh formed as independent state. Pakistani forces suffer bitter defeat, surrender in December 1971. Pakistan is demoralized as a country.

20 December 1971

(PAK) Z.A. Bhutto becomes 4th President of Pakistan. He also holds the title of Chief Martial Law administrator. He places Pakistan's nuclear program under his direct control.

January 1972

(PAK) Z.A. Bhutto establishes civilian authority over the military, nationalizes ten major industries.

20 January 1972

(PAK) Z.A. Bhutto meets with scientists and engineers at Multan to call for the development of a nuclear weapons program, appoints Munir Ahmad Kahn of the PAEC as head of the task force. This was Pakistan's initiative in response to what India was purportedly doing toward making an atomic bomb.

1972

(PAK) A.Q. Khan receives his doctorate in Metallurgy from Catholic University of Leuven, Belgium. He is employed by URENCO in Holland to work on gas centrifuges to produce commercial-grade uranium for light water reactors.

1972

(IND) Purnima research reactor comes online.

7 September 1972

(IND) P.M. Indira Gandhi approves the Atomic Research Center, Trombay, to manufacture a nuclear device and prepare to test it. The program underwent total secrecy and tight political control.

28 November 1972

(PAK) First nuclear power plant inaugurated (Karachi Nuclear Power Plant KANUPP-1) built in collaboration with Canada. A natural uranium and heavy water reactor.

December 1972

(PAK) Munir Ahmad Khan calls first meeting to design a plutonium-implosion type weapon.

March 1973

(PAK) Contract signed with French supplier for a large plutonium reprocessing plant to be built at Chashma.

March, 1973

Last U.S. troops withdraw from South Vietnam.

14 August 1973

(PAK) New Constitution. Z.A. Bhutto gives up position as President, becomes Prime Minister.

January 1974

(PAK) Z.A. Bhutto nationalizes all banks in Pakistan. The government establishes new rural and urban schools based on Islamic and Pakistani studies.

1974

(PAK) A.Q. Khan arrives in Pakistan after contacting P.M. Bhutto to offer his services in the development of a bomb.

18 May 1974

(IND) First test of fission device based on plutonium. Four to six kilotons, known as the "Smiling Buddha". Indian politicians state that test is "for peaceful purposes". The reprocessed plutonium came from the CIRUS reactor provided by Canada with heavy water provided by the U.S.

October 1974

(PAK) Contract signed with France for 2nd reprocessing plant.

December 1974

(PAK) A.Q. Khan meets with Bhutto, Munir Khan other scientists to discuss plutonium vs uranium for a bomb. They decide to pursue both avenues.

July 1976

(PAK) A.Q. Khan joins the new Project 706 now separated from the PAEC to work on uranium enrichment. A.Q. Khan brings stolen centrifuge secrets. Scientists start to look for a test site.

1976

(PAK) Abdul Quadeer Khan establishes the Kahuta Research Laboratories. He favors centrifuges to process Uranium.

24 March 1977

(IND) Morarji Desai replaces Indira Gandhi as P.M.

5 July 1977

(PAK) Z.A. Bhutto arrested in a coup by General Zia-ul-Haq.

4 April 1979

(PAK) Z.A. Bhutto hanged after kangaroo court finds him guilty of murder.

25 December 1979

Russian troops invade Afghanistan.

1980

(PAK) Engineers complete site development work at Chaghi and Kharana in Baluchistan. Munir Khan fostered the indigenous development of a plutonium bomb while A.Q. Khan develops one based on uranium.

14 January 1980

(IND) Indira Gandhi again becomes P.M. replacing Charan Singh.

7 June 1981

Israel jets destroy Iraq's nuclear site. Pakistan's Air Force went on alert to defend the country's nuclear development program against possible Indian attack.

1981

(PAK) Intelligence reports that Indira Gandhi issued orders to destroy Pakistan's nuclear facilities. Pakistan conveyed a possible counterattack to the Indians and the issue was dropped.

1984

Indian and Pakistani government officials finally agreed not to attack each other's nuclear facilities.

31 October 1984

(IND) P.M. Indira Gandhi assassinated. Her son, Rajiv Gandhi becomes P.M.

1986-87

(PAK) Munir Ahmad Khan serves as chairman of the IAEA Board of Governors. He also served as a Board member for 12 years.

1986-1987

(IND) Military "Brasstacks" exercise along Indian-Pakistani border in Rajistan state. Indian military tries to get Pakistan to attack in response. Not successful.

1989

Last Russian troops leave Afghanistan.

19 March 1998

(IND) Atal Bihari Vajpayee becomes P.M.

6 April 1998

(PAK) Ghauri missle tests.

8 April 1998

(IND) Prime Minister Vajpayee authorizes thermonuclear test.

11-13 May 1998

(IND) Five nuclear tests conducted at the Pokhran underground test site.

28 May 1998

(PAK) Five fission nuclear devices exploded in Chagai, Baluchistan in an underground tunnel constructed in the 1980's. Pakistan becomes the 7th country to successfully test nuclear weapons.

22 April 1999

(PAK) Munir Ahmad Khan dies in Vienna, Austria at 72.

February, 2004

(PAK) Abdul Quadeer Khan placed under house arrest by the Pakistani government after the U.S. disclosed that Mr. Khan had provided atomic bomb technology to other countries including N. Korea, Iran and Libya.

REFERENCES

A. Nuclear Weapons:

Perkovich, George. *India's Nuclear Bomb: The Impact on Global Proliferation*. Berkeley: University of California Press, 2001. Print.

Richelson, Jeffrey. *Spying on the Bomb: American Nuclear Intelligence from Nazi Germany to Iran and North Korea*. New York: Norton, 2006. Print.

Sagan, Scott and Waltz, Kenneth. *The Spread of Nuclear Weapons: An Enduring Debate*. New York: Norton, 2013. Print.

Ganguly, Sumit & Kapur, Paul. *India, Pakistan and the Bomb: Debating Nuclear Stability in South Asia*. New York: Columbia University Press, 2012. Print.

Brown, Michael et al. *Going Nuclear: Nuclear Proliferation and International Security in the 21st Century*. Cambridge: MIT Press, 2010. Print.

Google:

> Nuclear Non-Proliferation Treaty
>
> Third World Movement
>
> Indian Nuclear Weapons Development, History
>
> Pakistan Nuclear Weapons History

B. Autobiographies by CIA spies:

Gilligan, Tom. *CIA Life: 10,000 Days with the Agency*. Boston: Intelligence Book Division, 2003. Print.

Clarridge, Duane. *A Spy for all Seasons: My Life in the CIA*. New York: Simon & Schuster, 1997. Print.

Shackley, Theodore. *Spymaster: My Life in the CIA*. Dulles: Potomac Books, 2006. Print.

Paseman, Floyd. *A Spy's Journey: A CIA Memoir*. St. Paul: Zenith Press, 2004. Print.

Everett, James. *The Making and Breaking of an American Spy*. Durham: Strategic Book Group, 2011. Print.

Mendez, Antonio. *The Master of Disguise: My Secret Life in the CIA*. New York: Harper Collins, 2000. Print.

Kahlili, Reza. *A Time to Betray*. New York: Simon & Shuster, 2010. Print.

Crumpton, Henry. *The Art of Intelligence, Lessons from a Life in the CIA's Clandestine Services*. New York: Penguin Books, 2012. Print.

Moran, Lindsay. *Blowing My Cover, My Life as a CIA Spy*. New York: Putnam, 2005. Print.

Other:

Kessler, Ronald. *Inside the CIA: Revealing the Secrets of the World's Most Powerful Spy Agency*. New York: Simon & Schuster, 1992. Print.

Andrew, Christopher and Mitrokhin, Vasili. *The World Was Going Our Way: The KGB and the Battle for the Third World*. New York: Basic Books, 2005. Print.

Talbot, Ian and Singh, Gurharpal. *The Partition of India*. Cambridge: Cambridge University Press, 2104. Print

https://www.cia.gov

https://www.cia.gov/office-of-cia/clandestine-services/code-of-ethics.html.

Tradecraft: Google:

> Intelligence Tradecraft / Surveillance
>
> Agent Handling / False Flag Operations
>
> Intelligence Agent Meetings

C. India–Pakistan General:

Go to the Wikipedia site:

Sethna, Homi

Sino-Indian War of 1962

"Smiling Buddha" nuclear test of 18 May, 1974

Third World Movement

D. Indian Sights including those visited by Shiree and Ravi in the novel.

Go to the Wikipedia site:

Chandni Chowk

Delhi Gymkhana Club

Diwali Festival of Lights

India Gate

Humayun's Tomb

Jama Masjid, Old Delhi

Lodi Gardens

Qutib Minar

Parsi Tower of Silence

Red Fort

About the Author

James Glenn has enjoyed working in the corporate world of international business for 35 years. For nine of those years he and his family lived overseas, including four years in India and five years in Germany. He and his lifelong wife now live in the snow-capped mountains of northern New Mexico. They have three children and six grandchildren.

During his career Mr. Glenn has successfully sold and marketed at one time or another farm and construction equipment, power plant equipment, and plastics machinery in numerous countries including India, Germany, Finland, Holland, Sweden, Japan, China, Taiwan, Mexico, Canada, and the Soviet Union. He holds a degree in Mechanical Engineering from Cornell University and a Harvard MBA.

Made in the USA
San Bernardino, CA
13 August 2017